Mokomoko
Dannoura

Illustration: Chisato Naruse

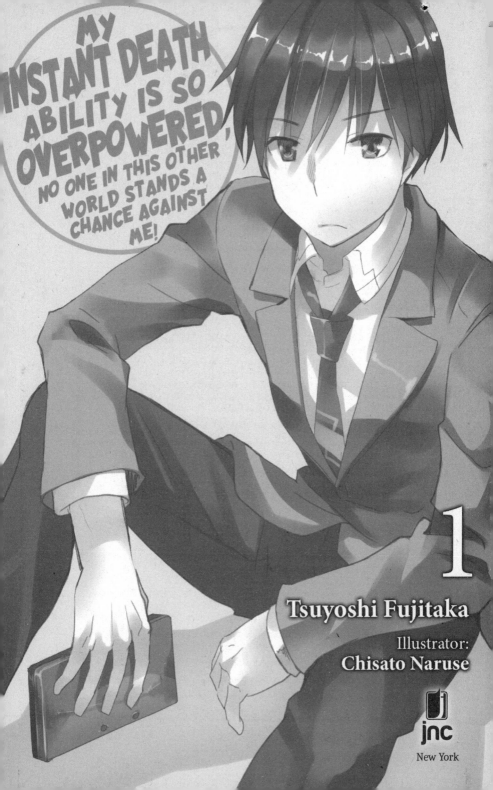

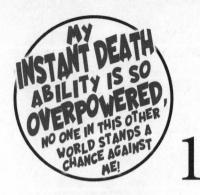

Author: **Tsuyoshi Fujitaka**
Illustrator: **Chisato Naruse**

Translated by Nathan Macklem
Edited by Tess Nanavati

SŌKUSHI CHEAT GA SAIKYO SUGITE, ISEKAI NO YATSURA GA MARUDE AITE NI NARANAIN DESUGA.
© Tsuyoshi Fujitaka / Chisato Naruse 2016
EARTH STAR Entertainment All Rights Reserved
First published in Japan in 2016 by EARTH STAR Entertainment, Tokyo.
English translation rights arranged with Earth Star Entertainment through Tuttle-Mori Agency, Inc, Tokyo.

English translation © 2020 by J-Novel Club LLC

Yen Press
150 West 30th Street, 19th Floor
New York, NY 10001

Visit us at yenpress.com
facebook.com/yenpress
twitter.com/yenpress
yenpress.tumblr.com
instagram.com/yenpress

First JNC Paperback Edition: June 2023

JNC is an imprint of Yen Press, LLC.
The JNC name and logo are trademarks of J-Novel Club LLC.

Library of Congress Cataloging-in-Publication Data is available.

ISBN: 978-1-9753-6830-2 (paperback)

10 9 8 7 6 5 4 3 2 1

LSC-C

Printed in the United States of America

Contents

ACT 3

MY INSTANT DEATH ABILITY
IS SO OVERPOWERED,
NO ONE IN THIS OTHER WORLD
STANDS A CHANCE AGAINST ME!

ACT1

Chapter 1 — Die

Yogiri Takatou awoke to the sound of shouting right beside him. Turning bleary eyes towards the voice, he found a girl with disheveled hair shaking his shoulders.

"Who are you again?"

A strange feeling came over him.

He was in the middle of a school trip, on a sightseeing bus. Since he was sitting by the window at the very back of the bus, there should only have been other guys around him.

"Tomochika Dannoura!" the girl shouted desperately.

It was one of his classmates, he finally remembered. He couldn't recall most of their names, but hers was a bit strange, so it had left something of an impression on him.

"Ah, Dannoura. Did we arrive already?" he asked, rubbing the sleep from his eyes.

Their bus was heading to a ski resort in Nagano. It was kind of odd for Tomochika to be the one waking him up as they had never spoken to each other before, but it was about the right time for them to have arrived.

"No, no! I just didn't know what to do!"

"I have no idea what you're talking about."

"How could you possibly sleep through everything that just happened?!"

Wondering what she meant by that, Yogiri looked down the aisle of the bus. The view before him had been twisted. The frame of the bus they were in had been crushed, and a white object of some sort had punched through the side of the vehicle, impaling one of the boys in his class.

"Ahh. Yeah, that's a hell of a mess, isn't it?" Satisfied that he had confirmed the source of Tomochika's hysteria, Yogiri continued to survey the scene. A number of holes were visible in the roof and walls of the deformed bus. A girl was lying in the aisle between the seats, covered in blood. Judging from the large hole in her chest, it was safe to say she was dead.

The rest of the bus was empty, so the other students had probably already fled. Aside from the two of them, the only living person left was the impaled guy, but that probably wouldn't last for long.

The object protruding from him looked like some sort of spear — white with a number of thin spikes on it. But it couldn't be something so inorganic. It was writhing. With the way it trembled slightly, stretching and recoiling, it had to be part of some sort of creature.

As far as what that creature might be, Yogiri didn't know of any animal with such an enormous, unsightly appendage.

"What's going on here?"

"I don't know! How would I know?!"

Apparently, Tomochika was upset. Yogiri looked out the window. Some sort of enormous, scaled creature had wrapped itself around the bus.

"A snake? No, probably more like a lizard?" In any case, it was kind of gross.

Picking up a karaoke microphone from the floor by his feet, Yogiri threw it at the spear-like appendage. The moment the microphone struck, a terrible screeching sound filled the air. The spear-thing quickly withdrew from the bus, dropping its captive to the floor.

As the startled, enormous creature distanced itself from the vehicle, Yogiri was finally able to get a good look at its entire body.

"Oh, it's a wyvern?"

A type of dragon, walking on two legs and with enormous wings. The appendage in question was situated between its legs, meaning it was likely the creature's genitals. As hard as it was to believe that an aroused dragon had attacked them, which is what the evidence seemed to point to, what they saw outside of the window was even more shocking.

All around them stretched nothing but bright grassland.

"Wasn't it night when I went to sleep? And wasn't there snow everywhere?"

"Who cares?! What if you just made it angry?!" Tomochika shouted, shaking Yogiri back and forth by his neck.

With his now shaky vision, he noticed something out of the corner of his eye. The dragon was glaring at them. As if its rage were taking physical form, flames began to leak from its mouth.

"Ah!" Yogiri blurted out, perking up with excitement.

"What? Did you find a way to get us out of this?!" Tomochika said, her eyes suddenly filling with hope.

"What? No, I was just thinking…I guess this is what dragon car sex looks like."

"What are you talking about?!"

Dragon car sex was a fairly unique but very real fetish. Yogiri opened his mouth to explain that, but before he could speak, the situation had already changed.

The wyvern roared. With a flap of its wings, the comically large creature lifted itself into the air and swooped straight down towards them.

"Well, this is a problem."

The seats and walls around them were warped, and the already narrow walkway was littered with corpses. Getting out in time seemed improbable.

I guess that's how it goes, Yogiri thought to himself. This was the way his life would end. His attachment to it was pretty thin anyway.

"No, I can't take it anymore!"

As Yogiri calmly gave in to his fate, Tomochika wrapped herself tightly around him. As her rather significant chest pressed into him, something changed.

Well, this isn't such a bad feeling.

No matter how antisocial he was, he was still a man. In a situation like this, even he couldn't help but develop a sort of urge to protect her. As such, he decided to use *that* power, though he had told himself he never would.

"Die."

With his target in his sights, Yogiri unleashed his ability. The dragon's wings instantly stopped moving and it spiraled downwards into the grass. The force of the impact threw dirt and debris up into the air as its enormous body slid across the ground.

The bus shook as the monster struck the side of it, although the friction from the slide had slowed it down and weakened the impact. Yogiri barely felt it.

"So, what do we do now?"

The danger seemed to have passed for the moment, but the situation they were in was still as bizarre as ever.

"We're safe, by the way, Dannoura."

"Really…?"

She continued to cling to him for a while, but when nothing more seemed to be happening, she timidly raised her head and stepped back.

"What? But…why? What even happened?" she said, her expression dumbstruck as she looked out the window.

"That's kind of what I want to ask, but there's no point while you're so flustered. We can talk after you've calmed down."

In deciding what they should do next, he would need to know the details of their current situation. For that, he would need her help. So until she had relaxed a bit, he figured he might as well wait.

Pulling out a portable game console from his bag, he switched it on. It was a fairly popular hunting game, but Yogiri himself had only started it recently.

"Are you actually playing *Monster Hunter* right now?! Seriously?!"

In spite of her obvious shock, Tomochika was unexpectedly composed. Maybe she'd be ready to talk sooner than he thought.

Chapter 2 — My Combat Level is Five Hundred and Thirty Thousand, You Know?

"Hey…why don't we go outside already?"

"And do what? It's not like we can guarantee it's safe out there."

"I appreciate the level-headedness of your response, but could you at least put down *Monster Hunter* while saying it?" Yogiri and Tomochika were still sitting in the rearmost seat of the tour bus. Yogiri was playing his game, waiting for Tomochika to calm down. "Also, I've been watching for a while, and aren't you really bad at the game?"

"It's kind of strange. Why does the third hit on the lance have so much windup? I was never this bad before."

"You're playing in Bushido style, right? Why not try switching to Striker style? That should remove the windup from the last hit of your three-hit combo."

"Wait, seriously?"

"Yeah, seriously."

As instructed, Yogiri switched styles. Sure enough, the controls immediately returned to what he was used to.

"Ooh, nice!"

"Also, you're far too reckless with your attacks. If you're going to use the lance, even if you can fit in three strikes, just do two instead. Or if you can fit in two strikes, do only one. You always have to be ready to block or evade." She paused for a moment, nonplussed. "Is this really the time to be talking about it, though?"

"What are you, Dannoura? Some sort of Lance God?"

"Seems like common sense to me..." she said, somewhat unconvincingly.

"So, have you calmed down a bit?"

"I guess. It feels wrong to be okay in a situation where people have died though, so maybe it's just some sort of shock? Even the smell isn't bothering me anymore."

If that was the case, she was probably okay, Yogiri thought to himself. Returning his game console to its sleeve, he turned to actually listen.

"Then why don't you tell me what happened?"

"You really march to the beat of your own drum, don't you? But fine, I'll explain. Basically, it seems we're in some sort of parallel world. There was someone who called herself a Sage, and she said we were all Sage candidates. Then Yazaki started dividing us all up..."

"Hold on, I don't get it at all. Can you start from the *actual* start?"

"Right. Okay."

Tomochika began to explain from the very beginning.

During the trip, the bus emerged from a tunnel and they suddenly found themselves in a grassy field.

"Huh?" Tomochika blurted out as she stared absentmindedly at the landscape from her window seat. Moments before, they had been passing by mounds of snow at night, but now they were speeding through grasslands in daylight.

Before long, the other students began to notice as well, and chaos erupted soon after.

"What's going on, Mikochi?" she asked Romiko Jougasaki, the girl sitting beside her.

"We're in some sort of field, I guess?"

"Yeah, I can figure that out by looking."

The tunnel they had just passed through was nowhere to be found, and the bus was now traveling through a thick field with no road.

As the confused students began to panic, the bus came to a sudden stop. Moments later, a woman in a white dress boarded the vehicle. She looked kind of dorky, like she was doing some sort of Magical Girl cosplay. That was Tomochika's first impression of her anyway.

"Greetings, Sage candidates. My name is Sion, granddaughter of the Great Sage."

Although Tomochika was normally one to butt in with all sorts of comments, this time her bewilderment left her speechless. That was probably for the best, though. Speaking carelessly would have been a mistake, as was soon demonstrated by their homeroom teacher.

"Who are you?! What are you —"

Despite the teacher's assertive attempt, he never managed to finish what he was saying. As he stepped towards her, Sion casually placed her hands on his head, which exploded with a light pop, showering the front rows of the bus in blood and brain matter.

"Everyone, please quiet down. Your best course of action at the moment is to bottle up all your feelings and just tremble in fear for a bit. Listen to me, and don't do anything stupid."

The students fell silent. In that one moment, the woman had displayed just how terrifying she was.

"I have no intention of harming any of you, but that only holds true if you don't upset me. Please pay careful attention. My combat level is five hundred and thirty thousand, you know?"

The students were frozen in place. Even Tomochika bit her tongue.

"Ah, I was hoping I could just smile here," she said, lifting her left hand towards the driver's seat.

From that hand, a light began to shine. In an instant, the driver — chair and all — was burned to a crisp.

"You see? It bothered me that it looked like he was trying to get away, so I ended up killing him."

As Sion spoke, with seemingly no regard for the lives she had just taken, the students shrank back from her.

"You may think me unreasonable, but this is simply the way of the world. 'Darkness is only a single step away,' and all that. Now, why don't I explain the situation to you? As you may have noticed, you are no longer in the world you call home. I have summoned you into a parallel world."

There was no way they could believe such a claim offhand, but despite the bewildering circumstances, the students didn't make a sound. They had decided it was best not to do anything unnecessary.

"I summoned you in search of candidates to become Sages. The Sages rule this world, but sometimes our numbers drop a bit, so from time to time our ranks require replenishment."

She raised her right hand towards the students. As the bus filled with light, Tomochika prepared herself for the worst — but no such thing happened. Timidly opening her eyes, she saw Romiko's body glowing with a blue light in the seat beside her. The students across the aisle were also glowing, in red and yellow. Standing up, Tomochika looked around the bus. Everyone was glowing in a full rainbow of colors.

What? What's happening? Wait, why aren't I glowing too? Not that I wanted to glow or anything...

But it felt like she was about to be separated from everybody.

Chapter 3 — Everyone! Listen to Me!

With the students glowing in a variety of colors, the inside of the bus had taken on a fantastical atmosphere.

"The color denotes the difference in your strength, but to put it simply, it's safe for you to assume that those of you who are glowing now are strong. After a short while, the light will disappear. I recommend that you keep in mind who among you looks the strongest, though. After all, if you gather the most powerful people around you, your chance of survival will increase."

As if taking Sion's warning all too seriously, the students began frantically looking around the bus. Although Tomochika wasn't the only one who wasn't glowing, there were very few like her.

"I've installed a system called Battle Song version 02.87.05.11 into all of you. If the installation was successful, you should see a number of license logos appearing in front of your eyes. It may seem annoying at first, but you will only see them on startup, so please bear with it for now."

Still standing at this point, Tomochika finally took her seat and began watching the space in front of her intently. But the only thing that she saw was the seat in front of her...nothing like what Sion had described was appearing.

"Mikochi, can you see anything?" Tomochika asked her friend, beginning to get anxious.

"Yeah, there are a bunch of colorful letters, but I can't read them. Oh, it says 'Status.' It's just Japanese? What is this?"

So everyone except her could see it after all. Tomochika was struck by another uncomfortable feeling. Being set apart from everybody else in a situation like this was…bad.

"This system is called the 'Gift' in this world. Using your Gift, please aim for the rank of Sage. I suppose we should set a time limit as well. For now, why don't we say one month?"

"U-Umm, excuse me!" Steeling herself, Tomochika rose from her seat again and called to Sion.

"What is it?"

"May I ask a question?"

"Of course," Sion replied with a gentle smile.

"Err, I didn't glow at all, and I can't see any logos or anything…"

"Ah, well then…" Sion's expression turned sympathetic. "Unfortunately, there are some people who just aren't compatible. There's nothing we can do about it, so please don't give it another thought."

Dismissed so quickly, Tomochika was struck speechless. The feeling that she was in a very bad situation was intensifying.

"Now then, let us continue. All of you will be working together as a single unit known as a Clan. From this Clan, you must produce at least one Sage. You can all work together to prop up one person, or everyone can try to get there by themselves. I'll leave the method entirely up to you."

"Excuse me! Why us?" As desperation began to settle in, Tomochika's usual belligerence was reemerging. The surrounding students began to turn sharp gazes in her direction, as if willing her not to speak out.

"It's just statistics. Our calculations suggested that this particular group has a high probability of turning out a Sage."

"Excuse me! What happens if no one can become a Sage?"

"Yes, that. I guess I'd have to turn you into livestock and use you to produce magical energy. You would all be put into a dark, cramped tank for the rest of your lives. So do your best to succeed, okay?"

Faced with a future even more tragic than she had imagined, Tomochika was once again speechless.

"But if even one of you attains the rank of Sage, then the rest of you will become their attendants, and will be accorded a degree of authority in this world. That I can guarantee. In one hour, we will begin your first mission. Try not to get wiped out right at the start, okay?"

With those parting words, Sion stepped off the bus. Almost immediately, the students erupted into chaos.

"What's even happening? I don't get it at all!" Tomochika said, falling back into her seat with a thud.

"Ah, the Mission Details are here," Romiko said matter-of-factly, as if completely unfazed by the circumstances.

According to Romiko, the details of the mission were as follows:

First Mission
Objective: Depart from your current location of the Dragon Plains to reach the city in the north.
Main enemy: Dragons (Average Level: 1000)
Advice: Humans are a dragon's favorite food.
If you exit the bus without any sort of plan, you will likely be attacked. In addition, you currently lack the power to defeat a dragon yourselves.
Until the mission starts, the bus will be protected by a barrier, so you will be safe.
Put a plan together so you will be ready to act when the time comes.

"No, no, no, a dragon would be…"
Tomochika looked outside the window. The landscape around them looked like nothing more than idyllic scenery, completely at odds with the idea of it housing such dangerous monsters.

"Everyone! Listen to me!"

As the chaos continued unabated, a single student stood up — Suguru Yazaki, one of the leaders of the class. Between his good grades, great looks, and extraordinary athletic ability, he was a boy with no faults. He could be rather inflexible at times, but that was likely a result of his penchant for justice.

When he raised his voice, the other students immediately fell silent.

"Although I have no idea what's going on here, it seems there's nothing we can do except try to clear this mission. For that, we all have to work together."

He had essentially just declared himself the leader, but it seemed most of the other students were okay with that. If they had held a poll, he almost certainly would have been chosen anyway, so there wasn't much in the way of objection.

"Is it really okay to leave it to Yazaki?" Tomochika whispered to Romiko, giving voice to her slight feelings of opposition.

"Well, we need someone to manage us for now, right? I think Yazaki is probably well suited for the job."

"That may be true, but..."

Even acknowledging that, she couldn't help but get a bad vibe from the way it had been so arbitrarily decided.

"First, I'd like to get a handle on everyone's abilities. Could you all write your names and Statuses down in this book?"

No one objected.

Chapter 4 — It's a Skill That Makes You Popular!

At the front of the bus, with Suguru Yazaki at the center of it all, an escape plan was being hatched. The students who, like Tomochika, hadn't glowed at all earlier had been sent to the back, where they were being totally excluded.

Besides Tomochika herself, there were three others suffering the same fate:

Ayaka Shinozaki: Rich and with a very domineering personality, she was disliked enough that she had no friends in the class.

Yuuichirou Kiryuu: In a word, a delinquent. He had a rather rough personality, so most people kept their distance.

Yogiri Takatou: Most of his time at school was spent sleeping, so he rarely interacted with his classmates.

"Is he honestly sleeping right now?" Kiryuu said, giving Yogiri an exasperated look.

Yogiri had been sitting in the back of the bus from the beginning, and the tumult that had struck earlier hadn't been enough to rouse him.

"Now that you mention it, he's always asleep, isn't he?"

"Who cares?! Why did I get stuck in this situation?!" Ayaka exploded at Tomochika, in response to her thinking out loud.

"Not like I know either…"

Tomochika looked towards the front of the bus. The discussion appeared to be proceeding smoothly. Rather than arguing, it seemed like everyone was eating up everything that Yazaki suggested.

After a while, the students began to get off the bus. It had been about an hour. Mission Start, or something like that.

"Pft. Not even a word to us, huh? Let's go," Kiryuu said, heading to the front of the bus.

"Takatou! Everyone's leaving! Wake up!" Tomochika said, shaking him lightly. But it didn't seem like he wanted to wake up at all.

"Just leave him. He likes his sleep, doesn't he?"

"Who cares about Yogiri anyway?" Ayaka turned to follow Kiryuu.

While she wasn't exactly happy about it, there wasn't much Tomochika could do if he wouldn't wake up. As she made up her mind to leave, she noticed the two in front of her had stopped at the front of the bus. Wondering what the delay was, Tomochika moved up behind them.

"What are you trying to pull here?" Kiryuu said, the threat heavy in his voice.

Standing in front of the exit was Yazaki and Asuha Kouriyama.

"Sorry, but we can't take you with us. We need you to stay here," Yazaki said, his tone anything but apologetic.

"Oh? Just cuttin' us clean off, are you? Who died and made you king?!"

"Not a king, just the General," Yazaki replied, casually pulling on the handrail by the exit. As he did, the solid metal bar changed shape.

"This is a General's power. For those of us who got the Gift, even being level one, our bodies have become this strong. Bringing normal humans like you along would just slow us down. You understand, right?"

Seeing Yazaki's clearly inhuman power, Kiryuu went stiff.

"B-But if you're that strong, you should have no problem keeping us safe, right?" Ayaka said with a hint of desperation.

"Please understand. We're not exactly happy about this. But thinking of the class as a whole, we have no choice but to leave you behind if you don't have powers."

"So then don't protect us. Don't even look after us. But you can at least let us follow you, right?" Tomochika pleaded. After all, they would be quite helpless if they were just abandoned here.

"We can't do that either. To be honest, leaving you here is part of our plan."

"Okay then, let's have you all looking nice and attractive! Charm Up!"

Before Tomochika could ask exactly what the plan was, Asuha made her move. Raising a hand, she held her palm towards them, and their bodies began to glow.

"What? What's happening? Asu, what did you do?"

The light soon dissipated, but there didn't seem to be any difference. There was no way that all she had done was make them glow for a bit, though.

"Her class is Beauty Coordinator, and Charm Up is a specialized buff skill. After going through everyone's abilities, we decided it would be useful as a way of managing Aggro. In short, we've decided to use you guys as bait."

"Bait?" It took a moment for what they were saying to sink in.

"Tomochii, you know this Charm Up skill I used on you? It will make you, like, super popular!"

"After using some of our other skills to search for nearby enemies, we found there's only a single dragon, somewhere above us. In other words, if it comes after you guys, then the rest of us should be able to reach the city safely."

"Are you saying everyone agreed to this plan?! What about Mikochi? There's no way she would have agreed to this!"

"By Mikochi, you mean Jougasaki? Of course she agreed."

"Sorry, but it's not like we're saying you have to die or anything. All you have to do is hold its attention for a while. If you stay in here, you should be all right." As if trying to convince herself, Asuha gave a short laugh before stepping off the bus.

Yazaki followed her, closing the door behind him by force. Kiryuu immediately rushed to the door.

"Dammit! I can't get it open! How strong is this guy?!"

"What do we do now?"

"How would I know?! What's going on?! Why is this happening to me?!"

As the three of them descended into a panic, a roar shook the air.

"That was…a dragon?"

They couldn't see it, but Tomochika's instincts told her that a sound like that had to come from something truly monstrous.

"The windows! We can get out through the windows, right?"

At Kiryuu's words, Tomochika approached the nearby window, only to find that it was sealed shut. Looking out, she could see her other classmates running away as fast as they could. The effort they exerted in doing so showed just how close the source of their fear was.

I have to do something quick!

Tomochika threw a fist at the window in an attempt to break it, but she never even made contact. The bus shook with enough force to nearly throw the vehicle on its side, sending her flying.

"Is everyone okay?!" Tomochika called out, pulling herself up from the aisle. The only answer was Kiryuu's terrified scream from the front of the bus where he had been thrown.

Between the two of them, Ayaka had collapsed, covered in blood. A long, thin, white object had punched straight through the roof and into her chest.

"Seeing Shinozaki get stabbed, I ran over here to get away. But someone was already back here, sleeping up a storm," Tomochika said with a hint of bitterness.

"A parallel world…? How am I supposed to charge my handheld, then?"

"Really?! That's the first thing that stood out to you about this story?!"

But as far as Yogiri was concerned, with his handheld's life on the line, this was now a serious situation.

Chapter 5 — It Looked Like an Adamski Type…

"Putting the issue of charging aside for now, I guess I didn't glow, so I was left behind?"

"Do you see something now that you've never seen before?"

"You mean like the logo and mission stuff you were talking about earlier? No, it all looks pretty much the same to me." He focused hard on his current field of view, but there was nothing out of the ordinary.

"That's what I thought. The people who glowed could all see information floating around. Like, a health gauge was always visible in the corner, apparently."

"That's pretty common in games, I suppose."

"I guess. Mikochi doesn't really play video games that much, so she couldn't explain it very well."

"This Mikochi is a friend of yours? And she just left you behind and went with everyone else?"

It wasn't hard for Yogiri to accept the fact that he had been abandoned by everyone else. Rather, it seemed natural. He had barely ever spoken to his classmates, after all.

But Tomochika should have been different. Sure, Yogiri wasn't particularly well versed in the interpersonal relationships of the class, but his impression was that Tomochika was someone who would have a lot of friends.

"I think Yazaki did…something," she answered with a bitter expression. Of course, she didn't want to believe that she'd been betrayed.

"If a Beauty Coordinator can manipulate someone's attractiveness, it's possible that a General can manipulate someone's behavior, I suppose. But with all this stuff about classes and levels and skills, it's sounding more and more like a video game." *It's interesting for there to be powers like that,* Yogiri thought. "If we believe General Yazaki's words, then there was only one dragon. In that case, it should be safe for us to go outside now," he continued, looking out the window at the massive body nearby. The creature was totally unmoving. Clearly, it was no longer a threat.

"Umm, actually…did you do something to it, Takatou?" Tomochika asked, her voice wavering slightly.

"It just fell and died on its own."

"Well, that's a lie if I ever heard one."

"Don't believe me, then. That's fine."

"Err…well, it's hard to believe you *could* do anything, but to think it just randomly died…"

While he wasn't particularly concerned about hiding his ability, it would have been a chore to explain it just then, so he decided to leave the conversation for later.

"The dragon really helps sell the idea of this being a parallel world. Or…maybe it does the opposite?"

"How could this not be a parallel world?"

"Well, some grossly rich guy could have kidnapped us and is putting us through some sort of snuff movie performance, right? It's easier to believe the dragon was made with genetic engineering than to believe we were transported to another world."

"Well, that's just because you didn't see the Great Sage's granddaughter. She was definitely using magic! Something came out of her hand and everything!"

Thinking it over, Yogiri had no way of knowing whether Tomochika was actually telling him the truth. But if he started doubting her, there would be no end to it, so he decided to believe her for now. If a problem arose later, he could modify his assumptions then.

"We're not helping anything by staying here anyway, so why don't we take a look outside?" Stepping over the bodies in the aisle, Yogiri headed for the exit. Although he had been told the door was unopenable, the dragon's attack had done considerably more damage. "Looks like we should be able to manage it. Er, something wrong?"

He was speaking as if Tomochika was right beside him, but there was no reply. Turning around, he found her hesitating by Kiryuu's body.

"I know there's nothing we can do if they're dead, but I still feel bad just leaving them here..."

"Ahh." Yogiri walked back down the length of the bus and put Kiryuu and Ayaka back into their seats. After that, he and Tomochika made their way to the exit. With one swift kick, the damaged door burst open with a loud noise. No point in trying to be stealthy now. Without hesitation, Yogiri stepped out onto the grassland.

"Looks like spring." A gentle breeze washed over the field around them.

"See? This is definitely a different world. It was winter up until now, right?"

"The Southern Hemisphere has different seasons than we do, though. It's still more believable that they put our bus on a boat or something and took it to another country."

"You're really stuck on this, aren't you?"

"I think it's stranger to immediately believe we're in a different world."

"There's plenty of proof, though...ah!" She had been looking around restlessly as they spoke, and it seemed she had found something.

Yogiri followed her gaze...and he saw, floating in the air, a flying saucer. With nothing to compare it to, it was hard to gauge the distance, but it looked to be at least a few kilometers ahead of them. There was also some sort of upside-down bowl-shaped object floating on top of the disk.

As they watched, it began to ascend. Following its flight into the sky, Yogiri was dumbfounded. Numerous rock formations were floating as well. Many of them were hidden by the clouds, so they must have been at quite an altitude. As the flying saucer approached one of these formations, it finally disappeared from view.

"See?! There are floating castles and everything! This is a different world for sure, right? There's a whole floating continent!" For some reason, she sounded rather proud.

"It looked like an Adamski Type, didn't it?"

"Why do you care about what shape it was?! Just admit it! This is a different world!"

"All right, I get it. Let's say it's a parallel world, then." The hypothesis that this was just a foreign country had been doomed from the start anyway. For now, he'd accept the theory that they were in a whole new place.

"But why a UFO?! Couldn't they find something more appropriate?!" Tomochika suddenly shouted at no one in particular.

"Glad you're doing well, Dannoura."

"So, what do we do now?"

"Well, I guess we need to get moving," Yogiri said, looking around.

The grasslands extended in every direction around them. The distant castle walls were probably the destination of the first mission that the others had set out on. If that was north, then the forest he saw some distance away must have been west. There were gently sloping hills to the south and east, so he couldn't see very far in those directions.

"City, forest, or hills. Three choices I guess. I suppose we should avoid the forest, at least."

Yogiri wanted to avoid forests wherever possible. For people like them, born and raised in cities, a forest would present far too many unknowns. On top of that, being in another world, who knew what kind of surprises such an environment might harbor?

"The city…if there are people, it might be the best choice, but…" That's where the classmates who had abandoned them would be. That might be a bit of a sticking point for Tomochika. "Let's find our luggage first. They all ran off in a hurry, right?"

"They did run off with nothing, yeah."

"There might even be a portable charger or something."

"What is with you? You are *way* too passionate about that game…"

Yogiri made his way to the storage space under the bus, where all their luggage was kept. The compartment, however, was locked.

"Doesn't look like we can open it. Dannoura, do you have any skill in lockpicking?"

"Do I look like a criminal to you?"

"I guess it's hopeless, then. It didn't look like there was much of value in the bus itself…shall we go look around on top of one of those hills?" He thought there might be something of interest just beyond them.

As Yogiri turned to make his way towards the hills, Tomochika pointed at the northern part of the sky.

"Hey. Something's coming towards us."

"Another dragon?" Or was it another UFO? Yogiri followed the direction of her finger.

There was definitely something in the air there, but it was too far away to make out. At the very least, it didn't appear to be a dragon.

"It looks like Higashida, Fukuhara, and Hanakawa are flying towards us."

"You've got a pretty good eye if you can see them from that far away," Yogiri said, impressed by her eyesight.

Of course, Yogiri himself didn't even remember the names and faces of his classmates, so it wouldn't have meant much even if he could see them.

Chapter 6 — What, You Just Want Me for My Body?!

"So, shall we kill them just to be safe?" Once he realized the objects flying towards them were their classmates, Yogiri figured that would be the best course of action.

"Yeah, if you find your classmates flying towards you, of course you kill them! *What is wrong with you*?" Apparently Tomochika thought he was being sarcastic or something.

"Well, what else are we supposed to do? Are you just going to be all friendly with the people who left you to die?"

"Wait. Were you actually serious about killing them?!" Of course she had thought it was a joke. Now that she knew he was serious, though, she was starting to look a bit anxious.

"Leaving us here was basically the same as trying to murder us. That's a crime the whole class committed, so they can't complain if we do the same to them, right?" It wasn't like he held a grudge against them or anything. But as far as he was concerned, he and Tomochika had earned the right to take revenge.

"Still…I'm not sure I can agree with that. Even if you could just snap your fingers and make them die."

"Even if I didn't want to kill them, I'm thinking there's always the possibility they will be hostile towards us." Tomochika blinked in surprise, as if the thought hadn't even occurred to her. "I wonder what they want if they're only sending three people."

"They said they had ways of looking for enemies, so maybe they found out the dragon died?"

"And…they thought maybe some of us survived and are coming to help? Kind of odd, since they're the ones who abandoned us with the excuse that we'd just slow them down."

"True enough." Recalling Yazaki's words, Tomochika immediately deflated.

"If they are acting independently from the rest of the class, then their objective could be the leftover luggage. In that case, if they've left the class behind, survivors like us would be in the way too."

"That's…just a guess, right?"

"Yeah. But it's a very real possibility. I'm trying to think of ways to keep you safe, so I'd like to keep the risk level as low as possible. I'm not trying to ignore your feelings or anything though. Let's just wait and see how things go."

"If their objective is the luggage, couldn't we just run or hide somewhere?"

"I'm sure they've already seen us. And trying to run away from people who can fly is pointless. For now, let's just find out who's who."

The three former classmates soon came close enough that even Yogiri could recognize them. According to Tomochika, the one on the left was Ryousuke Higashida, looking quite attractive, if somewhat superficial. In the center was a small, brown-haired Yoshiaki Fukuhara. And on the right was the plump Daimon Hanakawa.

The flying trio landed a few meters away from them.

"Tomochika yet lives?! But how?! This is beyond all expectation! My plan to turn her into a zombie slave and have my way with her is ruined!"

Hanakawa's honeyed voice was truly unpleasant. Yogiri was actually impressed by his ability to ruin a person's mood with so few words.

"I told you she might be alive, right? Charm Up doesn't last that long, so the dragon probably just left," Higashida said. Apparently, their ability to seek out enemies couldn't detect whether or not those enemies were actually alive. And as the dragon's body was on the other side of the bus from where they were currently standing, they hadn't seen it yet.

"It's better that she's alive anyway. The thought of controlling her as a zombie is kind of gross," Fukuhara said, poking fun at Hanakawa. Although he looked smaller and younger than the others, it seemed he had a bit of a cheeky streak.

"Do my ears deceive me?! Sir Fukuhara's ability is truly as pearls thrown before swine! Surrender it to me. I must engage in the procurement of a zombie harem!"

"I'm not really fond of killing people just to turn them into zombies, though."

"Hehe, I foresaw such an occurrence. Thus I have prepared this very slave collar! As they still live, I have no need of Sir Fukuhara's powers!"

"Gross. Why on earth would you make something like that?"

"It's not that bad, is it? Don't you think it's twice as much fun to break their spirits yourself?" Higashida chimed in.

"Well, my humble self is not so comfortable with such a bold assault…"

"Then get out of here."

"However, the act of cuckolding is a great pleasure of mine! For instance, doing it in front of the person they like…that thought alone gives such pleasure! Particularly if I might assume the role of providing gentle consolation after the fact."

"You really are gross."

"Leave it at that, guys. Look, Dannoura is totally shocked."

"Oh, I guess Takatou is here too. And look, he's even stepping forward as if to protect her. How brave!"

"Perhaps…is the boyfriend performing the cuckoldry?! I cannot allow it! Tomochika belongs to me alone!"

"Oh, that's a good idea. I was just going to kill him, but that's much better. I kind of want to see how someone who's always so spaced out reacts when his girl gets stolen from him."

"Great news, isn't it, Takatou? Looks like you get to live a little longer!"

The way they were talking, as if they could do whatever they wanted without consequences, was starting to get a little irritating. *Maybe I will just kill them*, Yogiri thought.

"I, uhh, don't really know what's going on here," Tomochika whispered, stepping closer to him, "but I guess it's safe to say we aren't going to be able to get along with them."

Yogiri considered what to do next. It would be easy enough to kill them, but then what? He would rather get as much information out of them as he could first.

I guess I'll start by trying to talk to them.

As Yogiri thought things over, Higashida made the first move, stretching out his right hand. Yogiri judged that there was no real danger in the action. Higashida had no obvious intention of killing them, and his palm was facing away from them anyway.

"Fire Ball!"

Higashida's hand began to glow, and in the next instant, something blew past Yogiri. That was it. Thinking it over, Fire Ball had to be some sort of flaming sphere, right? But Yogiri couldn't see anything like that, and there was no sound of it hitting the bus behind them either.

A few moments later, the sound of something heavy falling came from behind them. Turning around, Yogiri saw a bizarre sight. The rear half of the bus had disappeared.

The sound he had heard was the remainder of the bus falling over onto the ground. A straight line had been gouged into the landscape, the now naked earth carving a path towards the forest in the distance, where a large hole had opened up.

In short, whatever Higashida had fired, it had erased everything in its path without a sound. Who knew how far it had actually traveled before fading away?

"As always, Sir Higashida's Fire Ball truly beguiles the senses! No need to charge, yet displays such first rate power! In possession of such strength, he is confident enough to say, 'No, it's not Hellflame. It's Fire Ball!'"

Despite Hanakawa's flattery, Higashida didn't seem especially satisfied. While he didn't seem to have even considered the possibility of a counterattack, with an ability like that, it wasn't surprising that he would look down on everyone else as if they were trash.

"I can only use basic magic. So I went ahead and refined it as much as I could. I could even kill a Demon Lord with it now. I was the one who blew off the top of Mount Caluone, you know."

"So that was Sir Higashida! As expected of our hero!"

"Being a Hero sounds good, doesn't it? Quite a step up from me. Having the power to control the dead is really only useful for a Demon Lord's underling."

Yogiri had no idea what any of them were talking about. From the way they spoke, they made it sound like they knew quite a bit about this world and the Gift that the Sage had given them, but it hadn't been all that long since they had left the bus behind.

"That's how it is. You understand how strong I am, right? There's no point in resisting. Come on over, Dannoura. Takatou, you can watch from there."

He seemed to feel that his demonstration had been sufficient. The three of them showed no sign of expecting any sort of disobedience.

"Impressive," Yogiri said, looking over at the bus, which no longer held its original shape. Whatever this "Fire Ball" of Higashida's actually was, it appeared to have a diameter of about ten meters. Anything within that radius had been cleanly obliterated, but everything outside of it was essentially unaffected. Touching the frame of the bus, he found it was only slightly warm.

"Higashida! Why are you doing this?!"

"We already decided that, if the opportunity ever arose, we'd cut loose and do whatever we wanted. And surprise, that opportunity just came knocking. So there was nothing to do but grab it, right?"

"Right, and you had to be first, Dannoura. Ask anyone at school and they'll say the same thing."

"My humble self is already quite indebted to your lovely visage, which has brought me great pleasure on many nights!"

Looking at their vulgar expressions, it wasn't hard to guess what they were aiming at.

"So what? You're just after my body?" Tomochika said, wrapping her arms angrily around herself. Yogiri was impressed yet again. He'd expected her to be paralyzed with fear, but she was actually showing a lot of spunk.

"I'm impressed you've got the nerve to say that much right now. Whether it's a parallel world or not, I bet you could make it on your own anywhere," sneered Hanakawa.

"Looks like you two get along just fine," Fukuhara joked, although he couldn't quite keep the envy out of his voice.

It was certainly rather twisted, but it seemed their feelings for Tomochika were the real deal.

"For now, let's try and get them to talk to us," Yogiri said gently. Even though she was putting up a brave front, Tomochika must have been feeling uncomfortable. So the first step would be to shut them up and put her back at ease.

・・・

Chapter 7 — Eternal Force Blizzard, and They Die

"Die."

Yogiri unleashed his power.

"You fool! Simply telling someone to die like that speaks so ill of your vocabulary..."

Hanakawa must have thought that Yogiri's statement was nothing but vocal resistance. But as he scoffed at them, he noticed something was wrong.

Higashida had collapsed to his knees beside him, then proceeded to unceremoniously fall onto his face, motionless.

"Sir Higashida? Are you well?" Hanakawa cried, nonplussed.

"I told him to die, so he did. Even you should be able to connect those dots. So don't move. If either one of you does, another one of you drops," Yogiri warned them.

Ignoring him, Fukuhara moved to Higashida's side.

Pointing a finger at him, Yogiri spoke once again in that same clear voice. "Die."

Fukuhara must have been trying to find out what was wrong with Higashida, but he never made it that far. He abruptly fell over, collapsing on top of his companion, and never moved again.

"I told you to stay still. Move and you die. Do you get it yet?"

"Uh, er, umm…" Hanakawa had gone rigid.

There was no way he fully understood, and probably would have refused to accept it even if he'd had a better handle on things. But he did recognize that something was wrong, and seemed to realize that Yogiri was the source of it. *That should be enough to get him talking*, Yogiri decided.

"Now, let me explain my ability."

"Hold on a sec!" Tomochika shouted, once again full of energy. "I figured it was you that did something to the dragon, but you didn't seem to want to talk about it so I left it at that! Was this not actually a secret or something?!"

"It's not really a secret. I just thought it would be a pain to try and explain it earlier."

"You thought it would be a pain?!"

"And Hanakawa looks like an idiot, so if I don't explain it properly, he'll probably try and pick a fight with us, don't you think?"

"Fine. Go ahead then, tell us about your ability."

Yogiri had steeled himself to be chastised for killing the others. He had felt it was the correct course of action, but had still expected some resistance from Tomochika. It appeared, however, that she wasn't at all concerned about their former classmates.

"All right, but before I start, could you go confirm that those two are dead for me? Don't worry, I won't kill you for moving this time."

First, Hanakawa had to realize that they were actually dead, and then what that meant for him. If he didn't truly understand that he could actually die, he could come up with any number of justifications in his mind for attacking them.

Hanakawa knelt down beside his collapsed companions, timidly giving them a shake. Neither of them so much as twitched.

"Heal!" Hanakawa shouted something that sounded like it was supposed to be magic. It appeared to be some sort of recovery spell, but it clearly had no effect on the dead. The two bodies glowed briefly, but that was it.

"Heal! Heal! Heal! Haha! I am a Healer! No matter the severity of the injury or the extent of the disease, I can heal it in a moment! I've survived in this world with this cheat-like power, able to recover myself even when cut to pieces…wait, why aren't they moving?"

"Do you understand the situation?"

"No! Not at all! How could you do something like this?! Has something come loose in your head?!"

"I don't want to hear that from you," Yogiri said, rapping a fist against the remains of the bus. "That was quite a bit of power. Maybe he missed on purpose, but if he's going to throw around attacks that can kill people, he doesn't really have the right to complain when retaliation comes his way."

"E-Even so, Sir Fukuhara did nothing at all! And most importantly, I have done nothing either!"

"You have to know that's not going to work, right? No matter how you look at it, you three were all in this together. It's clear you both approved of what Higashida was doing."

Hanakawa was at a loss for words. Seeing that he wasn't going to protest for now, Yogiri continued his explanation.

"My ability is to 'invoke instant death at will.' The moment I want someone to die, they die. Instantly."

"That's absurd! What is that?! Eternal Force Blizzard, and they just die?!" Hanakawa shrieked. "Th-That's just not fair at all! That's too much to even call cheating! Normally such things need to be more indirect! Are you looking down on this world?! More importantly, you don't even have any Status, so how can you even do that?!"

"Status, huh? I'm more surprised that *you lot* were given any abilities." As far as Yogiri was concerned, their Statuses and Gifts and the like were far stranger than his own power.

"So, that's what you used to kill the dragon, right? Why did you blow your cover now, though?" Tomochika asked. She must have felt it was more advantageous to keep it a secret.

"So I can use it as a threat. If I want to use my ability to threaten or coerce people, I need to explain it properly for them to understand it. After all, just showing it off, it doesn't look like much is happening."

"That's true, I guess. Even I don't really believe it..."

"So do you understand my power? If you don't, it's probably more effort than it's worth to keep going this way, so I'll just kill you and get it over with."

"I understand! I understand! Please, don't look at me like some 'yare yare' cool protagonist! Don't look at me like you're actually going to kill me!"

Judging from the way he screamed the words, he must have thought he was about to die right then and there.

"Fine. Come over here. It's hard to have a conversation from so far away."

Yogiri sat down on the grass, leaning against the bus, and Tomochika took a seat beside him. But as Hanakawa tottered over to them —

"Okay, stop," Yogiri commanded.

"Wh-What is it?"

"You just tried something, didn't you?"

"Wh-Wh-What are you talking about?"

Hanakawa's reaction was clearly suspicious.

"I never said I only had one ability, did I? I also have the ability to perfectly detect any killing intent that's aimed at me."

"What?"

"So between these two abilities of mine, anyone who has any intention of harming me dies. Or rather, I can choose to kill them."

"Surely you jest! There's no way anyone could combat that kind of power at all!"

"That's not true. If you were, like, a super elite assassin who could perfectly conceal your intent to kill, and could attack in a way that my eyes couldn't follow, you'd at least have a chance. Regardless, from now on, I suggest you be very careful."

Hanakawa obediently stepped in front of them, nervously lowering himself to the ground.

"Okay, there're a few things I want to ask you."

"Understood. I will explain everything that is within the scope of my knowledge, even beyond what you may think to inquire of..."

"Just answer the questions, please."

Seized by a visceral terror, Hanakawa had lost all thought of arguing.

"Why were you guys so confident? It hasn't been that long since you got your Gifts, has it?" It was true that the Gift seemed to give them tremendous abilities, but they were far too comfortable for the short length of time they'd possessed them. And abilities like flying through the sky or being able to obliterate a huge chunk of a bus in a single shot didn't seem like beginner-level powers.

"Because this isn't the first time we've been to this world. We're on something like a New Game Plus..." Hanakawa began his explanation.

Chapter 8 — I'll Even Be Your Slave! I Definitely Won't Disobey!

"So…basically, you three defeated the Demon Lord and were sent back to our world," Yogiri summed up, drastically simplifying the embellished tale that Hanakawa had given them.

"Please refrain from describing my Alternate World Cheat Adventure in such a grossly childish manner!"

"I didn't much care while I was listening, but I guess there was some useful information in there. How did you guys get back to our world?"

While the current priority was to find a way to adapt and survive in this world, their ultimate goal would of course be to return home. Worst-case scenario, he hoped to at least be able to send Tomochika back.

"Ah, yes. In our previous adventure, we were summoned by the Magi of the Kingdom of Iman in order to defeat the Demon Lord, and once the task was accomplished, we were instantly returned. Unfortunately, I am unaware of how we would accomplish the goal of returning home this time…"

Yogiri turned to Tomochika. "I didn't know any of these guys before, but were they gone for that long?"

"Not that I remember. No more than missing a day here and there for being sick, at least."

"Our adventure spanned the course of an entire year in this world; however, upon our return, only a few short hours had passed. Perhaps the flow of time in our individual worlds is not entirely aligned?"

That would be good news, at least. It was very possible that they would be spending some time in this world, so he hoped they could keep the time they lost back home to a minimum.

"So what exactly was this Demon Lord? If you defeated him, shouldn't the world have become peaceful or something?"

"Kingdoms populated by the demonic are known as Demonic Kingdoms, and thus their rulers are Demon Lords. But such Demonic Kingdoms are rather plentiful. Our noble selves were called forth to dispatch the Lord of the Demonic Kingdom bordering the Kingdom of Iman. As such, I imagine the people of Iman have indeed procured some modicum of peace."

As an aside, the grasslands they now occupied were in the territory of the Kingdom of Manii. Apparently, it was quite a distance from Iman.

"So if we kill some Demon Lord somewhere, we'll be able to return to our own world? Well, I suppose that's a question for the Sage that summoned us."

Perhaps some conditions had been set for their return when they'd been summoned, but it hadn't been explained to them. And it was hard to believe that any such conditions would be easy to accomplish. The Sage was looking for someone who could become one of her own; there was no way she would let them escape back home that easily.

"Not that I am especially concerned with the endeavor of returning home…I have my dreams of an Alternate World Cheat Harem, after all…" Hanakawa grumbled, apparently having become rather complacent with his situation.

"So why did you guys act so normal when you were back in our home world?"

With the way they'd been acting earlier, and with the power they clearly possessed, it didn't seem like they'd have had much trouble doing whatever they pleased back home. But as far as Yogiri knew, they had done nothing that would disrupt daily life around them.

"Naturally, our first inclination was to put our powers to the test in our home world! But alas, they failed to produce results there."

"And when you were summoned again, your powers came back just as they were before? Was there anyone else like that?"

"Apart from our three noble selves, I am unaware of any examples."

But if there were three, it wasn't hard to believe that there could be more. Yogiri made a mental note of that.

"Can you see the Status of others easily?"

"Under normal circumstances, such a thing would be impossible, I imagine! One must refine their skill in Discernment as I have to receive such an ability!" With a proud smile, Hanakawa began to describe how he had increased his Discernment skill, but Yogiri had stopped listening.

Even if most people couldn't use the skill, he had to assume there were those who would be able to see his Status. It would probably be dangerous to try and bluff his way through this world by pretending that he had a Gift.

"What is the rest of the class doing right now?"

"They began their second mission. I was told they set their sights on the capital."

Apparently, upon reaching the city visible in the north, they had cleared their first mission and were immediately saddled with a second. The objective of their new mission was to accomplish great feats worthy of a Sage.

"What do you mean by 'great feats?'"

"Something incredible enough that they would be recognized by the general public for it. There are a number of such exploits that might qualify, but in any case, the cooperation of the royal family would be indispensable. They've therefore decided to make their way to the capital while they build up their own levels."

"So the three of you just broke off and left on your own."

"What meaning is there to us increasing our levels now? In our previous adventure, after finally defeating the Demon Lord, we had grand designs of building our own harem, yet instead we were forcibly transported away from this world! How could we not take this chance to finally do as we pleased?"

"As you pleased, huh? Well, fine. Are there any other cities nearby?"

"The closest would of course be the city to the north. There exists another to the south, but its distance would make the trek quite a challenge on foot."

Yogiri continued his barrage of questions for some time. The world, the Gifts…he asked about anything that came to mind, until he was satisfied that he had enough information.

"Well, that sums up my questions. Anything you want to ask, Dannoura?"

"Huh? Me? Hmm… Hanakawa, you guys were pretty strong, right? Why didn't you just fight the dragon?" Tomochika asked, giving him a bit of a resentful look.

She must have thought that if they had just killed the dragon, they wouldn't be in their current predicament.

"That was…out of fear, I'm afraid. Perhaps we might have slain a dragon, but that Sage! Truly a terrifying individual! It was the Sage's will that we clear that first mission of reaching the city, so there was naught we could do but comply."

"Sure, it was scary when she was shooting stuff out of her hands, but how were you *that* frightened? Aren't you guys pretty strong too?"

"A misconception that can be forgiven for you, dearest Tomochika, as you are unable to see her Status! Her level had surpassed one hundred million. And, even more terrifyingly, her level continued to rise by the second, even as we watched! There was no method by which we could stand against such a monster!"

"Well, that doesn't really help us, does it?"

Hanakawa describing the Sage's level as "over one hundred million" didn't help Yogiri pin down exactly how strong she was at all.

"Sir Higashida's level was perhaps around one thousand. My humble self is only at ninety-nine."

"After hearing she was at a hundred million, double digits sounds kind of pathetic, doesn't it?" Tomochika said, sparing him no compassion whatsoever.

Yogiri felt the same way.

"It is a thing beyond my control! For you see, the upper limit of a human being in this world is only ninety-nine! Without a particular skill to exceed that limit, or a class with no level limit to speak of, surpassing that number is simply impossible!"

"One more question, then. For everyone to quietly follow Yazaki like that, did he do something to them?"

"Ah, this is about Yazaki's skills, correct? Generals possess such skills as Charisma, Command, and Tactics. Should anyone accept his plan as logical or reasonable, they will find themselves unable to stray from it. Be that as it may, its compulsive force is only moderate, and thus it is rather ineffective on those who would be disadvantaged by the strategies set forth."

Tomochika's gaze dropped, frustration clear on her face. She must have been remembering her friend, Romiko Jougasaki. According to Hanakawa's explanation, that meant Romiko had accepted the plan to leave the powerless classmates behind.

"I see. I guess we'd be the epitome of 'disadvantaged' in a plan like his, but maybe we were just outside the scope of his skill in the first place?"

Most likely, the Command skill served to suppress unrest to a certain degree and promoted group cohesion. That meant those like Yogiri, who didn't receive a Gift, weren't a part of the plan in the first place.

"I imagine that would be the case."

As the discussion came to an end, silence settled over them. It soon became clear that they had no further use for their traitorous classmate.

Yogiri raised his right hand towards Hanakawa. His power didn't require him to speak, nor did it need any special hand motions, but it helped him to create the right image more easily, so that was how he did it.

"Wait! Please, wait! You do not perchance intend to slay me, do you? With your Eternal Force Blizzard?!"

"It doesn't have a weird name like that, but yeah, that's what I was going to do."

"Why?! For what reason?!"

"I feel it could be a problem down the road if we let you live."

"So flippant! Do you not place any value on human life?!"

"I just don't have any issues with killing people who intend to hurt me."

Yogiri's gaze flickered behind Hanakawa. The proof of the truth in his words still lay there, motionless.

"I won't! Really, I'm not going to hurt you at all! Please, please don't kill me!" As Hanakawa fell to his hands and knees, begging, his speech suddenly snapped from his haughty, pretentious style back to normal.

Yogiri hesitated. It wasn't like he was particularly set on the idea of killing him. He just felt like it might be a bit troublesome to leave someone alive when they knew about his power in such detail.

"I-I know! A slave!" Hanakawa suddenly blurted out a word rarely used in everyday life. "I'll be your slave! I'll totally do whatever you say!"

Chapter 9 — Because Your Boobs Were Soft?

"A slave? We're supposed to believe that you'd do anything we say?"

"Well, you see, this is another world, and we have something for that here!" With those words, Hanakawa pulled something out of thin air.

"Wait, what did you just do?" Yogiri was immediately on the alert.

Their adversary had been empty-handed just a moment before. But now, out of nowhere, he was gripping something tightly in his fist. Yogiri didn't feel any killing intent from him, so it didn't seem like they were in danger, but it looked as if there was still much more to learn about the full extent of the Gift. He would need to be more careful than ever.

"I just pulled something out of my item box."

"Can everyone do that?"

"Ah, this is also the result of a rare skill, so without that skill it's impossible. But it makes handling a Hero's belongings rather simple. Aha! If you let me join you, I can offer you this special service! With the item box, I can carry all of your luggage for you! With my recovery magic, I can heal any injury with ease! And since this is my second time here, I have plenty of knowledge about this world! Isn't it a great deal? I would definitely be useful! So please, don't kill me!"

Hanakawa bowed from his knees, pressing his head against the ground. "What do you think, Miss Dannoura? I wouldn't want to exclude you from this decision and leave it entirely in Sir Takatou's hands…" he continued, his gaze flickering back and forth between Tomochika and the ground.

She, in turn, thought it over for a moment. He was someone who had come here with the intention of attacking her. It must have been a complicated mix of feelings.

After having apparently gotten her thoughts in order, she spoke slowly.

"I'm only alive right now thanks to Takatou. I'm certainly not going to complain about how he chose to save me, and I don't feel that I need a say in how he deals with you, either."

"Noooooo! You're too cool about it! You should be getting more emotional, telling him he doesn't have to kill anyone without thinking of the consequences! It's not just about being a good person — that's the correct behavior for a proper Heroine!"

"Moving on. What's that in your hands?" Yogiri looked at the object that Hanakawa had retrieved. It was a simple metal circle and looked like a kind of collar.

"This is a slave collar. Whoever wears it can never disobey the first person they see after putting it on. It is an Ultra Rare magic item! See, you just do this!" Hanakawa did something with the collar, making it split in two. Then, fitting it around his neck, he immediately looked at Tomochika. "My master! What, pray tell, is your command? I would even lick your shoes should you instruct it!" Still on his knees, he began shuffling towards her.

"Ew! Stay back!" she shouted, and Hanakawa immediately stopped moving.

"I see. But it's hard to believe that you'll really obey anything. For all we know, you're just faking it."

"This feels kind of gross…no, it's extremely gross. Is there no way you can stop calling me 'Master'?"

"I don't want to! Truly, it is against my will! However, I cannot disobey your instructions…regardless of what happens, I will never be able to undo my being a slave, but it is theoretically possible to transfer the right of ownership to someone else."

"Oh. Well, in that case, Takatou can have it." Without the slightest bit of hesitation, Tomochika threw away that right.

"Noooo! Why?! WHY?! I thought at least being a slave to Tomochika would be something I could handle!"

"Even if you push that on us...fine. I won't kill you." Yogiri felt like things were getting ridiculous.

"Truly?!"

"But it's not like I plan on taking you with us. That's a forest over there, right?"

"Ah yes, the Forest of Beasts. Ruled over by the Beast King, it is a territory not in human hands. It was unrelated to our adventure in vanquishing the Demon Lord, so as such I have not had the experience of visiting it, but I am told there are prolific amounts of monsters within its confines. However, as the beasts within have resolved to distance themselves from humanity, so long as one does not attempt to enter, it presents no danger."

"Go wait there till I give you further instructions."

"Were you not listening to my explanation?! I was just saying how dangerous it — no! Stop! Why am I standing up?! My feet won't stop!" Just as he had been instructed, Hanakawa began walking towards the forest.

"Oh, right, I forgot," Yogiri said again, a new thought occurring to him.

"What is it?! Perhaps, after all, this instruction was just a clever joke?!" He turned only his head as he walked, his expression filled with hope.

"No, I just forgot the gag order. Don't tell anyone anything about us."

"That is all?! Wait, it's not too late! I will exert my fullest efforts in making myself an asset to you!"

"And one more thing."

"What is it?!" Once again, his eyes began to glitter. He must have thought that this time he would be saved for sure.

"Leave any valuables you have here."

"Now you rob me?!" Hanakawa began retrieving things from his item box, leaving them in the grass.

"See ya. Run along now."

"No, wait! Please, don't just send me off to my death after wringing me dry of information and money! Seriously, please!"

But no matter how hard Hanakawa screamed, his feet never stopped moving. As much as he hated it, he had no choice but to continue walking straight towards the forest.

Yogiri stood up and began collecting the objects that Hanakawa had left on the ground. There were various bits of gold, silver, and precious gems. He didn't know the economy of this world very well, but it seemed to be a significant amount of wealth.

"It would be nice to have something to put them in."

"Oh, I'll go find something. I think there was someone who had a big bag on the bus."

Tomochika went and retrieved two backpacks from the destroyed vehicle. Although they were clearly in an emergency situation, it was surprising how quickly she had accepted the idea of grabbing other people's belongings. And despite the fact that numerous students had died around her, she didn't seem to care. Of course, rather than her being particularly brave, it may have been that the reality of the situation simply hadn't hit her yet.

"All right, let's split it, then. Make sure you keep the expensive-looking jewels and stuff well hidden. Who knows, they might be useful someday." Putting the assorted valuables into the two backpacks, Yogiri sat down again. Maybe he had been standing up for too long...he was starting to get sleepy. "Next would be food. It doesn't look like there's anything here but candy, though."

"I guess we never got dinner, did we?" Tomochika pulled out a number of cookies and other snack foods. The original plan had been to eat dinner once they'd arrived at their hotel, so of course they were hungry. With the gathered snacks, they managed to have a crude meal.

"For now, all the pressing issues have been dealt with, I guess."

As Yogiri gave a relieved sigh, Tomochika looked at him in amazement. "Are you sure it's all right to leave Hanakawa like that?"

"I'm not fond of the idea of bringing him along. We have no proof that he's actually become a slave, and we have no idea when he might betray us."

"You're not very trusting, are you? It didn't look like he was acting."

"Even if he wasn't, we can't know how long it will last."

"And what about me? How do you know I won't suddenly betray you?"

"That would be fine. Deciding to protect you was just a selfish last-minute thought anyway," Yogiri admitted.

"Umm, I know it's probably kind of weird to ask, but the two of us have never really spoken before... Why *are* you willing to go so far to save me?"

"Huh? I wonder why..." Yogiri pondered the question. It had sort of gone without saying that he had to protect her, but now that she mentioned it, he wondered exactly what sort of thought process had led him to that point.

"No, no, no, there's gotta be something, right? Like I'm so beautiful that you naturally stood up to protect me without thinking about it?" Although she said it as a joke, a note of disgust still came through in her tone.

"Ah!"

"What? Did you think of something?"

"Maybe...because your boobs were soft?"

Tomochika's scream echoed across the field.

"Is there not a single decent guy in this whole damn world?!"

Chapter 10 — Interlude: They Do Die From Time to Time, Don't They?

Standing in front of Sion's door, Youichi felt as out of place as always. He still wasn't sure what sort of expression he should greet her with, now that she had reached the rank of Sage.

Had she really wanted to become one? It had been a sacrifice to protect the rest of them. Even now, she might still feel resentful about it. He couldn't help but turn that thought over and over in his mind.

Youichi shook his head. It was too late for that. All he could do now was the work accorded to him as the servant of a Sage.

He knocked on the door.

"Come in." Magic brought the words to his ears.

He opened the door. Inside was a room decorated in white and pink. The furniture was white with cat paw prints, and the curtains and carpet were pink. There was a canopied bed and a delicate chandelier with a flower motif.

In this room that smacked of the tastes of a young girl, the Sage Sion was lying on an enormous cushion. Relaxing comfortably in a loose negligee, it seemed she hadn't been expecting any guests at all.

"Oh? Youichi? Do you need something?" Seeing him enter the room, she looked a little surprised.

"You're the one who told me to come and give you a report on the situation, weren't you?" He couldn't quite mask his exasperation, but it was business as usual as he walked over to her.

"Youichi, please. Don't talk like that when it's just the two of us," Sion said with a sad frown.

He breathed a sigh. "Geez, fine. But if I don't talk like that regularly, I'm bound to slip up eventually."

"If I allow it as a Sage, there's no problem, is there?"

"A servant like me shouldn't be setting a bad example for the others."

"Well, anyway. What is the situation?"

"First, regarding the invaders. Santarou managed to fight off the Darkness, but the damage to the surrounding area was immense. The region around Altana has been turned into a desert. Fixing it would probably be impossible."

"You said 'fight off.' It wasn't defeated, then?"

"It managed to run away. It took a pretty severe beating, so Santarou said it wouldn't be coming back. But it's hard to say if something like that has feelings or intelligence in the first place."

"I see. Please continue." It seemed that she didn't approve of this news, as she spoke with a somewhat unsatisfied expression.

"Lain has also fought off the Wolf King."

"I understand when it comes to Lain. She's rather fond of animals, after all."

"The Hedgehog incident didn't go well. Yumehisa was sent to deal with it, but was killed. That's the second one this year. At this point, we're just uselessly stacking up the number of victims. Can we not ask the Great Sage to intervene for us?"

"I'm afraid that's impossible. Grandfather is incredibly busy."

Grandfather, my ass, Youichi thought.

Sion and the Great Sage had no actual blood relation. Being a "grandchild" of the Great Sage was only a title. It was nothing but a twisted game of pretend.

"Flirting with the slaves is far too important to him," Sion said, ridicule plain in her voice. Even Youichi knew that they couldn't expect the

Great Sage to help them. He had only thought to bring it up just in case. "I will put together a team myself to deal with the Hedgehog."

The only thing they really knew about the Hedgehog was its outward appearance. It seemed roughly human-shaped, slender and covered entirely in a lustrous black metal. Going by its behavior, it was assumed to be some sort of machine. Something like blades or needles fired out from its joints, so it had come to be referred to as the Hedgehog.

"That's it for the cases we couldn't classify. There are two that are clearly Angel types. One has appeared in Zabora, and the other in Ent. These were eliminated by Shirou and Yoshifumi, respectively. There was one point of interest with the Angels, though. Previously, it seemed their appearances were more or less random, but now that seems to be changing."

"You think they've found what they're looking for?"

"It doesn't seem like they know the exact location yet, but they appear to be gradually narrowing it down. I'm sure they'll find it sooner or later."

The only issue was that neither Youichi nor Sion knew what these Angels were even searching for. In short, they didn't know why they were targeting this world in the first place. It was believed that the Great Sage alone knew the reason, but he was too lazy to bother sharing it with his subordinates.

"Next, about the Sage candidates."

"Ah! I saw that the dragon died somehow. What happened after that?"

"Come on. Are you not concerned about how this dragon actually perished?"

"It was about level one thousand, right? They do die from time to time, don't they?" Sion said seriously.

For Sion, who had surpassed a level of one hundred million, a dragon at level one thousand was little more than a fly to her.

Youichi was struck by a complicated feeling. Sion likely didn't feel that she had changed at all. But whether she liked it or not, possessing such overwhelming power would begin to warp anyone. No matter how much she tried to keep herself under control, she still exuded an unquestionable sense of hubris.

"Ah, whatever, that's related to something else, so I'll set it aside for now. First, it appears they cleared their original mission. There were four casualties."

"Yes. It was probably the correct choice, but they cut off the four powerless among them fairly quickly. It's rare for the Install to be successful on an entire group, so it's a common strategy."

"About that...two of the casualties were those without any powers. The other two were from the five S-Rank candidates."

Sion had mentally sorted her candidates into four different ranks:

S-Rank: Those who had been to this world before. They had already had the Gift installed and possessed a considerable amount of strength. The most promising candidates.

A-Rank: Those possessing particularly powerful skills. Depending on their growth, they could potentially surpass the S-Rank candidates someday. The opposition.

B-Rank: Those who possessed only average skills, their abilities no greater than that of the natives. There was still a small possibility of some sort of growth, however faint. The pit.

C-Rank: Those who possessed the lowest level of skills, in most cases weaker than even the natives. In extremely rare cases, capable of growth, with those who did grow often surpassing the progress of the A and B-Rank candidates. The bottom of the pit.

Finally, those without any powers at all had no possibility of becoming Sages, and therefore weren't included in any category.

"That is unexpected. What are they doing now?"

"Using the powerless ones as bait, everyone else made straight for the city. From there, they decided to head to the capital for their second mission, as advised. But for some reason, three of the S-Rank candidates returned to the starting point, where two of them died, and the survivor headed into the forest."

"Why is that?"

"It's the same as with the dragon. They just died, suddenly and without warning. It was bizarre enough in the case of the dragon, but for these instant deaths to happen repeatedly at the same location is even stranger, don't you think? They expired almost immediately after making contact with the surviving powerless candidates from the bus. That, of course, makes me doubt whether those two are truly all that helpless, but the question then becomes, 'What can these *powerless* candidates do?'"

Their world was very much what one would call a Sword and Sorcery world. Due to the influence of magic, any number of peculiar happenings were possible. Even a single swing of a sword could split a mountain in two.

But that was only as a result of the Gift.

The powerless candidates who hadn't received the Gift should have been nothing more than generic, weak mortals. Weaker than even the natives.

"Looking at the phenomenon, it appears to be some sort of Instant Death ability...but back in our old world, I never came across a single person who could use magic. That goes for you too, right, Sion?"

"I wonder. The Japan we knew could have been a very different place compared to the Japan of today. Maybe it has undergone some significant changes."

"There's no way it changed that much...well, whatever. The problem is that someone who can use Instant Death Magic has now appeared in this world."

"It's not worth worrying about, is it? I assume you know why Instant Death Magic isn't all that popular."

"Hmm...because it's inefficient, right?"

Instant Death Magic was something that indeed existed. However, using it required an enormous amount of magical energy, so basically any other type of magic was far more efficient. And when using it against higher-level opponents, it could be resisted entirely. In short, it was only effective against weaker opponents who could just as easily be dealt with through much simpler means.

"Precisely. Anyone could learn to use Instant Death Magic. Yet barely anyone does. In our long history of war, the presence of Instant Death Magic is well known, and numerous methods of resisting it have been developed. It's common knowledge that an Instant Death Magic that works with a one hundred percent success rate doesn't exist."

"We have to be careful, though. Maybe we should change these last two candidates to C-Rank?"

"You worry too much. But if doing so will make you feel better, go ahead."

The way that she brushed it off, as if it were something so inconsequential, was only proof of the monster that her power had turned her into.

Perhaps this was a cause for optimism, though. Instant Death Magic only worked against weaker opponents. In that case, couldn't it mean that one of their "powerless" candidates might in fact be incredibly strong?

Without the Gift, such a thing is impossible... Even so, Youichi began to get a bad feeling about those two remaining otherworlders.

ACT 2

Chapter 11 — Okay! I Understand! Japanese My Specialty!

Yogiri and Tomochika reached the city in the north around sunset.

"That was pretty far. It was, what, an hour of walking? So probably around four kilometers, give or take."

"Man, I didn't think it would take us this long to get here," Tomochika said, her voice a shade angry.

Judging from the position of the sun, they had been brought to this world in the morning. Despite all that had happened since, the main reason it had taken so long to get to the city was that Yogiri had once again fallen asleep.

"I can't help it. I get sleepy when I use my power."

"Isn't that problematic?" Tomochika asked, a little concerned. After all, right now her safety was resting entirely on that power. It wasn't surprising that it would be a source of worry for her.

"Not really. It's not so bad that I couldn't stay awake if I really wanted to, and I can still feel people's intent to kill when I'm asleep."

"There really is no downside to it, is there?"

Leaving Tomochika to her grumbling, Yogiri surveyed the scene before them. The first thing that he saw was an enormous wall wrapping around the entire city. It seemed the entrances were all closely guarded.

In short, it was a fortress city, which strongly suggested they were protecting themselves from dangerous enemies on the outside.

"Hey, does it look like they're shutting the gate to you?"

"It's probably normal to shut the gates at night…"

"Hurry up, then!"

"I mean, I guess, if you want to."

Tomochika broke into a sprint, with Yogiri following after her.

"Excuse me! Would you mind if we went inside?!" Tomochika called out to the man at the gate. He was wearing western-style armor and carrying a spear. He must have been a soldier.

"@@@@@@@@@?"

"I don't understand a word he's saying!"

"I think it's normal not to speak the language when you arrive in a different world."

"A little, understand. You Japanese?" The guard spoke up again, this time in broken Japanese.

"Yes! Can we enter?"

"Wait. Lord, call."

The guard led them to a waiting room just inside the gate. After taking a seat and waiting for a while, a man who was clearly Japanese entered the room. The splendid clothing he wore indicated that he was the Lord that the guard had referred to.

"Are you two separate from the ones who came at noon? Man, what a pain. What do you want?" he said, not bothering to hide his annoyance.

Since, in this world, you were given an important position if you survived the process of becoming a Sage candidate, this Lord must have been one of the Sage's servants.

"We got separated from the group who came by earlier and are trying to catch up to them. For now, could we at least enter the city?"

After talking it over, they had decided to try and reunite with their classmates. Even if they had been used as bait, being trapped alone in another world was something that Tomochika wanted to avoid.

That said, even putting aside Tomochika's thoughts on the matter, Yogiri had felt the same way. If they wanted to get back to their own world, they would need to find the Sage and get the relevant information out of her. The best way to do that would be to stick with those who were trying to become Sages themselves.

The Lord clicked his tongue. "Normally, we charge an entry fee, but I assume you lot don't have money anyway. We were told not to get in the way of the Sage candidates, so I guess you can come inside."

"It seems like the others went on to the capital. Where should we go to follow them?"

"Let me rephrase that. The Sage told us not to get in your way, but she never said we had to help you. Figure it out on your own."

"Well, thanks, I guess."

It seemed there was nothing to be gained by staying there. Yogiri stood up, prompting Tomochika to follow suit.

"Ah, right, right. If you don't have any money, I guess you won't be able to find somewhere to sleep. If you want, I can put the girl up in my mansion."

"No, thank you!" Although the Lord's eyes had taken on a rather vulgar look, Tomochika didn't give him a second glance. Grabbing Yogiri's hand, she pulled him out of the room.

Once they had made it into the city, she finally stopped and let him go.

"You really dislike him that much, huh?" Yogiri was a little doubtful.

Tomochika seemed strangely flustered. "Of course he makes me angry, but the main thing I'm worried about is his life. I was worried you might end up killing him."

"What am I, a serial killer?"

"I'm kind of surprised you haven't noticed."

"Hey now. It's not like I'm killing people just because I don't like them. What do you think I am?"

Yogiri felt a little hurt. It wasn't a big deal, but it seemed like she thought he was just dropping people left and right for no reason.

Apparently unaware of his feelings, Tomochika had already moved on and was excitedly inspecting their surroundings. "Hey, look! This is totally a classic fantasy city, isn't it? Oh! There are even people that look like cats! Beastkin, I guess?"

A stone road ran through a town of stone-crafted buildings before them. It was a scene that Yogiri had long grown accustomed to — that of medieval European cities from his video games.

"Looks like they don't have electricity. I guess charging this thing is really going to be impossible."

"Are you still on about that? I think the more important question is, what are we going to do now?"

"Well, whatever we're doing, I guess we should do it while we still have daylight. Any ideas?"

"First, I think we should get some weapons!" From her tone, it appeared that Tomochika thought this was a matter of great importance.

They couldn't read the language of this world, of course, but they used the pictures on the signs to eventually locate what appeared to be a weapons shop. Yogiri and Tomochika made their way inside.

"I'm not sure we really need weapons to protect ourselves."

"But if we rely solely on you to protect us, you'll just flat-out kill everyone we come up against."

"Live by the sword, die by the sword, you know? That's what they get for attacking us."

"But if we have weapons, maybe it'll discourage people from attacking us in the first place."

"I wonder about that. I don't think that having weapons will make much of a difference." It was highly unlikely that a pair of amateurs wielding daggers and the like would deter anyone who truly meant them harm.

The inside of the store was quite luxurious. Apparently, there was a significant demand for weapons, which likely meant a corresponding level of local danger.

A wide range of gear was on display within, and a number of customers were browsing the wares. Behind the counter were what he assumed to be several particularly high-class items.

Among the customers were beings who were clearly not human. Other than the cat-eared people that Tomochika had pointed out, there were also those covered entirely in fur or scales. It seemed there were a number of different races in this world.

"What about this?" Tomochika asked, handing Yogiri a sword with a blade about thirty centimeters long. From the way she handled it without any hesitation, he guessed that she was somewhat used to dealing with them.

Yogiri took the sword from her. It was lighter than he'd expected and felt comfortable in his hands, but he didn't think it was something that he'd be able to use effectively.

"If we want it for intimidation purposes, shouldn't we get something a bit more dangerous-looking?"

"Walking around with something heavy will be difficult. And you don't look all that strong."

"Maybe I don't need anything after all. I think it's just going to get in the way." Trying to use a weapon that he wasn't familiar with would only open him up to lowering his guard.

"Oh. Well, I'm not going to force you or anything." She began looking around for a weapon of her own. "Hmmm, walking around with something big will be inconvenient, but the smaller ones won't have much of a range...could I put a nock spear on this...?" Picking up the bow, Tomochika continued to mutter to herself.

"Not to interrupt, but how do you plan on talking to the clerk?"

"I can just show them the weapon and hand over some money, right?" You could call it excessive optimism, but she was pretty brave. She didn't seem at all bothered by the obvious language barrier.

In the end, she picked a small bow and quiver and brought them over to the counter.

"Excuse me, do you speak Japanese?"

"Okay! I understand! Japanese people my specialty!" He was hardly fluent, but the natives of this world had likely grown used to dealing with otherworlders.

As Tomochika pulled out a handful of money, the clerk's expression turned to one of surprise. Apparently, she had taken out a whole lot of it. But all the pair had on them were coins and jewels that looked fairly expensive. As it was too much of a nuisance to try and count it all out, she handed it all to the clerk and left it at that.

"Buying it is all very well, but aren't bows kind of hard to use?"

"It's fine, I'm used to it."

"Oh, were you in the Archery Club?"

"I wasn't in any club, but yeah, something like that," she said, putting the bow into her backpack. After that, they left the weapons shop behind.

Standing just outside the store was a girl with cat ears. From the way she was staring, it seemed she had been waiting for them.

"You guys from Japan? First time seeing you around here. You having any problems?" She called out in fluent Japanese — although her speech was peppered with bizarre, cat-like "meows" between each word.

Chapter 12 — All the Bad People Seem to Be Japanese, Though!

An off-putting cat-eared girl.

That was Yogiri's first impression of the stranger. She was about the same height as Tomochika. With bits of armor here and there, and a sword at her side, she appeared to be a warrior of some sort.

"Wow, your Japanese is so good!"

Tomochika was unreservedly impressed. But there was always that first impression to deal with. Yogiri couldn't help but be on his guard against someone who had singled them out for no apparent reason.

"But of course! The girls here all study Japanese, after all!"

"Why?"

"To get along with the Japanese boys, of course! They have great future prospects and are famously easy to seduce."

"Awfully blunt, aren't we?"

"Why not? Not like it's something worth hiding."

"But isn't that the same for men? Why aren't they as good at Japanese?"

"Japanese girls don't pay much attention to normal folk here. They're always looking at nobility or royalty, so the men are doomed to fail even if they try."

"I don't think that's necessarily the case...although I can understand why it would be."

"So, what do you want?" Yogiri interjected.

"Ah, right. I was wondering if there's anything you needed help with. Just one more step on the path of the husband hunt! Of course, I have no intention of splitting you up from your girlfriend, but making friends like this is the secret to broadening my scope, you know?"

"Oh, I'm not his girlfriend or anything, but I wouldn't try anything with this guy if I were you. He's pretty messed up."

"Is that so? He looks good enough to me."

"What do you mean by 'helping' us?"

"I could give you a tour of the city, that kind of thing? I figure if you've just arrived, you probably don't know your left from your right."

"And all you want in return is to be friends?"

"Yup!"

"Well?" Yogiri asked, looking at Tomochika. In truth, he thought it was highly suspicious, but it didn't seem like she was trying to take advantage of them yet, so he figured he'd leave it up to his companion.

"She's right, we have no idea where anything is around here."

Finding the weapons store so quickly had been sheer luck. If there was somewhere else they needed to go, asking a guide for help would definitely make things easier.

"All right. Could you show us around then?"

"Thank you! My name is Mireiyu. Outside the city, I work in transportation, but inside I'm just looking for marriage options. Can I ask you your names?"

"Yogiri Takatou."

"I'm Tomochika Dannoura. Nice to meet you."

Mireiyu gave a slight nod. "Yogiri and Tomochika. Got it! So, where did you want to go?"

"I'd like to see a bunch of things before it gets dark..."

"Then I'll start by showing you what's right around here, and we'll go grab dinner afterwards. How does that sound?"

And that's exactly what happened.

After shopping around at a variety of stores, they ended up at a nice restaurant for dinner.

"It seems so cheerful here, doesn't it? Everyone looks like they have everything they could ever need."

Tomochika had changed into the clothes that she'd bought in the city. She was now wearing a light blue tunic with shorts. It would have stood out quite a bit in Japan, but it seemed to fit with this world's fashion trends.

Yogiri was still wearing the same clothes, although he had removed his blazer. It was a look that stood out in this world, but there were so many different styles of clothing worn by the locals that it didn't draw too much attention.

The city was quite a comfortable place. All the necessities of life seemed to have been put together with Japanese people in mind, but maybe that was to be expected. It almost felt like the two of them could slip into a normal routine practically overnight. Even the food they had eaten wasn't all that different from what they'd have had back home.

"Well, that's just limited to cities of a certain size, you know? If you go out into the country, things get pretty bad."

"What do you mean?"

"Small villages and those types of places don't have the protection of the Sages. It takes everything they have just to defend themselves against the monsters, so they have no room to grow and develop."

This world, they had learned, was populated by a number of monsters. The regions protected by barriers that the Sages had constructed were safe enough, but anywhere else was fairly dangerous.

"Speaking of Sages, did the two of you not get a Gift from them?"

The Gift was apparently something that could be inherited from others, and it was normally passed on from parent to child. On top of that, while it had a wide range of uses, the Gift given by the Sages was rather unique, and those otherworlders who could use it well were seen as being quite special.

"What makes you think that?"

"Well, of course I can tell. My Discernment skill isn't especially high, but I can assess, generally, how strong someone is. And you two are definitely 'super weak.'"

Hanakawa had told them that it took a high level of Discernment to be able to read others' Statuses, but apparently a low level was enough to determine their overall standing. Yogiri was sure that he would have this conversation more than once while they were there. He would need to come up with a plan to deal with it.

"Ah! Are you aiming for a Gift from a Swordmaster? In that case, I could definitely understand. But finding a Swordmaster without a Gift in the first place will be almost impossible."

Yogiri continued to eat his dinner, content to let Mireiyu fill in the gaps herself.

"Hmm, I kind of figured it would end this way."

Shortly after dinner, Yogiri and Tomochika had ended up in a dead end back alley. The exit of said alley was now blocked by a crowd of beastkin. The pair had been following Mireiyu to what was supposed to be a place for them to stay for the night.

"Oh, you did? Sorry! I thought you were such good kids, just following me without a thought after I was a little nice to you."

Tomochika, a little surprised at first, didn't take long to fall into a sulk.

"Well, life just isn't that easy, is it?" Mireiyu said, standing amid the crowd of beastkin like it was the most natural thing in the world.

It was well into the night, but the bright moonlight meant visibility around them wasn't bad. Their would-be assailants were comprised of ten male and female beastkin, as well as one human. All were armed and seemed extremely comfortable with their weapons. Yogiri figured this type of criminal activity was simply business as usual for them.

"Can we talk about this?"

"You seem pretty laid back. What do you wanna talk about?" someone who looked like their leader scoffed, taking a step towards them.

He looked Japanese through and through. Likely in his early thirties, he had a large build and a violent air about him.

"You're after money?" Tomochika asked. Mireiyu had seen them in the weapons shop. She must have noticed how much they were carrying.

"We'll be taking your money, of course, but it's not just that," said the leader. "Our main interest is in powerless otherworlders like you two. Thanks to our kind wreaking havoc on this world, the nobles here have come to hate us. But there's nothing they can do about the strong ones. So powerless interlopers have become quite valuable. They make great punching bags!"

"There really are no good people in this world, are there?"

"You say that, but it sounds like all the bad people here are Japanese!"

Yogiri couldn't help but agree with Tomochika's assessment. "Okay, I get it. I'm just going to kill you all then, is that okay?"

"Ah, you can relax. It's not like we're gonna kill you or anything. Though you'd probably be happier if you did croak right now!"

The crowd of beastkin laughed along with their leader's sneer.

All right, killing these people definitely won't be much of a weight on my conscience.

Yogiri was relieved.

Chapter 13 — Let's Start With Killing the Ones Behind Us

"Mireiyu! We'll let it all slide, so please leave! I know how he looks, but Takatou is actually really strong! There's no way you guys can fight him!" Tomochika must have known there was no way they'd listen to her. But even so, she couldn't just stay quiet and do nothing.

"Oh? Bluffs like that won't work on me, you know? In this world, the Gift is everything. There's nothing the two of you can do without it."

"And I have a high level in Discernment," their leader added, "so I can tell for sure that you don't have the Gift."

As they were speaking, five of the beastkin walked around behind them. Yogiri took stock of their opponents' equipment. Most of them seemed to be using swords. Those who were barehanded may have had some sort of magic. There were also those with weighted nets. No doubt their objective was to capture them.

"First of all, let's have you five die."

All at once, the beastkin that had circled around behind them collapsed. Yogiri had cut their numbers in half right from the start. Now it was time for an experiment in mercy.

During their walk to the city, Yogiri and Tomochika had discussed the way in which he used his power. While she was still troubled by it, she did eventually accept the idea of killing in self-defense. But, thanks to the overwhelming advantage that his power gave him, Yogiri had a tendency to be overly reliant on it. Tomochika had asked if he couldn't show a bit more restraint.

"Wait, what did you do…?"

In an instant, the leader of the beastkin realized that something was wrong. Of course, if he had figured out that much, he should have already been running away. Instead, he was standing stock still, hyper alert. He seemed completely unprepared to deal with a situation like this. The best course of action was to beg for his life. There was no guarantee it would work, but it was the best chance he had. After all, whether they ran away or tried to attack him head-on, Yogiri still planned on bringing all of them down.

There were six left now. He quickly decided on a suitable order in which to kill them off.

"Half of you, die."

He pointed at a beastkin who looked like a tiger, causing him to immediately drop to the ground. His target had been only the creature's lower body. This was one of the ways he had thought of to "go easier" on his opponents.

Yogiri's ability was to kill anything he targeted. In that case, if he divided up a target, could he kill only one part of a person? Having never considered showing mercy before, he honestly had no idea how it would turn out.

The tiger man screamed something in a language he couldn't understand. It appeared he was still alive, but before long, his screams abruptly cut off.

Well, perhaps that was to be expected. If you lost the lower half of your body, it was only natural that the rest would follow suit. He didn't know exactly what was going on inside the target's body when it happened, but regardless, it seemed that killing half of the body was too much. He decided to limit the scope further.

"Right ankle."

This time, his target was a sheep beastkin. But the experiment failed. Maybe it was just inexperience, but he couldn't successfully restrict the power to that one small place. As a result, his victim died instantly.

"Left arm."

He next targeted a leopard man and was much more successful. But in the end, it still led to the total death of the target. He had completely stopped the function of the left arm. Certainly, there were those who could survive losing an arm like that, but it was equally normal for someone to die from the shock of the experience.

"This approach doesn't seem to be working very well..." Yogiri muttered to himself. At this rate, it would just be easier to kill them without overthinking it.

"Eyeballs."

His target this time was a dog-like creature. At last, he achieved something approaching actual success. Although it was a smaller body part than the ankle, perhaps it helped that it was a more distinctive one. With a howl, the dog man fell over, holding his hands to his eyes.

"Nose, ears."

Yogiri continued to unleash his power. If the beastkin possessed similar senses to that of a dog, he couldn't leave the ears or nose intact.

Another success. But killing three of the dog man's five senses didn't feel particularly merciful.

"Wh-What is happening?! What the hell are you?!" Mireiyu began to panic. In only a few moments, her group had been reduced to three — the Japanese leader, Mireiyu herself, and a lizard beastkin of unknown gender.

Although barehanded, the lizard was radiating a clear intent to kill. But whatever it had been planning, Yogiri's counter was faster, killing the creature instantly.

Now there were only two.

"Well, that settles that. I don't think there's much point in explaining myself further."

Unlike with Hanakawa, Yogiri had no need to extract information from them. As such, there was no need to explain the threat in further detail.

Yogiri turned to Tomochika. She had a pained expression on her face but showed no signs of trying to stop him. It seemed she was ready to do whatever it took.

"W-Wait! Please, don't kill me! I was only doing what this guy told me to! My little brother is starving, waiting for me at home! My father abandoned us to chase after some woman, and my mother needs expensive medicine for her illness! I needed the money!"

It appeared her bizarre, cat-like manner of speaking up until then had all been to curry favor with them, and she had now decided, correctly, that it would have the opposite effect. Yogiri had certainly found her weird inflections extremely annoying.

"Oh, really?"

"Yes! Yes! It's true! So please —" Mireiyu grasped desperately at the single thread of compassion she saw in Yogiri's words. Stepping away from the leader of their group, she began to approach the two of them.

"Not really a good enough reason for robbing and kidnapping though, is it?"

Mireiyu's expression immediately filled with despair, her feet stopping mid-stride.

"What...what are you?... You're supposed to be powerless..." The leader shrank back, terror plain on his face.

"Well, it seems I can go easy if I want to, but it's pretty inefficient. I don't see much of a point to it, either." His words did little more than fan the flames of their fear, although that hadn't actually been Yogiri's intention.

"We're both Japanese, right? *Right?* Please, don't kill me! This is the only way to get by in this world!"

"Don't act like we're the same, please." In the end, Yogiri had no doubt this guy would simply run away and continue his criminal lifestyle without a second thought. Letting them live would only be a nuisance later.

"Die."

He unleashed his power at the two of them. He didn't especially want to kill them, but the experiments had to continue.

Nothing happened.

"Ha, haha! Looks like it failed!"

"Now's our chance!!"

The two of them immediately broke into a run, fleeing from the alley.

"Wait, what? Are we really letting them go?!" Tomochika may not have been particularly happy about the way Yogiri had been dealing with things, but even she recognized the danger it presented if their would-be abductors escaped.

"I didn't let them go..."

But even as he said that, the two thugs were running full tilt into the depths of the city, disappearing into the night.

Mireiyu ran with everything she had. Leaning forward, she dropped to her hands and feet, soaring down the stone road on all fours.

"Hey! Don't leave me behind!" Whatever her former leader was saying, Mireiyu ignored him. There was no way she was slowing down for him.

Taking one turn after another onto numerous side streets, she eventually bounded up the wall of a building, coming to a stop only when she had decided she was far enough away to be safe. Crouching low on the roof of the building, she could feel her heart pounding from the exertion of her escape.

"What was that...that monster...?"

She didn't understand at all. With only one or two words from Yogiri, her companions had all collapsed. It was like some sort of elaborate practical joke. There was no impression of reality to it at all. But its lack of realism only served to strengthen her conviction that an equally irrational death had been waiting for her as well.

They were supposed to be worthless. Powerless. Those with no abilities were less than slaves in this world. And otherworlders with no powers were extraordinarily rare. When she had seen them at the weapons shop, she had felt incredibly lucky. After an easy kidnapping, she could sell them to some noble for a great price. That should have been the end of it. So how had it ended up this way? She simply couldn't accept it.

But none of that mattered now. She had escaped. That in and of itself was worthy of celebration. For the moment, she just had to focus on calming down.

As these thoughts ran through her mind, Mireiyu realized how unnaturally quiet it had become. There wasn't a single sound around her. And when she finally understood what it meant, it was like a rod of ice stabbing her in the back.

Her heart had been racing up until that point, yet she realized she could no longer feel it now.

Mireiyu gave one last groan. She couldn't breathe.

Her heart had stopped.

Her vision was rapidly growing dark.

Desperately, she extended her claws, trying to dig into the roof below her, but at this point it was meaningless. The strength left her limbs, and her consciousness began to fail.

I should never have gotten involved with them...

And then, Mireiyu slipped away into darkness.

"I already explained this on our way here...the effects of my power are irreversible. Once it's been activated, there's no way to stop it. They will definitely die."

"Yeah, I remember you saying that."

"The timing is somewhat flexible, though. I won't claim that delayed death actually qualifies as 'taking it easy' on them, but I had never tried it before and figured I'd give it a shot."

"So..."

"They're dead, somewhere out there."

From Yogiri's perspective, he had merely retaliated against a band of common thieves. Tomochika understood that to some degree, but she seemed unable to simply leave it at that just yet.

"Anyway, let's get out of here. Even if there's no evidence, it could be bad if we're here when the bodies are discovered."

"R-Right! If someone sees us, they'll think we're the culprits!"

Without hesitation, they left the alley behind. Or at least, they tried to.

As they made their way to the exit, a figure stepped forward to block their path.

"Halt," it commanded them in stern, fluent Japanese.

"What's up?" Yogiri asked, stopping in front of the figure.

"We're with the City Guard. I have some questions for you," said the armor-clad woman. Behind her were a number of other soldiers, so she must have been the highest ranked among them.

"All right. But we just came across this scene when we got lost and ended up in this alley by chance," Yogiri replied smoothly, sweeping his gaze around him.

"Nice try," said the soldier with a snort, her voice brimming with confidence. "Unfortunately, we've been watching from over here from the start."

"And now they think we're the culprits!" Tomochika cried.

Chapter 14 — I'm Not Sharing a Room With a Guy That Goes to Love Hotels

"Wait, hold on a second! If you're a guard, that means your job is to keep the city safe, right?!"

"Yes. And?" the soldier responded without batting an eye. Blonde hair framing an attractive, blue-eyed face made it clear that she wasn't Japanese, but she still spoke the language like it was second nature to her.

"Then what do you mean you saw everything from the beginning?! We were being attacked! Why didn't you help us?!"

"You've got to break a few eggs to make an omelette, right? I can't blame you for being upset when you haven't seen the whole picture. We're investigating a particular criminal organization, trying to smoke out the nobles who are running things behind the curtain."

"In other words, you were planning on waiting to see who they sold us off to?" Yogiri asked, making sure to keep his tone polite. There wasn't any reason to start a confrontation.

"Precisely! Even if we had arrested the whole gang just now, it's unlikely they would have told us anything. We've tried that a number of times already, after all."

"Takatou...it looks like this world really *is* full of nothing but terrible people..."

While he certainly agreed, Yogiri was more concerned with how freely the guard was sharing this information. It was surprising that she would speak so openly about an official investigation.

"Well, for some reason they all started collapsing one after another. So what do you want from us?" Yogiri continued to feign ignorance. Killing the soldiers would be easy enough...but this time he was up against public officials. If he could talk his way out of it, that would be a far better option.

"That's the thing! From where I was standing, they all seemed to fall over on their own. I can't imagine what could have happened. Since the two of you were so close, I thought you might be able to clear it up for us easily enough."

"Did it not occur to you that we might have done something to them? In which case, wouldn't it be dangerous for you to be close to us right now?" Maybe he was taking it a step too far, but Yogiri couldn't help himself.

"Oh, of course there was a high probability that you did something to them. After all, you were just about to be kidnapped! However...we have the blessings of the Sage. The Gift rendered to otherworlders is ineffective against us. Ah, from that look, I'm guessing you didn't know that, did you? You're starting to get a little worried, perhaps?" The guard broke into a grin, as if she had just pinned them into a corner.

If the Gift was a power granted by the Sages, it made sense that the Sages would have a system to counter it. There were probably a fair number of otherworlders who had received these Gifts. As such, those in charge of keeping the peace would need a way of dealing with them. It would also make it difficult for those granted power by the Sages to turn that power against them.

Yogiri felt that he had finally caught a glimpse of the way this world truly worked. The Sages summoned candidates, and from them new Sages were born. Those new Sages then summoned more candidates. In this way, they had built a layered structure where those at the bottom could never disobey those above them.

"No, I'm not all that worried since the two of us don't have the Gift in the first place."

"Wait, what?! Hey, Jorge! Inspect them!"

"Yes…as they say, they don't possess the Gift," a man standing just behind the leader answered. He also spoke in perfect Japanese. "In addition, I see no traces of magic in the vicinity. The probability that they did something themselves seems rather low."

"What is going on here?!"

"Not sure what you expect me to say," Yogiri quipped.

"Then why did you lie?! Can't you see how suspicious that looks?!"

"I thought explaining would be a pain. I'll apologize for lying, but we really don't know anything. It's not like you would have believed us if we'd simply said that they all started collapsing on their own."

"Dammit! Fine! Let's go — inspect the bodies!" Sulking like a child, the captain led her retinue into the alley.

The guard named Jorge stopped beside them as they passed. "My sincere apologies. I'm sure being accosted like this is quite frustrating, but Captain Edelgart isn't such a bad person. I guess you could say she has a tendency to get tunnel vision."

"As long as her suspicions have been cleared up, it's not a problem. If I may be blunt, did you actually intend to let them kidnap us?"

"Yes, and it pains me to admit it," he replied apologetically. "It appeared they had no intention of killing you just then, so our plan was to observe and follow."

"Well, all's well that ends well, I suppose."

"I'm afraid we can't simply allow you to return home like nothing happened, though. Could I trouble you to accompany us to headquarters? I'd like to take down a written statement."

"Sure. And, not like I'm asking in exchange or anything, but could you show us somewhere we can stay for the night? We were actually on our way to find a hotel but were led here instead."

"Of course. I can at least do that much."

"Hey! One of them is alive!" the captain shouted, as if she had made some great discovery.

It was the dog beastkin, the only one that Yogiri had decided to spare.

Maybe I should kill him after all... Yogiri thought briefly. But after going through the trouble of keeping him alive in the first place, as irritating as it was, he decided to let it be.

After giving their statements, Yogiri and Tomochika were released at once. Yogiri was half expecting to be arrested on the spot, but apparently the request for a written statement had not been a cover. It seemed the people of this world had an absolute trust in the Gift. The two of them, possessing no obvious abilities, simply didn't qualify as viable suspects.

As promised, Jorge introduced them to a number of hotels, from which they picked the most luxurious. A cheaper option might have had problems with cleanliness and safety, and they had an abundance of money at the moment so there was no reason to be stingy. The two of them had agreed on that immediately.

"Wow! What is this?! This is amazing! It's like a castle! Not that I've been inside a castle before..." Tomochika began gushing the moment she stepped inside.

The lobby was bright as day, lit by numerous shining objects. At a glance, all of the fixtures were clearly expensive items, but none of it seemed overdone. The place was perfectly clean, and not a speck of garbage was visible anywhere.

"Does this look kind of like a Love Hotel to you?"

"Hang on, you've been to one before?!" Tomochika's surprise continued to grow.

"Yeah, I hid in one once. It was a lot like this."

"Well now I can't help feeling that all this gaudy stuff makes it look cheap!"

"So, what are we going to do for rooms? Just one for the both of us?"
On top of being in a high-class hotel, this was a whole other world. There

was no way of knowing what could happen. When it came to safety, it was in their best interest to stay as close to each other as possible.

"No way I'm sharing a room with a guy that visits Love Hotels."

"Then I'll see if I can get us adjacent rooms." His suggestion hadn't been all that serious anyway. Being in the room immediately next to hers was probably good enough for protection purposes.

Heading to the front desk, they filled out the paperwork. Perhaps because it was such a high-class hotel, they had no problem doing so entirely in Japanese.

The two of them decided to meet up in the lobby the next morning.

Tomochika stepped into her room.

The interior was rather bright at first. But whether it was magic or electricity, it seemed she had free control over the light levels. Despite being a single room, it was a remarkably large and luxurious space. The bed was big enough that the two of them could have slept side by side with plenty of room to spare.

"Ugh, what am I even thinking?!"

As it was, Tomochika was already relying on Yogiri for everything. Without his help, there was no way she would have made it this far. She was plenty thankful for that. So if Yogiri came to her now, she felt it might be difficult to turn him down.

"But I wonder. Is he really all that interested in me? Or does he just like my boobs?"

While she wasn't happy with the idea of him suddenly coming on to her, if he followed the right steps, then...

As that kind of vague feeling tried to creep its way into her head, it was immediately blown away by the sudden realization that she was not alone.

"Who are you?!"

A moment before, she had been looking at an empty room. But now someone was floating in the air right in front of her.

"Chiharu?!"

She should have immediately run to find Yogiri — that was the best course of action, she knew, but she just couldn't bring herself to do it. Because she had seen this person before.

But perhaps saying that about her own sister was an understatement.

Chapter 15 — My Guardian Spirit is the Strongest; This World Doesn't Stand a Chance!

Tomochika was speechless. Wrapped in a Japanese kimono, her own sister was floating in the middle of her luxury hotel room. While that in and of itself was strange enough, it was made all the more bizarre by the fact that they were in another world. There was no way her sister should have been there.

"You *are* Chiharu...right?"

Maybe she had been summoned to this world as well? Or had she died, and this was her ghost? Either case seemed equally likely. And how had she learned to float in the air that way? Her sister, Chiharu Dannoura, was an existence that defied common sense.

Please don't confuse me with her!

A voice echoed in Tomochika's head. But even as it said the words, she couldn't think of the voice as belonging to anyone but her sister.

"No, no, no, you *have* to be my sister, right? I don't know why you're wearing a kimono, but there's no way anyone else could look as strange as her."

Short and wide, far exceeding what one could call plump — that

was her sister. For someone so identifiable from her silhouette, seeing her clearly like this left no room for doubt.

I am Mokomoko Dannoura! Wife of the son of the founder of the Dannoura School, the one who revived the family line! I am the Guardian Deity of the Dannoura School, your ancestor, your watchful protector, your guardian spirit!

"Slow down, please! I can't keep up like this! Uhh…if you revived the family line, you didn't really revive it too much, did you?"

Heh, pathetic! Your snark leaves me unfazed!

"Now my jokes are being criticized by a ghost?!"

At that point, Tomochika accepted that maybe this wasn't her sister after all. Chiharu was always one to play the fool, so she would never have complained about the quality of someone else's jokes.

"So…you really aren't my sister?"

I am Mokomoko Dannoura!

"Why are you here?" Even if she said she was Tomochika's guardian spirit, such things didn't usually appear without warning, did they?

As your guardian spirit, I'm usually limited to protecting you from the attacks of evil spirits. However, in a situation like this, such a restriction seems meaningless, so I thought I would help more directly. But there is no need to have this conversation standing up. Set down your luggage and have a seat.

With a sigh, Tomochika complied. As suspicious as this Mokomoko was, she found it hard to disobey her. Maybe because she looked like her sister, it was hard to think of her as a stranger. Laying the bags she was carrying on the floor, Tomochika took a seat on the bed.

"I have a lot of questions. Is that okay?"

Ask to your heart's content!

"Why did you show up now? If you were planning on saving me, shouldn't you have shown up earlier?"

I was waiting for you to be alone. That boy is truly dangerous!

"That boy…you mean Takatou?"

Correct. If I were to carelessly appear before him, he could erase me in an instant. So I would be very grateful if you could warn him of my existence in advance tomorrow.

"That's fine, but you're a ghost, right? How could his power even hurt you?" Yogiri's abilities were certainly impressive, but Tomochika wasn't so sure it would work against ghosts.

As a high-level divine spirit, I instinctively got a "this guy is dangerous" vibe. That is all. I felt it very strongly from him.

"Well, he'll understand if we just talk to him…I think. I'll let him know, so I'm sure it'll be okay. And what do you mean by 'saving me?'"

Ah, yes. If I were to put it into modern web novel terms, the title would be "My Guardian Spirit Is The Strongest, This World Doesn't Stand A Chance!" Or something along those lines, I guess.

"I have absolutely no idea what that means."

It was a rather bizarre example coming from a ghost from the Heian era.

I suppose I should make it clear that, as a spiritual being, I can't offer you physical assistance. My primary focus is on spiritual defense. Actually, I have already been doing just that. There was some strange system called the Gift, correct? I am the one who prevented it from reaching you.

"That was your fault?! Why couldn't you have just left things alone?!"

Oh? Were you interested in such a vague, suspicious power?

That put Tomochika at a loss for words. True, if she had received the Gift, she wouldn't have been split up from her classmates. But she had no way of knowing whether that would be better than her current situation.

Of course, it has its benefits. The Gift is a thing designed for battle. By having it installed, one becomes more aggressive, the fear of death is suppressed, and aversion to slaughter is reduced.

"Um, that actually sounds a bit dangerous."

Should a monster appear before you, being scared of every little thing will only get you killed, no? If you wish to live in this world, combat cannot be avoided. The main benefit of the Gift is that any fool can gain the ability to fight.

"So you don't think things like classes and skills are important?"

Little more than gambling. Even the Sages don't know what sort of abilities will arise when they hand out the Gift. There are some abilities which are truly detrimental.

"So, if those are the advantages, what are the disadvantages?"

It is a fundamentally untrustworthy thing. It eats into the depths of your soul. I do not know precisely what it does there, nor to what end. But the moment one accepts that power, the Sages have uncontested control over your life and death.

Tomochika had difficulty picturing something like her own soul, but it wasn't hard to grasp that being freely manipulated by someone else was a bad thing.

"Thank you. I suppose I should say that much, shouldn't I?"

Yes! Shower me with your appreciation!

Although she had started out by speaking politely, Tomochika's usual frankness was gradually slipping back into her speech. Luckily, Mokomoko seemed to have no particular qualms about that.

"Hey, does this mean that others who failed the Gift installation have guardian spirits as well?"

Such knowledge is beyond me. The only spirit that was able to accompany your class to this world was myself.

Mokomoko's expression became rather proud. It was hard to say at this point, but Tomochika wondered if there was in fact some reason that the installation had failed on those who died on the bus.

"You said you were the guardian deity of the Dannoura School, right? Doesn't it make more sense for you to be with my sister?" Tomochika's older sister Chiharu was the true successor to the Dannoura School. If Mokomoko was going to protect any of them, it made more sense for it to be her.

She is rather feeble, I'm afraid. Not suited at all to be a successor. It is therefore necessary that you return to our world alive.

The Dannoura School of Archery. A comprehensive martial art developed during the Heian era, it was still passed down through generations of the Dannoura family today. Tomochika was knowledgeable enough about it, but in a world with dragons, magic, and superpowered skills, she found it hard to believe that some ancient form of archery would be much help.

"Of course I want to go back, but right now all I can do is rely on Takatou..."

Well, with your current education in the Dannoura School, such a task seems almost impossible. So! I shall personally instruct you in the true arts of your family!

Mokomoko's smile was smug as she spoke. Tomochika was anything but reassured.

Tomochika looked rather exhausted when she stepped into the lobby the next morning.

"Good morning. Couldn't sleep last night?" Yogiri had had no such difficulties and looked perfectly well rested.

"Something like that. It's complicated. So, what are we doing today? Information hunting to find out where the others went?"

Their immediate goal was to reunite with their classmates, who had headed to the capital. To do that, they'd need to find out how to get to the capital themselves.

"Well, about that. I kind of already did."

"What? When?"

"Last night."

"What, were you out walking around by yourself?"

"No, I just asked her. Apparently she's a concierge." Yogiri pointed to a corner of the lobby. Standing there was a woman wearing a suit. As Tomochika turned to look at her, she gave a short bow. Her flawless beauty made Tomochika feel a sort of irrational pressure.

"She looked up where our classmates were, showed me a number of ways to get there, prepared some items to help with the language barrier and hiding our Stats, and found a solution for charging my handheld, too."

"This concierge is too much! Is there anything left for us to even do?!"

All of the problems that Tomochika had been racking her brain over, this concierge had solved in a single night.

Chapter 16 — You Can Just Make a Charger

They were now sitting in a corner of the lobby. Yogiri and Tomochika were across from the concierge, with a map spread out on the desk between them.

"My name is Celestina, and I am working as a concierge for this hotel."

"Ah, nice to meet you." Now that Tomochika had arrived, the concierge was explaining everything to her as well.

"From the city of Quenza, where we are now, the capital city of Valeria is about one hundred and forty kilometers as the crow flies. In more familiar terms, I'd say it's roughly the same distance as Osaka to Nagoya."

"In a way, this is so easy to understand that I'm getting more confused!" Celestina's Japanese was flawless. Maybe it was to be expected that she would also have a thorough knowledge of Japanese geography.

"Osaka and Nagoya, huh? I wonder which is the capital."

"Takatou! Could you please avoid saying things that sound like they'll start a war?!"

"There are numerous routes that could take you to the capital, but it appears your classmates have departed on foot. If they are intending to build up combat experience along the way, it is highly likely they will be passing through the Haqua Forest."

Yogiri looked at the map. If one walked in a straight line to the capital, they would pass through the Haqua Forest, Garula Canyon, and Meld Plains, in that order. But they had no way of knowing where their classmates were within those areas.

Celestina placed a number of sheets of paper on the desk before them.

"This is a distribution of the monsters that are currently within the Haqua Forest, and this is a calculation of the probability of encountering each one, taking into account their individual properties and behaviors. Even at a low level, Sage candidates are stronger than ordinary soldiers. Factoring that in, plus combat and rest time, we can surmise they will be around this area," she said, pointing to a spot on the map.

A symbol was marked in the middle of the forest. It was a spot about ten kilometers away from their current position in Quenza.

"After a whole day, they only made it that far?"

"That forest is particularly dangerous. All things considered, they are actually moving quite fast."

"So, there are a number of routes we can take to catch up to them, but Celestina recommended going by steam engine."

"Yes. The tracks take a wide detour around the forest. Hanabusa Station is between the Haqua Forest and the Garula Canyon, so it should be possible to get ahead of them. It is also possible that they have taken an entirely different route, but even in that case you should be able to reunite with them at the capital itself. Chasing after them would probably be quite a nuisance."

"That's awfully frank of you..." Tomochika muttered.

"How long would it take them to reach Hanabusa?"

"It's impossible to give a precise calculation, but assuming they continue to train as they travel, I would expect it to take them a week at the bare minimum."

"So we need to get to Hanabusa in less than a week. Sounds like that should be no problem if we're going by train." Once again, Yogiri looked at the map. He didn't know exactly how fast these steam engines traveled, but given the distance, he thought it would only take them a matter of hours.

"Unfortunately, I would advise you to leave as soon as possible. The train schedules are fairly irregular. If everything runs smoothly, it will only take three hours. But there are instances where the journey can take multiple days as well."

"That's quite the range."

"This world is very dangerous beyond the city walls. The existence of monsters does a lot to hamper the running of the trains."

"Well, regardless, we should leave as soon as we can, then. I'm fine with that."

And so the plan was set.

Celestina placed two slips of paper on the table. "Here are tickets to the capital, departing at noon."

"Wait, you can just pull something like that out of your pocket at any time?!"

"Our hotel maintains guaranteed seats on all trains."

Perhaps if they asked for companions or equipment, she could pull those out as well.

With their discussion of travel plans concluded, Celestina pulled a pair of necklaces off a shelf right behind her and placed them onto the table. "Mr. Takatou mentioned that money is no issue for you, so although it was a little expensive, I've managed to prepare these necklaces for you. They are magic items that should handle the problem of translation. I cannot recommend relying on them too much, however, so I suggest that you also make use of these."

She placed two books onto the table beside them.

"These are dictionaries for translating between Japanese and the language of this world. The pronunciation guide is written in Japanese as well, so you should have no trouble using them for studying purposes. While it is certainly possible for me to teach you myself, it would take a considerable amount of time, so I believe this will be more effective. My apologies."

"You don't have to apologize for something like that!" Tomochika was flabbergasted by the deep bow that Celestina gave them.

"Next, these rings can be used to conceal your Status. I have customized them to display fairly harmless results." As she spoke, she placed a pair of rings on the table. They were unadorned bands of silver. "Ordinarily, their only function is to display a fake Status to those who look, but considering your situation, I've prepared this double fake option for you. Normally, they will display the Status of an ordinary person. Should someone see through the first layer of that disguise, they will then see the Status of a Sage candidate."

"I see. So it looks like we're Sage candidates who are trying to blend in. If someone sees through the first layer, they should be satisfied upon seeing the second."

"Of course, penetrating the first layer of the disguise will be no easy task, either."

"When you say it like that, it seems unlikely that anyone will be able to see through the first layer anyway..."

"It is also possible to change the displayed Status at will. If you tap the ring three times, it will flash red for a moment, indicating a switch to Sage candidate mode. Repeating the action will cause it to flash green, returning to the Status of an ordinary person."

If they came up against someone who was deeply suspicious, that person could potentially see through both layers of the disguise, or just make them take off the rings. But if they were under that degree of suspicion, their cover would already have been blown, so they would need to think of a potential response to such a scenario regardless. The main selling point of the rings would be the ability to avoid getting wrapped up with problematic people around town.

"Finally, this." Celestina placed a cube on the table. It was a box about fifteen centimeters on each side, with a small metal lever along one edge. "Unfortunately, design is not my specialty, so it looks rather unseemly. My sincerest apologies."

"Wow, are you saying you made this, Celestina?"

"Indeed. When you turn this lever, the device will produce electricity. Please use this cable to attach it to your game console."

"You can even create charging devices…" Tomochika's amazement continued to grow.

"Magnets are easy enough to come by, so producing electricity in and of itself is not particularly challenging. The primary difficulty is adjusting the output level to match the necessities of the individual device. This size is the best I could do in a single night." Celestina spoke with an air of frustration, as if she could have made it even more compact if she'd only had more time.

"What about this cable?" It was, by all appearances, premade. No matter how amazing she was, expecting her to make a cable with all the appropriate connectors in a single night was too much.

"Although rare, goods from other worlds occasionally make their way into ours. Acquiring a charger itself would have been best, but unfortunately I was unable to do so. Instead, I collected a number of other objects and used their parts to create this. Is it not sufficient?" Despite the device seeming perfect in every way, Celestina suddenly seemed uneasy.

"It's way too perfect. Thank you."

Sensing Yogiri's heartfelt gratitude, she gave a small smile. Last night, Yogiri had decided to speak to the concierge on a whim, just to see if she could offer any help at all. He had never imagined that she would provide them with so much.

"Back home, I heard that concierges can never say no, and I guess it's the same in this world…" Tomochika's shock had turned to admiration.

Yogiri immediately picked up and put on one of the rings and one of the necklaces. He then went to put the charger in his backpack, only to find it full of money and jewels. Without hesitation, he began removing some of the contents, making enough space to put the charger inside.

"Um, Takatou. What are you doing?"

"Well, it didn't fit. Oh…Celestina, could you take these for us?"

"Understood. I shall take responsibility for these." Despite the rather impressive amount of money, she seemed entirely undaunted.

"Are you sure about that? I mean, I know I've got some too, but…"

"I didn't give her all of it, don't worry. Oh, hey. Could you actually invest that for us?" Yogiri asked as the thought suddenly occurred to him. He figured if it was left in her hands, it would work out somehow.

"Are you sure? I can't guarantee that any investments will bear fruit."

"If you end up losing it all, that's fine. I'll leave everything to you."

"Takatou, even if she's a concierge, asking that much is kind of —"

"Understood."

"You still can't say no?!"

Even Yogiri was surprised when she agreed to do it.

Chapter 17 — Who Cares About the Eyeball?

As Yogiri and Tomochika boarded the train at noon, Jorge and Captain Edelgart of the First Battalion of the City Guard were visiting the local lord's castle.

The ten-story stone structure towered over the center of the town. With most of the buildings being only one or two stories tall, it stood out rather conspicuously. The roof of the castle was a flat, open space where Jorge, Edelgart, and the lord now stood.

The two guards had shed their armor and were wearing only their uniforms. The lord wore clothes that spoke loudly of his frivolous spending habits.

"Was the incident last night truly serious enough to require the attention of a Sage?"

Edelgart's only concern with the incident was her failure to get a lead on the organization that she had been pursuing. While notoriously good at covering their tracks, they had gladly snapped at the bait of two powerless otherworlders. But in the end, her investigation hadn't managed to produce a single clue.

"Is it so strange that they would take an interest? An entire group of people were killed by causes unknown, after all," Jorge replied, surprised at Edelgart's lack of concern. In the middle of their investigation, ten of the people they'd been tracking had died mysteriously right in front of them. Such an abnormal incident would be huge in and of itself, even under normal circumstances.

"You think they care at all about some random criminals dropping dead?"

"The issue is how they died, not who was killed. There are already numerous possibilities, from disease to poisonous gas. I don't think it's strange at all for the Sages to be interested in finding out what happened."

"Even so, I can't imagine them taking such a personal interest. But there's no point in us arguing about it. There's no way we can guess what the Sages are thinking anyway!" Edelgart spoke with her chest puffed out proudly, although Jorge had no idea why.

"Make sure you guys shut up when we're in front of the Sage," the lord standing beside them said.

There was no direct hierarchical relationship between the lord and the City Guard. That was because the City Guard also held the role of keeping the local otherworlders in check. In short, being Japanese himself made the lord a target for the City Guard's activities.

"I'm quite sure that we were the only ones who were ordered to greet her," Edelgart replied.

"Well, she's arriving at my castle. I have to at least welcome her, don't I?"

"Is that all?"

An unpleasant silence settled between them. After a while, a silver disk descended.

The majority of the Sages lived on the floating continent. They moved to and from the surface primarily by way of aircraft.

The disk landed on the roof of the castle. As its hatch popped open, a woman in a dark red dress stepped out. It was the Sage named Lain. Bearing the title of the Great-Granddaughter of the Great Sage, she was the one responsible for protecting this territory.

"Thank you for meeting with me," Lain said with a haughty air as she stepped towards the lord. "It's been a while, hasn't it, Masahiko? Have things been going well?"

"A pleasure to see you again, Miss Lain. There have been no issues."

Apparently, Lain and Lord Masahiko had known each other since their time as Sage candidates.

"So you're Edelgart? I read your report. Take me to the survivor."

"Yes, ma'am! The survivor is currently being held within the castle," Edelgart replied with a salute before guiding Lain inside.

The group soon reached one of the castle's smaller rooms. The beastkin in question had been restrained and was lying on a simple bed, the lone survivor of the previous night's incident. He had no particular external injuries, but with his eyes, ears, and nose completely nonfunctional, there was no way to interrogate him. Approaching the dog man, Lain stared at him intently.

"Hmm. At first glance, nothing appears out of the ordinary." Pulling back the beastkin's eyelids, she saw no signs of damage. But even the light from the nearby window shining directly into his eyes sparked no reaction.

"We attempted treatment in order to proceed with our interrogation, but our efforts have proven fruitless."

"Your report said that even healing magic failed?"

"That is correct."

Listening to Jorge's reply, Lain held the beastkin's eye open as she pushed a finger into his eye socket.

"Miss Sage?!"

"I can't tell what's happening unless I see for myself."

Naturally, the prisoner began to struggle, letting out an agonized scream as Lain plucked out one of his eyes with her bare hands.

"Quiet."

At that one word, the beastkin froze. He was supposed to be deaf, but even so, he had immediately stopped moving. Perhaps the threat of her words had somehow penetrated in spite of his inability to hear.

Tearing the optical nerve off, Lain held the eyeball up to her face. She inspected it thoroughly but it looked like a perfectly normal eye.

"Nothing out of the ordinary. Masahiko, would you mind if I swapped one of your eyes with this one?"

"Wha —?! You can't be serious!" The lord's face instantly paled, but it wasn't long before he realized she was, in fact, only joking. Her words hadn't been an order. But that didn't mean he could relax, either. There was no telling when Lain might change her mind.

"Well, who cares about the eyeball itself. This is the real test. *Heal.*" Discarding the useless organ in her hands, Lain turned her healing magic on the beastkin. As she did, the now empty socket began to change, and within moments, a new eye had appeared.

The powerful abilities of the Sage could recreate a missing body part in an instant — but there was still no indication that the newly grown eye could see at all.

"Hmm. Seems like he still can't see. The organ itself was perfectly reconstructed, but the function hasn't been restored. So...how about this?" Lain lifted the corners of her mouth, and her canine teeth began to extend. Once they were long enough, she sank them into the beastkin's neck.

"Wh-What are you doing?!" Edelgart shouted in surprise.

"Didn't you know? Sage Lain is a vampire."

"But she was perfectly fine standing in the open sunlight on the roof!"

Being undead, vampires were weak to sunlight. That was just common sense.

"Miss Lain's class is Origin Blood. As the highest rank of the undead, she is also known as the Queen of Undeath. For someone of her level, sunlight is nothing to be concerned about."

"You seem to know a lot...I thought the Sages were simply powerful mages."

As Edelgart worked through her shock, Lain finished feeding. As soon as she took her mouth off the beastkin's neck, his body began to change. His claws began to grow and his muscles started to ripple. His lips curled back and fangs began to grow. With a single movement of his arms and legs, the ropes binding him to the bed were ripped apart and he fell to the floor.

"Kneel," Lain ordered the creature now lying at her feet. At her words, he began to thrash around, but that was all. He seemed to recognize that he had been given a command, but in spite of his desperate efforts to comply, he had no idea what he had actually been ordered to do.

"Apparently even being in the same bloodline doesn't help," Jorge muttered. "Interesting that not even telepathy works."

Vampires increased their numbers by drinking the blood of others. Those new vampires could then communicate with each other via telepathy, but in this case it had failed to get through.

"Well, I've made him part of my bloodline now regardless. Do you mind if I take him with me?"

"V-Very well. Understood," Edelgart agreed.

In truth, Jorge was relieved. He'd been wondering how they would even deal with a suspect in this sort of condition on their own.

"Now then. It seems this individual has been put into a rather interesting state. And the ones who did this were Yogiri Takatou and Tomochika Dannoura, correct?"

"Um, actually, those two have no powers, so I can't imagine they were involved."

"Don't be stupid, Edelgart. Ten people died and only those two were left unharmed. Are you saying you have another suspect?"

"Th-That may be true, but if they did something, I have absolutely no idea what it could have been. And without any evidence, we can't just arrest them."

Jorge steeled himself to meet his end. Edelgart must have been feeling the same way, but she made no excuses for their actions. If she didn't know what had happened, then she didn't know. That was all there was to it. She wasn't clever enough to come up with a bunch of justifications for her choices.

"Sorry, I teased you a bit too much. Forgive me. The truth is, I already knew about those two beforehand," Lain said with a smirk. Once again, Jorge felt relief wash over him as he realized his life wasn't yet in danger.

"Is that so?"

"Sage Sion has an attendant named Youichi. He told me about them. Apparently, they used something along the lines of Instant Death Magic to kill a dragon. He was pretty vague with the details, but it was enough to make me curious. And then I received this report from you."

"I see. Then how did those two...?"

"About that —"

Lain started to say something, but the rest of them couldn't hear what it was. A tremendous explosion rocked the building, shaking the walls of the castle around them and throwing the room into a state of confusion.

Edelgart grabbed Jorge and flung him to the ground, rolling into a corner and out of the way.

"Wh-What's happening...?!" Jorge lifted his upper body off the ground as he asked.

"It's him!" Edelgart pointed towards the door. Standing on the threshold was a man with a sword, showing no gaps in his defenses despite being in the middle of the afterswing of his attack.

The ground beneath his feet was riddled with cracks. Although hard to believe, it seemed the massive vibrations had been a result of his footsteps. Half of the door, now split cleanly in two, had fallen to the floor. His sword had shaken the entire room when it slashed its way in.

A red line now ran straight through Lain. The intruder's sword didn't seem capable of reaching anywhere near her, but even so, she had been cleanly cut in half.

"A Hero..." Jorge instantly activated his Discernment skill.

"What?!"

"That's what my skill is telling me! I don't know who he is, but his class is Hero!"

The two of them could only stare in shock.

Chapter 18 — Mokomoko Is Watching

A strange scene was developing in front of Jorge's eyes. It was a fight at a speed the eyes couldn't track, clearly well beyond the level of ordinary humans. But no matter how one-sided the battle appeared, it showed no signs of ending.

With each strike from the Hero, the castle shook and broke apart. The countless swings of the Hero's blade sliced apart Lain's body, and bright white bolts of energy scattered her insides. Lightning fell from the sky, striking her dead on. As one would expect, the state of Lain's body was horrifying to behold.

But, in the next instant, Lain was standing in the middle of the room as if nothing had happened. The only indication that she had been attacked at all was the sorry state of her clothing.

And still, she did nothing.

Making no attempt to dodge or defend herself, she calmly absorbed the full force of each and every attack. Even as her arms were severed and flung away, her head smashed to pieces, her entire body engulfed in flames, it took only an instant for her to re-form.

"What is going on here...?! Is this what a Hero's battle...no, is this what a Sage's battle looks like...?" Edelgart's voice shuddered as she spoke.

Jorge and Edelgart could do nothing but watch the fight from the corner of the room. As if to say he was only interested in fighting the Sage, the Hero was making a small effort not to harm the others around him. If it hadn't been for those small efforts, Jorge and the rest of them would have been killed at the start. That being said, they still had to protect themselves from the waves of shrapnel and debris raining down on them.

"Is this even a battle? It seems like the Sage isn't attempting to defend herself."

"Perhaps the Hero's Gift is being nullified?"

Jorge found it hard to believe that, given the scene before them, but he could understand the need to rationalize what they were witnessing. That's how unbelievable the situation was.

"No, the Hero's Gift is from a Swordmaster, so it doesn't fall under the Sages' authority. It appears she is actually taking the attacks head-on and simply regenerating afterwards."

The Gift was something that had to be given, so those who handed it out had full control over those who received it. But since the Hero's Gift was from a different line, it had no connection to the Sages.

The Gift given by the Sages had a tendency to lean towards magical disciplines, while the Swordmasters' Gift tended towards physical attacks. In keeping with that trend, the Hero's primary weapons were swords.

As the two guards commented on the fight, the Hero broke off his attack for a moment. He must have realized that he wasn't making any progress.

"Hmm. If you plan on giving up and going home, that's fine with me," Lain said, still without a scratch on her. At some point she had even used some kind of magic to repair her clothes.

"You monster!" Even as the Hero seethed with rage, he recognized that it was pointless to continue his blind attacks. He settled on glaring at her instead.

"If we're going to take a break, mind if we talk?" Lain spoke without a care in the world, as if she hadn't just been handily dismantled multiple times in a row.

The Hero didn't reply. But the fact that he was holding back may have merely been an effort to buy some time.

"You seem to be a Hero. Why is a Hero attacking me? Isn't there some Demon Lord somewhere that you should be fighting?"

Jorge had also wondered the same thing. The Sages were the ones who ruled over and protected the world. What point was there in trying to kill them?

"Like hell! You people are nothing but a blight on this world!"

"Maybe it's not so convincing coming from me, but I feel like the Sages are doing a pretty good job. The amount of intervention varies from Sage to Sage, but you still have a considerable amount of freedom, don't you? And above all, we're the ones protecting you from outside enemies. What will getting rid of us accomplish? Aren't you better off using us to protect yourselves?"

"What freedom?! Just how many people have died thanks to your pointless whims?!"

"Well, I suppose that's true. But without us, considerably more people would have died, you know?"

"What reason is that to forgive your tyranny?!"

"Hmm. I thought Heroes fought for the sake of bringing about peace, but you seem to be different. Was someone close to you killed by a Sage? Or were they taken away? Manipulated somehow? At any rate, attacking me won't help your cause. I barely spend any time on the surface. There's basically no chance that I've personally done anything that impacted you."

"I will eradicate the Sages! What you've done personally is irrelevant!" Apparently content with whatever time he had bought, the Hero once again fell into a fighting stance. Lifting his sword, he hurled it forward. The wide blade pierced the ground at Lain's feet — but he hadn't been aiming at her at all.

The sword began to shine. At the same time, the ground around her began to glow as if in response. Around Lain's feet, numerous smaller blades sprouted from the floor. Each reflected the light of the glowing sword, and in short order, beams of light stretched out from each of them to draw a complex pattern around the Sage.

"It doesn't matter if you're immortal! I'll just have to incinerate you all at once!"

The pattern carved into the floor began to expand, building up into a three-dimensional figure. All at once, the lines snapped together to form a cage around Lain.

Reaching out with his trembling right hand, the Hero grabbed his own left hand and pressed it down. It was clear that he had been pushing himself to the limit from the very beginning of the exchange, but there was nothing Jorge or Edelgart could do about it. No matter how open the Hero may have looked to attack, the difference in their abilities was just too much. The moment they tried to approach, they would have been blown away.

"Take this!" the Hero roared as the prison of light began to shine brighter.

It only lasted for an instant. When the light subsided, the cage it had formed was empty. The small blades protruding from the ground, the storied longsword that the Hero had been wielding, the beastkin lying on the ground, even Lain herself — they had all simply vanished. Whatever had vaporized them had also melted the floor, turning the stone into a bright red liquid reminiscent of lava.

"Ariel...finally...I've killed one..." Muttering to himself, the Hero fell to his knees. He appeared to have completely exhausted himself. It didn't look like he could even muster the strength to stand.

"What...should we..."

"You idiot! Killing a Sage is a capital crime! Arrest him immediately!"

With Edelgart not thinking straight, Jorge was at a total loss. No matter how shocked he was, he knew there was no way they could simply arrest a Hero. Jorge looked over to the lord, who was standing by the wall opposite them.

If you're one of the Sages' attendants, then please, do something!

Jorge wanted to say it out loud, but the lord was already shaking his head. There was nothing they could do.

"So, was Ariel your lover or something?"

And then there was no need for them to do anything. Lain was once again standing in the same spot that she had occupied moments before. The Hero's face twisted in despair.

"How did you avoid it…?!"

"I didn't avoid anything. I just don't die. So what would be the point of moving?"

"Impossible…at a temperature high enough to completely destroy the Holy Sword Cartena, there should be nothing left…"

The truth was that Lain had, in fact, been completely incinerated.

"If leaving nothing behind was enough to kill me, I'd be a lot better off. Immortality like this is honestly more of a curse than anything else at this point. How much longer am I going to have to live this way? Every time I think about it, I lose all hope."

"Kill me…" The Hero had fallen into despair.

"Why? You're the one who attacked me. What reason would I have for killing you?"

Lain's answer was tinged with disbelief. Apparently, being attacked out of nowhere wasn't reason enough in her mind for killing someone. Even someone as tolerant as Jorge couldn't help but feel she was showing a bit too much lenience.

"Umm, if that's the case, then what are we supposed to do?" Jorge asked. Killing the Hero would solve a lot of problems but it didn't seem like that was going to happen.

"Just deal with him like any criminal. Breaking and entering, murder, property damage — there's plenty of grounds for an arrest, don't you think?"

"But…he's a Hero. There's no way we could arrest him against his will."

"Hmm. Then let's do this."

Lain reached down and grabbed the Hero's arm. She then spun on

the spot, hurling him through a hole in the wall as if he were no more than a piece of trash.

"Wha—?!"

"You guys can't arrest him and I don't feel like killing him. In that case, having him around is just a pain in the ass. So why don't we act like he was never here in the first place?"

She may have said that she hadn't felt like killing him, but this room was fairly high up. Any ordinary person would die instantly from the fall.

"Very well. No one ever came here, then."

A Sage's word was absolute, and that was more convenient for them anyway. Jorge was relieved yet again.

"Well, it seems the dog beastkin was completely annihilated, so I guess that's it for today. Edelgart, about what we were discussing earlier... Go track down this Yogiri Takatou. Contact me once you've found out where he is."

"Understood!" Despite the circumstances, Edelgart seemed relatively undaunted.

Jorge gave a bitter smile. It had to take an impressive dullness to be so nonchalant in a situation like this.

Three days after they'd left the city, Yogiri and Tomochika were still on board the train. Unlike back home in Japan, the trains here didn't operate on set schedules, but even so, their destination should only have been a few hours from their starting point.

"Why do I have to be stuck here, spinning the charger while trapped in the stomach of some fat ghost?!" Tomochika complained from inside Mokomoko's translucent form, still spinning the device connected to Yogiri's handheld.

Oblivious to her discomfort, Yogiri was happily enjoying his game once again. "Well, the battery is dying. If you don't charge it for me, I can't play."

And I do not occupy physical space, so there is no need to worry, is there? I certainly don't mind.

"Well, I feel like I'm being smothered! If you don't care, then go sit on Takatou!"

No, he's far too scary.

The tickets that the concierge had given them were for a luxurious personal compartment with seating sufficient for four people. Yogiri and Tomochika sat opposite each other, and Mokomoko was technically sitting beside Tomochika. But as wide as she was, she covered most of the other seat as well. Therefore, the two of them were basically overlapping.

"Why don't you just go float over there, then?!"

That would not do. If I were to try to float in a moving object, I may be left behind. I need to maintain a solid image, which requires that I be sitting on a seat.

"Man, ghosts are a pain! Why don't you just go back to being invisible then?!"

It's not that I'm actively showing myself to you. You are simply able to see me now.

Apparently, at some point Tomochika had developed the ability to see spiritual entities.

"That's mostly because she became aware of your existence, right?" The moment Yogiri had been made aware of Mokomoko's existence, he had also been able to see her immediately.

Precisely! Like when you first meet a person, you think nothing of it, but when you notice their ear hair, you can't see anything else! Actually, that makes me seem like I'm just ear hair, doesn't it?!

"Are you on the level of ear hair, then?"

No, forget I said anything. I'll think of a better example.

Mokomoko folded her arms and sank into thought.

"Well, I kind of owe you a lot, so just spinning the charger isn't that big of a deal. But this train is really taking its time, isn't it?"

"Apparently the monsters aren't normally supposed to approach the barrier."

One of the Sages' attendants was on board the train, maintaining a barrier to protect it. That sort of deterrent was normally enough to make most monsters lose interest the moment they took sight of it. But for some reason, the monsters this time around had formed ranks and attacked the train anyway. They had managed to pull through to the next station, but it had completely exhausted the resources of the mage protecting them, so they were stuck in place for the moment.

Apparently, this was a regular enough occurrence that there were emergency stations set up along the train line. These stations had lodgings for the passengers, so that's where they had stayed. At around noon on the third day, they had finally managed to get moving again. Now their goal of Hanabusa was a short distance away.

"It's a much more dangerous world than I first thought," Tomochika said, looking out the window.

A sharp sound reverberated from the barrier as another monster bounced off it. It was common for one or two monsters to attack at a time.

Turning her gaze forward again, Tomochika saw that Mokomoko had begun spinning in the air, arms still crossed.

"You're so annoying! Why do you have to spin like that?!"

"Why don't you just come sit beside me, then?"

"Oh, yeah!"

There was plenty of space for Yogiri and her to sit side by side. For some reason, she had gotten it into her head that they needed to be facing each other. The moment that he suggested it, she jumped across to sit beside him and began watching the screen of his handheld. As always, he was doing terribly. His passion for the game wasn't the least bit matched by his skill at it.

Tomochika suddenly realized just how close Yogiri was, almost pressing up against her. Just as it hit her, Yogiri suddenly stopped playing his game and looked up.

"What is it?!"

As Tomochika began to panic, he pushed her over.

"Hey! Stop it! What are you doing?! Mokomoko is watching, you know!"

Oh, don't mind me. As a guardian spirit, I'll always be here, so you might as well get used to it.

"Wait, you too?! Are you seriously always going to be around me, Mokomoko?!" As Tomochika grew more and more flustered, something passed by overhead. "What...?"

Over Yogiri's shoulder, she could suddenly see the sky. The roof of the train car had been blown away. Looking around, even the top halves of the seats they had been sitting on were gone. If Yogiri hadn't pushed her over, Tomochika's head would probably have been gone along with them.

"Why don't you just explain what you're doing?!"

"I suddenly saw the line of killing intent." The killing intent that Yogiri spoke of was just a placeholder term. Yogiri could see a concrete image of any danger to his own body. "I wonder what that was. I can't imagine the two of us are being specifically targeted."

They had no way of knowing what sort of attack it was, but the train appeared to have been struck by a number of objects all at once.

At that moment, the engine ground to an emergency stop and a loud siren began to blare.

Chapter 19 — Like Nobunaga Oda or Enchou Sanyuutei

This is an announcement to all passengers. It appears a Sage is in combat with the nearby aggressor. In accordance with official policies regarding warzones, all contracts for transportation are hereby null and void. For a refund of the full ticket price, please inquire at any station.

After making its announcement, the voice that was coming from nowhere in particular abruptly cut off.

"What does that mean?" Tomochika said from under Yogiri, her mouth agape.

"'It's none of our business anymore, do whatever you want.' Something like that, I guess?"

"They aren't even going to evacuate the passengers?!"

"If the same thing that just happened is going to happen again, the staff won't have the ability to do anything for their customers anyway."

"Well, could you at least get off of me? If another attack hits, it's not like this will help."

For the moment, there was no indication of an attack coming their way. As requested, Yogiri let Tomochika sit up. Looking around the car, it was clear that the train had suffered significant damage. A number of unidentified objects had passed through it, cleanly cutting away everything in their path.

It reminded him of Higashida. The result was similar to the Fire Ball he had used. Whatever this attack was, several passengers had been caught up in it. None of those who had been struck had survived, leaving their lifeless bodies scattered about the scene. There weren't any entrails or blood, however; just the stench of burnt flesh thick in the air. Those who had survived the attack were now hurriedly disembarking from the train per the announcer's instructions.

"If another one of those things comes for us, getting off the train isn't going to help much. But I suppose there's no point in staying here either, so I guess we should get ready to leave too."

The train had sustained critical damage. Even after the Sage's battle was finished, it was hard to believe that it would ever be able to move again.

Gathering their luggage, Yogiri and Tomochika stood up. Once the rest of the passengers had left, they took their time disembarking. Mokomoko followed them. As Tomochika's guardian spirit, they probably didn't need to worry about her.

The tracks they had been following ran between the Haqua Forest and the Garula Canyon. The forest was situated on the left side of the tracks, with the canyon to their right. Yogiri looked towards the canyon, where he figured the attack had originated.

Some distance away from the tracks was a cliff, at the bottom of which flowed a large river. Beyond the canyon were mountains bare of any vegetation. The river below split off in a number of directions, carving a complex piece of scenery into the landscape.

"So what even happened?" Tomochika asked, looking in the same direction.

It didn't take long for them to find a likely source for the attack.

"Look! A robot!" she shouted.

A giant was clinging to one of the mountain faces. Its frame was clearly made of metal, and it had some token bits of what Yogiri guessed were supposed to be armor fastened to it. It had four arms, the two on its left clinging to the rock, and the two on its right holding an enormous sword and shield. Perhaps its horned head was heavier than its size suggested, as it maintained a hunchbacked posture. As Tomochika had pointed out, it looked like some sort of machine; there was nothing about it that looked organic.

"So that's the aggressor they were talking about. What about the Sage?"

"Maybe over there?"

Looking over to where Tomochika was pointing, Yogiri saw a small speck in front of the enormous automaton.

"You really do have a good eye, don't you?" Yogiri was impressed. As he had noted before, her eyesight was truly exceptional.

The Dannoura body is uniquely made. As with a certain historical battle manga, the blood of legends runs through Dannoura's veins! Those like Nobunaga Oda and Enchou Sanyuutei are all mixed in!

"Wait, really? What kind of abilities do we get from the blood of a *rakugo* storyteller?" Apparently, this was the first Tomochika had ever heard of it.

The overall result is good, so don't worry about the little details.

As they were speaking, the battle by the canyon resumed. The Sage fired off a number of bolts of light, which the giant blocked with its shield. The bolts glanced off it, scattering in random directions and blowing away chunks of the nearby mountain. The damage to the train must have been caused by those bolts.

The giant swung its sword down at the Sage. A weapon of that size must have been tremendously heavy, but the giant slashed through earth, stone, and air alike, as if the blade weighed nothing at all.

And then the giant suddenly disappeared. As the mountain it had been clinging to collapsed, it reappeared on another nearby peak. Using its right arms, it pulled a rifle-like weapon from its back, firing off a few shots in quick succession. More mountains exploded and huge gouts of water were blasted upwards from the river below.

Each time Yogiri blinked, the canyon had completely changed shape. Neither combatant was sparing a thought for their surroundings.

His optimism was starting to fade away. A number of stray bolts of light struck the ground around them, cutting off — as well as cutting straight through — some of the fleeing passengers.

"Hmm, this is problematic. Even running away doesn't seem like a very good option."

"You say that, but you don't sound all that worried."

Yogiri pulled out their map. Considering the time they had spent traveling and the landmarks nearby, he tried to pinpoint their precise location. It seemed they were fairly close to Hanabusa Station.

"Looks like it's about ten kilometers. But walking there while dodging stray magic attacks seems a bit too risky. Maybe we'd be better off heading into the forest for a bit."

The other passengers on the train had split into three groups: those who were following the rails, heading towards Hanabusa, those who were fleeing to the forest, and the stragglers who had yet to decide on a course of action and were standing around in a state of confused panic.

"Hey! Why don't you just get rid of that monster?"

"Why?"

"What do you mean 'why?' It's in our way, isn't it?" Tomochika looked surprised, as if the reason was perfectly obvious.

"If that's the only excuse I need, I could say the people walking in front of us on the street are in the way, so I might as well kill them too."

"But it tried to kill us earlier! Bullets were flying at us and everything."

"It's not like it was targeting us personally. It only happened once, so it was probably a mistake."

"Geez, how are you so calm about this?! And it fired multiple shots, by the way!"

"If I don't follow some set of personal rules, I'm going to end up killing people just because they annoy me. I'd like to avoid that, if possible."

Tomochika deflated a little. "Oh. Well...sorry, I guess. That was kind of naive of me..."

"I'm not criticizing you or anything, so don't worry about it."

The fighting was going on fairly far away, so Yogiri figured if they were careful, they could avoid most of the trouble. Killing everyone they came across would be more trouble than it was worth, anyway.

"It doesn't look like it's going to be difficult to avoid their attacks, so if we move carefully —" *There should be no problem*, is what he had wanted to say. But before he could, the sound of an explosion filled the air around them. At the same time, an intense gust of wind kicked up a huge cloud of dust. It took a moment for Yogiri to process what had just happened, but once he noticed that everything had gone dark, he understood instantly.

Something was blocking the sun.

As the dust dissipated, Yogiri looked up to see the giant looming over them. Standing on the train, its feet had completely flattened the cars beneath them. Although the giant had been quite a distance away just moments before, it had closed the gap between them without warning. In an instant, they had found themselves in the most dangerous possible place.

"You bastard! You can't run from me!"

One step behind, the Sage came flying over. His enormous cloak accentuated just how small he was, adding an unbalanced appearance to his image. Floating in the air, he was glaring at the giant. And then, without warning, he snapped out his hand.

"Dannoura, can you step over here for a second?"

Grabbing Tomochika's hand, Yogiri pulled her towards him. With a short cry, she jumped back just in time to see something strike the ground where they had been standing.

The earth had been completely buried in hail, covering an area about a meter wide. Each chunk of ice was only a few centimeters long, but there were so many of them, stretching out as far as Yogiri could see.

Unsurprisingly, such an attack had no effect on the giant, but the ordinary humans in its path weren't so lucky. The passengers who had hesitated and failed to run were now scattered about in a tragic, gruesome display.

"But...why...? Why would you even do that?!" Tomochika shouted as she saw the carnage before them.

Hearing her, the Sage turned. "What? You were all lined up so nicely that I figured I'd take you out in one go...but some of you survived?" Keeping an eye on the giant, he glanced over at Yogiri and Tomochika.

"I don't understand either. Why are you attacking us? We have nothing to do with this, right?"

The boy before them was supposed to be fighting the giant. There wasn't any reason for him to be killing the passengers of a passing train.

"Are you talking back to me? Why are you even looking at me? You should be bowing with your face in the dirt when you see a Sage, you disgusting peasants!"

Yogiri was relieved. The Sage's behavior simplified the issue. "You're the disgusting one here," he replied, unleashing his power as he spoke.

The boy fell. A dull thud marked his impact with the ground. It looked like his neck had broken from the fall, but that would hardly be an issue for him now.

"Did you kill him?"

"Yeah. That was the right reason to kill someone, don't you think?" There was no need to hesitate against an enemy who was happy to attack them without a second thought.

Yogiri looked at the giant. He had no idea how it would react now that the Sage it had been fighting was dead. As he considered whether or not to take it down preemptively, the giant spoke.

"Wait. I. Intend. No. Harm."

A sound like a chorus of people speaking in unison reverberated from the massive creature above them.

It appeared to be the giant's voice.

Chapter 20 — This Robot Knows Too Much!

The creature was about the size of a ten-story building. About thirty meters tall, if Yogiri judged correctly.

"It really is a robot, no matter how you look at it," Tomochika muttered to herself.

As they got closer, it was quite clear that it was a machine of some sort, but it also gave the impression of being a living monster. It had four arms and an armored skeleton. Apparently incapable of standing up straight with its thin frame, the parts that constructed its spine were bent from the hip upward. An enormous horn sprouted from its head. It had a single piece that looked like an eye, which glowed with a dull light.

"Seems about as unrealistic as the dragon, doesn't it?"

As Yogiri and Tomochika spoke, the giant slowly crouched down. That may have just been its standby state, but either way it seemed quite nimble. There was no guarantee they were safe just because it was crouching.

"So, you don't plan on fighting us?"

"Correct. I have no intention of partaking in a battle I cannot win." It had been speaking in rough, broken sentences at first, but its chorus-like voice gradually took on a more natural tone, as if it was fine-tuning itself on the fly.

"Wait, is there a girl in there?!"

The giant's voice had changed to that of a young female. Their translation necklaces weren't active just then, so it had to be speaking Japanese all on its own. No doubt it had chosen the language after hearing Yogiri and Tomochika's conversation.

"I have no passengers. It would be acceptable to consider me an autonomous robot."

"So then why did you make your voice sound like that?"

"I am attempting to curry favor. According to my database, it is more likely for this type of voice to garner positive reactions when facing human males."

"Talk about being calculating!"

"Three hundred million possible courses of action have been reviewed, including continued combat. It has been decided that the most efficient course of action for completion of my current mission is to behave modestly. To that end, it is necessary to explain my thought process honestly in order to build trust. Retreating in this context bears the risk of being perceived as a threat and thus risks a forced interruption of all functions. Acquiring your understanding has become necessary for continued operation."

"This robot understands people too well!"

As a robot, it could be perfectly logical with no wishful thinking mixed in, Yogiri surmised. It was rare that someone was so guarded against him; the vast majority of people he had come up against, even after seeing his ability firsthand, were unable to fully comprehend it.

"Well, if you don't plan on fighting us, that's fine. But can I ask you some questions?"

If the giant left now, it wouldn't be a real problem, but they would still have no idea what had actually happened here. If the boy that Yogiri had killed earlier was truly a Sage, it would likely impact their future actions significantly.

"I shall answer anything within the scope of my knowledge."

"Why were you two fighting?" Yogiri asked, pointing at the fallen boy.

"I was attacked. It is my conjecture that he was taking defensive action. His kind refer to us as 'invaders.'"

"Apparently, he was a Sage. Did you know that?"

"I lack any particular knowledge of this individual."

"*Are* you an invader?"

"If by 'invade' you mean 'the attempt to subvert the sovereignty or dominion of the present ruler,' then I have no such intentions. In completion of my mission, however, I do not avoid combat. From their perspective, taking defensive action against us is logical."

"What's this mission you keep talking about?"

The giant suddenly fell quiet. It didn't seem to feel like talking about it.

"Okay. Whatever you're doing, it has nothing to do with us. If you don't plan on attacking us, then go ahead and finish your mission or whatever."

"I request a negotiation. If there is any assistance I can offer, I shall do so. In return, I request that you refrain from attacking me. Do you accept?"

"Hmm. I suppose it's hard to trust someone who says they'll let you go, so you want to ensure that it's worth our while?"

"Geez, this robot is a pain! We said we'd leave you alone, so that's that, isn't it? More importantly, can you even harm a robot like this?"

"Is there a reason I shouldn't be able to?"

"What? Well, robots can't really die, can they?" Tomochika was once again caught off guard by Yogiri's reply.

"Even a robot can live and die, don't you think?"

"Oh, now we're getting philosophical?"

"I won't know until I try, but the thing's been talking like it can be killed from the start, hasn't it?" As Yogiri pointed at it, the giant's lone eye blinked on and off.

"I do not know what you believe I am, but I do consider myself to be alive."

"Actually, now that I think about it, if you're an invader, where did you come from?"

"I came from beyond this world."

"Oh, would you happen to know how to get back? We were actually brought here from another world against our wills."

"Unfortunately, the only world that I can return to is the one I originated from."

It would have solved an awful lot of problems if the robot could have taken them home, but clearly that wasn't going to happen.

"What if we asked you to take us back to your world, then?" If they didn't have any direct way home, they might as well explore other options.

"Impossible. There are two reasons for that. One, my existence is not solely located in this world. A portion of myself remains in my original world, to which I am connected. As such, I am able to return. But the entirety of your existence is located here."

"I see. So you've got a sort of lifeline connecting you to your home."

"An acceptable metaphor. Additionally, this world exists in the lowest strata of energy potential. Descending to it is rather simple, but ascending from it requires a tremendous amount of power."

"So Hanakawa and the others probably got back the first time because they still had a connection to our world."

But Yogiri and Tomochika had no such connection. The Sage that had summoned them obviously had no intention of sending the candidates home.

"The power required to return me to my home is located within that world. To return you to yours, the precise coordinates of your world and a tremendous amount of energy would be required."

"Coordinates and energy. So if you have those, you can travel between worlds. Is that right?"

"Correct."

"Suppose we had those…what would we have to do? We have no idea what the actual process is for getting back."

"Advice on the method is possible. In comparison to those two main issues, all other problems are minor."

"Then let's use that for our exchange. Thanks."

Such a deal was plenty valuable to Yogiri, who had no idea how to even begin trying to return to their original world.

"Is that truly sufficient?"

"Sure. So what's the second reason you can't take us with you?"

"I would refuse to carry a being as dangerous as you to my home world. Such a concern is more pressing than my individual life."

"Is there anything you want, Dannoura?"

"I have no idea what a robot like this could even do for me," Tomochika said with a troubled expression. "What could I possibly ask for?"

Yogiri understood...it wasn't particularly easy to think of something you could ask a robot from another world for.

Well then, allow me to offer a suggestion!

As Tomochika pondered over her answer, the ghost of Mokomoko entered the conversation.

Edelgart and Jorge of the City Guard's First Battalion were rigid with shock.

Following instructions from Sage Lain, they had accompanied a construction crew out to the area by the Garula Canyon. There, they found the body of another Sage.

"What happened here?!" Edelgart cried.

Jorge had no answer for her. "This is...Sage Santarou, correct?"

The train was completely destroyed, the rails had been ripped up, dozens of people lay torn to pieces, and the landscape of the canyon itself had been changed. It was clear that something out of this world had taken place, but that wasn't particularly rare where the Sages were concerned. Whenever one was locked in combat, these kinds of things tended to happen.

But the Sage that had brought all that about was now dead, his neck bent at an impossible angle. While that was likely the cause of death, Jorge couldn't bring himself to believe it. The Sages were absolute. There was no way one could just be lying here, discarded like trash.

"What the hell happened here?!"

But of course, there was no one there who could answer the captain's question. The only ones alive and moving were the construction crew that had accompanied them. The passengers of the train were either dead or had long since fled the scene.

"It seems he fought something here...in which case, there is a possibility that those two were involved..."

Jorge and Edelgart had come this far in pursuit of Yogiri Takatou and Tomochika Dannoura. And that pursuit had led them to a destroyed train and a dead Sage. Beyond the strange powers they seemed to have, it was now possible that they were involved in the death of one of the world's all-powerful protectors.

"I have no idea what's going on here! There's nothing we can do but report what we've found to the Sages."

This was a situation that a pair of city guards couldn't hope to deal with alone.

Chapter 21 — You Can't Kill Someone Who's Already Dead

A pigeon began to speak in Edelgart's voice.

It was a carrier pigeon. These birds, born as magical creatures, upheld an important corner of the world's intelligence network. While magic could be used for long-distance communication, it required both parties to be fairly accomplished in the magical arts, and thus was not something ordinary people could use.

This was Lain's residence, a white-walled mansion on the floating continent. In a reception room that gave no hint of its master's nature as a vampire, two Sages sat opposite each other.

One was the master of the mansion, Sage Lain. The other was the one responsible for bringing Yogiri and his classmates to this world, Sage Sion.

While Edelgart's voice was rather panicked, her main point was still communicated clearly — Sage Santarou was dead. And what's more, Yogiri Takatou and Tomochika Dannoura may have been involved.

"This is why I called you here," Lain said. She had felt the need to run this information by Sion.

"Oh? Did the candidates I summoned do something?" The management of Sage candidates was a responsibility that fell on the one who had summoned them. Dealing with another's candidates was somewhat taboo among the Sages.

"Now that a Sage has been killed, it's not something I can ignore. They have long since exceeded the capacity of simple Sage candidates. On top of that, the problems they are causing are within my jurisdiction."

Santarou's jurisdiction was around the capital of Manii, but in this case, his pursuit of the invader had led him into Lain's territory. When it came to dealing with invaders, the distinction between territorial jurisdictions wasn't especially important, but now that a Sage's death was involved, things had changed. As the one responsible for the territory where that death had taken place, a certain amount of responsibility fell on Lain as well.

"There's no proof they did anything, is there? Santarou was sent to fight off a large robot. Are you sure he wasn't killed by that?"

"It's possible. But even if there is only a suspicion that they might have the ability to kill a Sage, they can't be left to wander on their own." Lain had taken a personal interest in this mysterious power. She had intended to watch and see how things unfolded for a while, but the circumstances would no longer allow for that.

"If they are able to kill a Sage, they are well outside the bounds of a Sage candidate. That's enough to make them into a Sage on the spot. I reviewed them all personally and didn't see anyone even approaching that level."

"Then how did Santarou die?"

"Santarou's specialty was his ability to use the magic of all elements, correct? Among the Sages, he had the greatest range of abilities. With those abilities, he could adapt and be effective on any battlefield, but as a result, the individual power of his spells was somewhat lacking. In short, he was a jack of all trades but a master of none. A single mistake in battle could be enough to get him killed."

"You make it sound so easy. But Santarou's body had no external wounds. Some of his bones were broken, but that likely happened after his death. The cause of death is still unknown, but I heard from your attendant that those two have something like Instant Death Magic."

"Youichi is a bit of a worrywart," Sion sighed, as if to say "what of it?" "But even if you think they are the culprits, what reason would they have to kill a Sage? Santarou had no visible injuries, you said? So there is no evidence they removed his Philosopher's Stone."

"No, there was no report of his stomach being ripped open. While it's certainly bizarre that they would simply kill and leave him there, there's no way we can guess at their motives. Regardless, I'm going to deal with those two. I know I don't need your permission, but I figured I'd let you know."

"You'll deal with them? And here I thought you were a pacifist."

"I don't recall ever boasting such absurd principles. Unlike the other Sages, I just don't kill people without reason. If there's an actual need, I have no problem taking lives."

"Then fine, do with those two as you please. But really, I thought you had called me here for a different reason."

"And what would that be?"

"It's also related to Santarou...and the Darkness. I was told he managed to drive it away, but it's still lingering somewhere in this world. I thought it might be about that."

"You're wondering who will go out to fight it next?"

With Santarou dead, the territory he was responsible for was now vacant. The responsibility for that territory would most likely fall on someone whose jurisdiction bordered it — in this case, either Lain or Sion.

"Ah! Now that I think about it, you owe me a favor, don't you?" Sion clapped her hands together as if she had suddenly come up with a great idea.

"All right, I'll go deal with it."

Someone would have to anyway. Lain didn't have any particular reason to avoid handling it herself, so if she could clear up her debt to Sion at the same time, it was the most convenient option.

"Well then, please allow me to excuse myself." With her business concluded, Sion wasted no time making her exit.

"Masayuki," Lain called out to the empty reception room.

"You called?" A moment later, a male voice replied from behind her.

"Take the Immortals to Hanabusa. Find Yogiri Takatou and Tomochika Dannoura, and kill them."

"Wait, are you serious? Just those two? What on earth are you thinking?"

"Those two absolutely have to be dealt with. It seems they can use something akin to Instant Death Magic. There's a possibility another unit might not be able to take them on."

"Ahh, I see. That makes the Immortals perfect for this job. It's not like you can kill someone who's already dead, right?"

The Immortal Corps had about a hundred members, and it was almost entirely composed of undead, golems, and other such entities that didn't qualify as 'alive.' In other words, it was an entire unit consisting of beings immune to Instant Death Magic.

"But still, wouldn't I be enough by myself?" Masayuki was a member of Lain's bloodline. As a vampire who could be called one of her children, he was also a high-ranking undead.

"In order to guarantee their deaths, we need numbers like that. If you still don't have enough, recruit from the locals."

"Whoa, whoa, whoa! Are you saying it's okay to destroy Hanabusa?" An unmistakable joy filled his voice. Masayuki had instantly gotten on board.

"Only if it's necessary. Don't do anything you don't have to."

"Don't worry. I'll make absolutely sure we get them." Despite Lain's warning, he didn't seem to be particularly concerned.

"I'm planning on going out. There's a need for me to face down an invader." While dealing with a Sage murderer was important, the invaders were a more pressing threat.

"I'll leave those more complex enemies to you. I'm much better suited to tearing apart people with blood and guts."

With Masayuki and the entire Immortal Corps, the death of two Sage candidates was more or less guaranteed. If Yogiri and Tomochika only had Instant Death Magic on their side, they wouldn't stand a chance. If they somehow survived against the entire Immortal Corps, however…

That possibility wasn't even one in a million. And yet Lain couldn't help but secretly hope that they would.

Chapter 22 — Interlude: You Came to Get Me, Right?

He had no idea where he was, or where he had come from. But when Ein came to, he was walking down a familiar road. Far off from the village, it was a slightly overgrown path. This was the road to his own house.

Though he had barely been able to drag his ruined body around earlier, at some point it had begun to heal. He hadn't done anything in particular — the rare healing power he possessed had already knit closed most of the wounds inflicted by the Sage. It was a wonderful power. Despite falling from such a height, not only had he not died, but he'd started to heal automatically.

Yet Ein had nothing but derision for himself. So what if he could heal? He couldn't beat a single Sage in combat.

It was supposed to have been the perfect chance. The Sages were elusive, unpredictable in when and where they would appear. There was normally no way to know where they would be at any given time, but his agent had infiltrated the City Guard and managed to secure that information. He had known both the place and time that a Sage would appear.

Ein had been confident in his abilities as a Hero. If he could confront a Sage, he knew he could beat it. He had believed that from the bottom of his heart. But here was the result. The Sage had taken every single one of his attacks without resisting or even batting an eye.

He had slain Demon Lords. He had saved entire kingdoms. Even the Sage's attendants were easy prey. But he couldn't beat an actual Sage. He had exhausted every option and still hadn't found even a clue as to how he could fight them.

So what could he do now? He was the Hero of the Resistance, who bore all their hopes on his shoulders. He'd had every intention of honoring those hopes, but now he felt crushed beneath the weight of them.

By the time he had fully recovered, he was standing in front of his house...a ramshackle ruin on the verge of total collapse, completely abandoned. He didn't know what had brought him here, but something was off.

There was someone inside. There was someone in the house that should have long since been abandoned. It wasn't just his imagination, either — a Hero's senses were far too reliable.

Ein stood frozen. It couldn't be. But even as he thought that, the door swung wide open.

Ariel.

The sister he had been searching for, who had disappeared so long ago, was standing right in front of him. Expression full of hope, she immediately looked towards Ein.

"Lord Mitsuki! You came to get me!" The name was totally unfamiliar to him. As Ein wondered who she was talking about, the girl's face immediately lost its hopeful glow. "Oh, I'm sorry. I thought you were the Great Sage. Oh! Are you one of Lord Mitsuki's messengers? Something's wrong here! When I woke up, I was suddenly in this dirty house. I have no idea what's going on!" And her eyes immediately began to shine again. The way her expressions changed in the blink of an eye was just like he remembered her from so long ago.

"Ariel..." Ein immediately embraced her. Her behavior was rather strange but he didn't care. The fact that she was alive, that she was back, was all that mattered.

But Ariel began to struggle. "Please, stop! Let go of me! Someone!

Help!" With unbelievable strength, she desperately tried to break free from the Hero's arms. At this rate, she would hurt herself, so Ein let her go.

"No! No, no, no! My body belongs to Lord Mitsuki! No one else is allowed to touch it!" Ariel wrapped her arms around herself, crouching down.

As Ein watched her, dumbfounded, another person stepped out of the house. A woman, wearing glasses and a cold gaze.

"Hello. I am the secretary of the Great Sage. Please call me Alexia."

The Great Sage. The moment Ein heard that name, he immediately fell into a fighting stance. Although he had lost his holy sword, that was only one part of a Hero's power. Even barehanded, he had plenty of combat strength remaining.

"As the Great Sage has grown tired of her, I have brought her back."

"What…?"

"The Great Sage is a terribly kind person, so he would never say something so hurtful. But watching him every day, his feelings were clear. As such, I have returned her. Of course, we wouldn't be so callous as to take her life simply because our use for her was finished. That would make the Great Sage unhappy. As such, she has been returned home. I have come to explain this to you. Unfortunately, those who are taken away from the Great Sage inevitably feel the loss, as they've become rather obsessed, but there is nothing to be done about it. Such is the magnificence of the Great Sage."

As the secretary prattled on, Ein could do nothing but listen in awestruck silence. His shock rapidly turned to rage, and he ended up reflexively throwing a punch at the secretary, but his hands passed through her like she was nothing but air.

At that point he realized the truth — there had never been anyone there besides his sister.

"Unfortunately, I am not physically here. I have only appeared to explain Ariel's situation, that it might not be a hindrance to her in the future."

As if that was all she had come to say, the woman who called herself the Great Sage's secretary suddenly vanished.

"Lord Mitsuki! Where are you?! You! Did you hide him from me?!" Ariel stood back up and punched Ein. Still in shock, he took the blow to the face and was instantly knocked flat.

He jumped back to his feet, staring at Ariel in disbelief. Even if he had been caught off guard, there was no way Ariel should have had the strength to send a Hero like him flying. But taking a closer look, he saw that her arm was strangely swollen. It was almost like the arm of some monster had been crudely grafted onto her. Ariel brandished that arm, staring at Ein with ragged breath and bloodshot eyes.

A pang of fear urged him forward. Quickly closing the gap between them, he punched her in the stomach. The strange sensation of that contact sent another chill through him, prompting him to throw another blow. And with each blow, Ariel transformed further.

How long did he spend punching his own sister? By the time he came back to himself, Ariel was motionless at his feet. The strength left his knees and he collapsed over her. She was still breathing, if only barely. But so what? What could he do now?

Ein was at a complete loss.

ACT 3

Chapter 23 — As Expected of My Master!

From the remains of the destroyed train, they had walked about ten kilometers west. While it was a bit slower than the pace of your average healthy high school student, the main cause of their slowness was Yogiri.

"This is why I told you to get the robot to carry us," Tomochika sighed, looking down at him. Having found a conveniently placed fallen tree, Yogiri was sitting to recuperate his strength. Despite the fact that their backpacks were basically the same weight, Tomochika was still brimming with energy.

"I really want to avoid stirring up as much trouble as we can. What would we do if someone saw us being carried here by that robot?"

The giant had been called an "aggressor." Although they didn't know exactly what sort of basis their necklaces used to translate, it apparently meant "invader." That almost certainly made the robot an enemy of the people of this world, so being seen together with it would have cast them in the same light.

"That robot didn't seem like such a bad guy, though. Are you really that out of shape? You seemed strong enough when you pushed me over earlier," Tomochika said, a hint of displeasure in her voice.

"I was forced to exercise regularly, so I'm not totally hopeless. I'll admit my stamina is kind of lacking, though."

Yogiri had been all for hurrying when they'd first set out, but as they'd progressed, he had slowed down bit by bit and began to regularly ask for breaks.

"Well, you never know what might happen, so maybe you should work on that," Tomochika said, sitting down beside him. "Or at the very least, we should have gotten a vehicle or something. Was there a reason for us to run away so fast like that?"

I agree. If we had stayed a bit longer, we could have gotten a lot more out of that robot.

Mokomoko was floating alongside them.

"Because I saw the shadow. I told you I can sense danger, right?"

"Yeah, you said you can see something. Kind of like Morihei Ueshiba?"

"Who?"

"He's an Aikido master. He can even dodge bullets, but apparently he can see something like a ray of light that shows where the bullets will go before they're even fired."

"I guess it's something like that. But instead of light, it's more like a black line or a kind of shadow. Earlier, I saw a huge shadow hanging over the entire area around the train, so things were getting pretty intense there. The danger level was around thirty percent, maybe."

"Okay. I have no idea what you mean by a percent, but I'm guessing it's something like a weather forecast?"

"Something like that. Where we are now, it's below one percent, so this area should be much safer."

"You make it sound like we're only resting now because we got to a safe place, but you really just wanted to rest because you're tired, right?"

"We've basically made it to the city anyway, so it's fine."

They'd known there was a station between the forest and the canyon. Hearing that, Yogiri had assumed it was some small settlement tucked away in the wilderness, but the truth had been quite different.

Despite its isolated location, he could see numerous skyscrapers. It seemed like a rather large city.

"It looks like there are no city walls. Does that mean they don't get attacked by monsters here?"

"I doubt it. The cities in this world that don't have the Sage's protection all seem to be in constant danger."

"You say that, but we just walked along the rails without a care in the world."

"That's only because I kept killing all of the enemies."

"What?!"

"Yeah, we were targeted by some monsters and bandits and stuff on the way."

"Tell me, then! Now I look like an idiot for just strolling along, humming a tune without noticing anything!"

Most of the enemies had come from within the forest. The monsters were likely attracted by their scent. And apparently the trains were regularly attacked by bandits, so a gang probably had a stronghold nearby as well.

"I didn't think it was worth mentioning."

"This weapon is really going to be pointless, isn't it?"

It has a number of different shapes programmed into it, but I suppose it isn't proving too useful.

A sword had suddenly appeared in Tomochika's hand. One of the robot's internal functions was to reproduce materials in any shape it desired. Apparently, this function was mostly used to produce things like muscle fibers for itself. They were much softer than the exterior of the robot, but from a human perspective, the material could be used to make things that were more than solid enough to qualify as weapons.

When Mokomoko had asked for a weapon, this was what the robot had produced. Normally, it camouflaged itself as a piece of clothing, but at Mokomoko's command it could change shape, doing so at such a speed that it looked like it was being summoned on the spot.

"Aren't you supposed to be a ghost from the Heian era? How come you can use such a science fiction-y weapon so easily?"

The Dannoura Style of Martial Arts can evolve to suit any circumstance! Recently, the main focus has been on electronic warfare. Did you not know?

"Not even a little! Who would have thought an old-fashioned martial art would go in that direction?!"

"Honestly, it's good to hear that you're good at things like that, Mokomoko. You said you'll be able to analyze the Gift as well, right?"

Indeed. I managed to get about a million credits from that robot. I was able to use that to purchase the rights to the middleware used by that Battle Song system. The original Battle Song is now open source, so by putting those together I can reproduce a kind of counterfeit version of it. The Gift has changed considerably from the original, however, so it will take some time to analyze the newer version. If I can do that, it should make understanding this world a lot easier. It may even be possible to hack it to some degree.

"I feel like this conversation is completely leaving me behind! I have no idea what you guys are talking about at all. Who are you that you can even do something like that?"

Yogiri had been wondering the same thing. What were those credits she was talking about? How and where did a ghost like her buy something with them? And if the Gift was a program, where was it developed? Mokomoko hadn't explained that at all, so they were completely in the dark.

As a result of my long lifespan, I have evolved into a high-level divine spirit, an information-based life form, giving me awareness of and access to higher levels of information layers! Even in a different world, the upper-level information layers fundamentally remain the same, so knowledge of it gives me a working knowledge of all worlds, in a general sense. Accessing that layer also allows for the use of value exchange media, known as credits. That robot's home world must be one where information-based life forms are rather common. He considered someone like me to be an ordinary being, after all. In short, by manipulating the parts of that robot, I could even interact with the material world —

"You're not explaining anything at all!" Tomochika shouted as Mokomoko's explanation continued to make things more confusing.

Once they had finished resting, the two of them entered Hanabusa. There were no walls or anything that looked like official entry points. It seemed they weren't limiting access to the city at all. There were, however, a number of poles around to indicate the city's boundaries. They must have been there to show how far the Sages' protection extended.

The roads were paved in asphalt, and the buildings were constructed from concrete. It had a completely different atmosphere from Quenza, the city they had visited earlier. While Quenza was a medieval fantasy metropolis, Hanabusa looked more like modern Japan. The streets were bustling with people, coming and going with an overflowing energy.

"So…we're waiting here for everyone else, right?"

"Either that or we head to the capital and wait for them there. What do you think?"

"The capital is pretty close by train, isn't it? Why don't we wait here for a bit?"

"In that case, we'll need a base of operations. Celestina told me about a good hotel, so let's go check it out."

"Oh, if Celestina told you about it then that's good enough for me." It seemed Tomochika had developed an unconditional trust in the concierge.

Following the map that Celestina had drawn for them, they found the hotel in no time at all.

"Wow, this is amazing!"

The building was enormous, tall enough that from street level, you couldn't even see how many floors it had. The outside was rather unrefined but its height alone was enough to impress. Even in Hanabusa, it must have been one of the tallest buildings. Pushing through the revolving door at the entrance, the two of them entered the lobby.

"It looks gorgeous, but thanks to you, I still can't see anything but a love hotel. Why did you have to say that?!"

"Not much I can do about it now, even if you complain."

The bright, open lobby was filled with gold fixtures throughout, lending it a high-class yet cheap-looking feel. It was crowded to the point of overflowing. While most of the people present were likely guests, a number of them seemed to be using it more as a meeting place.

As the pair looked around the lobby in amazement, a group of people began walking towards them. When they stepped aside to make way, the group instead turned to approach them.

"I thought so! It's Dannoura!" The speaker was plainly a Japanese boy. Yogiri didn't remember him in the least, but if he knew Tomochika, he must have been one of their classmates. Behind him were five women who all seemed to be natives.

"What? Tachibana?! Why are you here?"

Their classmates should have still been making their way through the forest. There was no way they could have reached Hanabusa before Yogiri and Tomochika, who had traveled most of the way by train.

"I'm so glad you're safe! I decided to split off from the others. There was no point participating in their absurdly slow way of leveling."

"Oh, really? Not that I know anything about that."

Having encountered one of their classmates so unexpectedly, Tomochika was at a sudden loss for words.

One of the girls behind Tachibana, a blonde with hair tied up in twin tails, immediately showed her displeasure. "Who is this woman? And why is she acting so friendly with Yuuki?!"

In the face of her sudden and blatant hostility, Tomochika was even more confused. She had no idea why she was being attacked.

"Stop it, Erika. This is one of my classmates."

"If you say so…" Reluctantly, Erika backed off.

"As expected of my master! Your tolerance shines so much brighter in the light of your companions' rudeness! Truly yours is a heart fit to be king!" This time, a girl with wavy brown hair had spoken up.

"Takatou, what is up with these people?" Tomochika murmured.

"I have no clue." The girls all seemed to be obsessed with Tachibana, but he couldn't say why.

"Oh, I've got an idea!" Tachibana said, as if a brilliant thought had just occurred to him. "Meeting here must have been fate! Why don't you become my lover, Dannoura?"

The moment the proposal left his mouth, the adoring gazes of the collection of women behind him turned murderous.

"Excuse me?" Tomochika's bewilderment continued to grow unabated.

Chapter 24 — At This Point, It's Starting to Get Funny

The three unexpectedly reunited classmates had moved their conversation to one of the lobby's meeting spaces. Yogiri and Tomochika sat beside each other on a sofa, across from their classmate Yuuki Tachibana, with a table between them. The five girls following Yuuki now stood arrayed behind him. It had only been four days since he had arrived in this world, but he already had a group of his own companions.

"Umm, to be honest, I don't really know what this is about, but this isn't just a confession of love, is it?"

"Why don't you become my lover?" wasn't the kind of line one would expect from a high school student. Even Yogiri, who was completely deprived of friends to joke around with, felt the same.

"If you don't decide quickly, I'm not going to offer such great conditions again. Do you think you can make up your mind in two minutes?"

Pressing her for an answer, Yuuki set a harsh time limit. A classic move in trying to guide someone to a particular answer. But that would only work if there was some value to the offer. Yuuki, at least, seemed to believe wholeheartedly that there was.

Tomochika, of course, flatly refused him. "I don't really care about your conditions. What I want to know is what you're doing here."

The girls standing behind Yuuki immediately began to glare

daggers at her. There was an unquestionable thirst for blood in their eyes, but it wasn't accompanied by any impression that they might carry out their violent wishes. Yogiri decided it was best to see how things played out for the moment.

"Are you sure? If you ask to join me later, you'll be at best a mid-tier slave. This is a great opportunity for you."

"I don't understand *anything* that's going on right now!"

Even as she said that, Yuuki somehow managed to look more surprised than Tomochika herself. Apparently, he had thought his position quite strong.

"Ah! See, slaves are divided into four tiers: top, middle, lower, and labor. But as my lover, you'd be special. It's an Eternal-tier slave, above all the others—"

"No, I don't care about any of that!"

"Then…what do you want?"

"Well, to start with, who are all these people behind you?"

Becoming more and more flustered by the conversation, Tomochika turned her attention to the girls accompanying Yuuki.

"Ah. I guess I haven't introduced them yet. These are my bodyguards, chosen specially from my most qualified slaves. Hey, introduce yourselves."

As Tomochika stared at him in disbelief, hearing him casually referring to the girls as slaves, they began their introductions. The first was the girl that had lashed out at Tomochika earlier. Her long blonde hair was tied up into twin tails, and her sharp eyes hinted at a strong personality.

"Bodyguard Unit, Position Five. Erika. Honestly, I'd never give my name to someone like you, but if Yuuki tells me to then I guess I have to. Of course, I'll never let you become an Eternal slave!"

The second to speak up was the brown-haired girl, her soft wavy hair giving a calm impression. "Bodyguard Unit, Position Four. My name is Stephanie. I have nothing to discuss with someone who would reject our master's invitation, but orders are orders. Even being a mid-tier slave would be more than you deserve."

The third was the youngest of the group. Wearing a black frilled dress, she held a teddy bear in her arms. "Position Three. I'm Chelsey. Could you please die for me?"

The fourth had long silver hair, which was a striking contrast to her darker skin. "Position Two, Euphemia. Honestly, it hurts just to look at you. Could you please leave?"

The fifth was the oldest of the group. Wearing a white dress, the way she gently smiled matched her overall more mature impression. "First Position, with the honor of being Captain of the Bodyguard Unit, my name is Riza. Please don't take Yuuki's offer seriously. You may be excited by his promise to make you his lover, but please try not to think so highly of yourself — such a thing is clearly beyond you."

"Geez, just one after another with you people! Tachibana, can you please keep them under control?" Tomochika's irritation at being talked down to by the other girls was starting to show.

"Yuuki! Hanging around people like this is just a waste of time! We were supposed to go shopping today!"

"Please don't act all high and mighty simply because he's your classmate! Just hurry up and become a slave so we can make you a plaything for the labor-tier slaves!"

"Yuuki, can we kill these guys?"

The bodyguards continued to layer on the complaints. But when Yuuki raised his hand, they all immediately fell silent.

"Sorry about that. I'm not good at being strict with girls, but I think they went a bit too far. Everyone be quiet for a while."

"Understood!" the five girls responded as one. But even so, they continued to glare at Tomochika.

"Maybe it was too forward of me to ask you to be my lover out of the blue like that. Oh, are you worried about Takatou? Normally, I only take men on as labor slaves, but I can make him a lower-tier slave instead if that will make you feel better. He is one of our classmates, after all."

"At first, this whole thing was pretty annoying, but at this point it's getting kind of funny," Tomochika muttered under her breath, her previous irritation apparently gone.

"Up until now, there hasn't been any killing intent," Yogiri whispered back. The vibe he was getting was more like desire. He turned to Yuuki and continued. "There's no way we can join you without any explanation of what you're up to. Could you tell us exactly what you are doing here?"

"I suppose that's fair. Okay, I'll explain it to you. But you'll regret it. You would have been better off just accepting my offer right away," Yuuki happily replied, his voice becoming serious. "First of all, please relax. We were told that if no Sage came out of our class, we'd become livestock for generating magical energy, but that's impossible. I'm already guaranteed to become a Sage, after all."

"Wow, I've never seen such a smug expression before!"

But Yuuki's confidence in himself was enough to let Tomochika's jab slide. "So...even if you do nothing at all, you'll be safe. But I'm not going to offer any rewards to classmates who don't contribute. That's only fair, right?"

The entire class had been meant to act as a single group — a Clan. That Clan had been given the mission of producing a Sage. If a Sage was born, the rest of the Clan would become his or her attendants, and their treatment from that point on was up to their new leader. So the appearance of a Sage in and of itself didn't guarantee them any safety. Those who couldn't become Sages needed to get in good standing with those who could, so that once one of them "ascended," their own positions would be secure.

"And that 'contribution' is becoming your slave or lover?" Yogiri had no intention of beating around the bush. He simply asked the questions that came to mind.

"That's the best you two can offer, isn't it? To be clear, that doesn't just go for you guys, either. I'm strong enough that everyone else in the class is dead weight in comparison. The best that any of you can do is help to entertain me."

Yogiri was impressed. Yuuki seemed to genuinely believe the things he was saying.

"This is only the fourth day since we were summoned here, right?

I don't know what kind of power he received, but his personality has really come a long way in a short time," he whispered to Tomochika.

"No, not really. Tachibana has been that way from the start."

"Wait, seriously?"

"He's been a narcissist since forever. He was always popular with the girls, so it's kind of understandable, I guess. Didn't you know that?"

"Seems like high school was a more interesting place than I thought..." Yogiri was struck by the feeling that maybe spending all his time at school sleeping had been a wasted opportunity.

"Hm? Is something wrong? Ah, is being my lover not enough for you?"

"Not even slightly appealing," Tomochika replied in a flash.

"Unfortunately, that's the best I can do. In the end, I'm a very honest person. If I'm going to spend the rest of my life with someone, I have to test them thoroughly. Of course, I'm most likely to pick a wife from among my lovers and top-tier slaves, so becoming my lover now is as good a start as you'll get."

"I'd appreciate it if you could rethink what it means to be an honest person," Tomochika said, exasperated. She had heard that he'd always been like this, but it definitely couldn't have been to this degree. "Why are you so confident in yourself? Everyone in the class is training but you, aren't they?"

Yogiri felt that Yuuki's self confidence was on the same level as the three who had already been to this world before. Tomochika must have been thinking the same thing.

"I don't need any training," Yuuki declared proudly. "My class is Dominator — the strongest class, fit to rule over everyone."

Chapter 25 — Support Types Are Way Too Strong

Rewinding time a little, we come to a period shortly after the class-mates that had left Yogiri and the others as bait had made it to the city of Quenza. The class had gathered in a bar, similar in atmosphere to the pubs of their original world. The first floor of a house had been converted into a wide open space, with a number of tables lined up throughout.

The class had reserved the entire bar. The reward they'd received for clearing their first mission was rather sizable, so an expense like this was well within their means. Now they were discussing what would happen next.

Although they had put their trust in General Yazaki to clear their first mission, now that they'd had a chance to calm down, a number of them had begun to fear that they would be cut off next. Among them, Yuuki Tachibana sat alone. That was likely because of his class, Dominator.

While they were developing their plan to clear the first mission, all of their classes had become common knowledge. Although the exact details of those classes were still unknown, Yuuki having such an over-bearing class name was enough to make people distance themselves from him.

Dominator was a powerful class, capable of controlling people and monsters alike. But there was a process that had to be followed for that control to set in. It wasn't something so simple that he could simply control anyone who happened to get close to him. However, there was no way that his classmates would know that.

So, after being summoned to this world and thrust into a situation where he understood almost nothing, he had been further isolated. While that would normally have been cause for panic, Yuuki was still acting as carefree as ever. There was no basis for it at all, but he was convinced that he was special, so his thoughts ran in an optimistic direction. This was likely because he had never experienced a serious setback in his entire life. He had no understanding of the concept of failure.

So now, not thinking about the future in the least, he sat at a window table to watch the women walking by outside. Although most of them appeared to be locals, every once in a while a Japanese-looking person would pass by as well. As Yuuki was deciding that he liked Japanese girls better after all, one of his classmates approached.

"Yo. Can we talk for a bit?"

"Sure. What's up?"

Haruto Ootori. The only other guy in the class as popular with the girls as Yuuki himself. While Yuuki boasted a perfect, model-like appearance, Haruto had a more aloof, intellectual air.

As if he hadn't considered that he might be rejected, Haruto had already taken a seat before Yuuki could even answer.

"I just wanted to give you some advice."

"Oh? That's right, your class was…what was it again?" Yuuki tried to recall the name but it wouldn't come to mind. He just didn't care that much about the other guys in the group.

"It's Consultant. I specialize in providing advice for resolving problems, I guess."

"Right, right, the Consultant. So what are we consulting about?" He remembered now that Haruto had been the one who had reserved this bar for them. It was pretty impressive to be able to handle that kind of negotiation with strangers in a city and world that he'd never been to before. There might be some value in listening to his advice.

"It's about how you use the Dominator power. You don't really understand it yet, do you?"

"That's true, but I'm more of a hands-on kind of guy. I'll figure it out once I try it for myself." He wasn't making excuses; it was what he honestly believed. He was ultimately a true optimist at heart.

"For you, that actually might work out. But I wouldn't overlook my advice either way."

"Oh? All right, let's hear it, then. I'll decide whether or not to listen after you tell me what you have to say."

"The strength of the Dominator class lies in the number of underlings you have. That means the first course of action for you would be to gather subordinates, but there are some restrictions on the types of people you can control. The first is that you can only control those of a lower level than yourself. The second is that they have to agree to being put under your control."

Yuuki already knew that much. That was why he hadn't immediately set out to begin collecting subordinates. His current level was only one, and there were hardly any people who would choose to be his subordinates willingly.

"But there is a special exception to the second rule. They don't necessarily *have* to agree. Otherwise, it would be pretty useless against things like monsters, who can't really understand you."

"That wasn't in the explanation at all," Yuuki said, his interest now piqued. When they'd received the Gift, they had also received a basic understanding of how to use their abilities. But this was the first that Yuuki had heard of an exception to the second rule.

"Right. It's almost like a video game, in that they wanted you to figure it out yourself. The way you bypass that second restriction is by stepping on someone's head when they're close to death. That will put them under your control."

Yuuki wasn't the least bit suspicious about how Haruto would know that. Just knowing his class was Consultant, he was more than happy to accept it as fact.

"With that in mind, the best course of action for you is to pick up as many level one slaves from this city as you can. You should be able to find some that have been rejected for one reason or another for fairly cheap. Whether it's because they are close to death or disabled in some way doesn't really matter."

"What does that have to do with the Dominator class?"

"If you buy slaves, you'll be able to control them with your power. Slaves are already bought and sold without their own will taken into account, so it works the same as them agreeing to be under your control."

"I see. It's an easy way to get subordinates. And what am I supposed to do with them?" Not interested in thinking things through himself, he continued to ask for Haruto's advice.

"Divide them into groups of five, then send them out of the city to start hunting monsters. Once they are under your control, you can give them orders. No matter how stupid they may be, they'll do exactly as you say. Even slaves that are close to dying can hold the monsters down for a while. So if you send them off on a suicide attack, they should at least be able to bring weaker monsters close to death. Then you step in and take control of those monsters as well. If the beasts end up dying, it's not a real issue. The threat of monsters in this world is significant enough that, at worst, you'll earn money by killing even the weakest ones."

"Wait, I don't have to step on their heads myself?"

"Yeah, that's the amazing part about the Dominator class. Your subordinates are basically extensions of you. And what's more, if they defeat any monsters, half of the experience points go to you instead of them."

"I see. So basically, if I buy some slaves and send them out into the fields, I'll automatically start gaining experience and building up a large army." An ordinary person might hesitate at the "buying slaves" part, but Yuuki had no such compunction. From the beginning, he had thought of other people only as support for the main character that was Yuuki himself.

"Once you've finished your initial preparations, I recommend you head to Ectel. It's a mining town that has made prolific use of slave labor

for ages. There should be an abundance of slaves to choose from there. After that, continue on to Hanabusa. There are ruins nearby that are completely overrun with monsters, so it should be perfect for leveling and building your army quickly."

"It feels like you're trying to get rid of me."

"There are certainly those in the class who are uneasy about you. Many people are saying that you'll get in the way of the group's cooperation."

"I don't really see the class getting along that well just by getting rid of me, though." In truth, the class was already fracturing into separate factions. At that point, you couldn't call them a single group anymore.

"I agree. But there isn't much of a reason for them all to cooperate either. Everyone doing the same thing seems suicidal. If we want to produce a Sage, we need to take a number of different approaches. This is part of that. Basically, I'm singling out those who have the best chances and offering them advice to increase the probability of their success."

Yuuki looked around the bar. A number of their classmates had already left. Perhaps the ones that Haruto had spoken to had already taken his advice and moved on.

"Is there anyone in the class that you feel like making into a slave? I can probably handle the negotiations if it's only one person." Haruto made the offer even though he was unsure of what Yuuki's reaction might be. The class had already sacrificed four of their own to get this far. If there was a chance for Yuuki to do well, one more sacrifice wasn't asking that much.

"Don't worry about it. There's no one here I'm all that interested in."

The first one he had thought of was Tomochika Dannoura, but she was no longer with them. Yuuki rose from his seat. Now that he had decided on a course of action, sticking around was a waste of time.

"Well, feel free to consider yourself safe, Haruto. Because I'm definitely going to make it to the rank of Sage."

With a bold smile, he left the bar behind.

"Support types are way too strong in this world!" Tomochika cried out after hearing Yuuki's long explanation. She may have been remembering Celestina as well.

"So even as you're sitting around here, you're still growing your army and gaining levels," Yogiri mused.

If that was the case, his overwhelming self-confidence wasn't that strange.

"That's right. And the Consultant didn't figure it out, but I found an even better method," Yuuki replied, pausing for effect. "Bugs. The number of them can't even be compared to the number of humans and monsters around. So I figured I'd start controlling them! While individually they are awfully weak, their numbers are effectively infinite. Using insects, I can take control of even more insects. This isn't even comparable to something like rats multiplying. My power is growing at an unbelievable rate!" Although it wasn't a power he'd had from the start, and the basic idea for how to use it had come from someone else, he still spoke with pride. "So how about it, Dannoura? You regret not becoming my lover, don't you? It's too late for that now, but if you want to become a mid-tier slave —"

"Not even a little," Tomochika cut him off. "And those girls behind you are incredibly good looking. It seems you've got lots of girls like that around. Why are you interested in me at all?"

"Hm, to be blunt, I'd say I'm just after your body. Even before we came here, I always had my eye on you."

"Well, that's the worst confession of love I've ever heard."

"You're awfully popular, aren't you?" Yogiri said to Tomochika, legitimately impressed.

"Oh yeah, I guess those other guys said something similar, too..." Tomochika hung her head at the realization that all the bad people seemed to have a thing for her.

"Didn't you know?" Yuuki continued. "You're pretty famous in our school. People are always saying that you look like a gravure model, or that you'd be phenomenally beautiful if you just stopped talking, or that if they knocked you out you'd even be above average overseas."

"Seems like there are an awful lot of opinions about me!"

"Well, maybe asking you to join me now was a bit too sudden. But I'm pretty lenient. Feel free to think it over as much as you like. I'm living at the top floor of this hotel, so come on over any time you change your mind."

Yuuki stood up, taking his bodyguards with him as he left the hotel. Given his unfailing confidence right through the end, he seemed sure that Tomochika would break if only given enough time.

"Wow, he's annoying," Tomochika said once Yuuki had disappeared from view.

"Well, it's not like he's coming after us as enemies, so I guess there's nothing we can do but let him be." If they stayed in Hanabusa they might come across him again, and while that was certainly irritating, there wasn't any real harm in it. "Anyway, becoming one of his companions doesn't sound like that bad of a deal. You'd probably be safer than if you stuck with me."

"Don't you start, too."

"Oh. Well, sorry, I guess?" Seeing how quickly she became angry, he immediately apologized.

"Not sure how I feel about that kind of apology, either. But there's no way I'd stick with someone who just came out and said they were after my body —" Tomochika cut off in the middle of her sentence, a sudden realization causing her to raise her voice. "Except that you said the same thing about my boobs!"

Chapter 26 — Let Him Give Them a Good Rub

Two days had passed since they'd arrived at the hotel in Hanabusa. Yogiri had spent the entire time sleeping in his own room, so Tomochika was stuck in hers as well.

For now, they passed their time in peace and quiet. The temperature of the room was always comfortable, and the lights could be freely controlled. They could call the front desk to have any food they wanted delivered.

As an aside, while a telephone network had been set up within the city, it didn't extend beyond it. Apparently they hadn't developed wireless communications yet.

The bathrooms were fully equipped with plumbing, the faucets produced water when turned on, and they even had toilet paper. If they stayed there, they could live just as comfortably as back home. It really didn't feel like they were in another world at all.

"How long can we sit around here, though…"

Staring absentmindedly out the window, Tomochika spoke to herself. Her room was on the fifth floor of the hotel. From here, all she could see was an array of dreary buildings, so it wasn't particularly appealing scenery. As expected, being cooped up in a single room by herself was causing her mood to dip.

Until the boy wakes up, I imagine, Mokomoko answered from where she floated beside Tomochika. The ghost had warned her against going outside on her own, and while that was a danger she well understood, it didn't make her any less bored.

"Could you go see how he is? You can walk through walls, right?"

While I certainly could, I will not. He's far too scary.

"All you have to do is take a peek."

He is much worse when he is sleeping. Entering his room without permission would be inexcusable. Who knows how he would react?

"He never told us not to wake him up."

Our best option is to wait for him to wake on his own. It's best to let sleeping dragons lie. In this case, that means letting the child sleep.

"But even if he wakes up, we're still just sitting around waiting."

They had come to Hanabusa to reunite with their classmates. They didn't have anything else to do here, so all they could do was hang around.

What would you even do if he was awake, with both of you stuck in these rooms? Hm? Mokomoko floated closer, a sly grin rising to her face. As Tomochika realized what she was implying, her face flushed red.

"What are you talking about?! We're not like that!"

What do you mean? You should be clinging to him as much as you can so he doesn't dump you.

"Dump me? We're not dating or anything." Tomochika wasn't quite sure how to describe their relationship.

He already said he's interested in your chest, so why don't you let him give it a good rub?

"Are you stupid?! Why on earth would I do that?!"

Oh? I would think using your body to entice him would make it go rather quickly. And I'm sure it would increase the value in protecting you for him as well.

"Well, I do feel bad that he's always protecting me, but I don't know what I can really do to pay him back."

You can entertain him with your body, can't you?

"Do you have to say it like such a pervert?!"

There's no need to be afraid. We did all kinds of night crawling in search of strong blood for our family in the past.

"Isn't that kind of backwards? I'm so sorry, ancestors!" Tomochika suddenly felt the need to apologize to the great men of history. They must have been terrified by the approach of such a rotund woman.

Even if it's your first time, I'll be sure to teach you thoroughly!

"Don't make me look up how to do an exorcism!" Tomochika shouted as the worst possible scene came to mind.

Well, I suppose if you absolutely insisted, I could give you two your privacy.

"What do you mean you suppose?!"

It would be a much bigger issue if I could be separated from you so easily as your guardian spirit, don't you think?

This conversation wasn't going to go anywhere pleasant. Tomochika sighed, looking out the window once more.

"Looks like I'll really be stuck in this room the whole time. Even if I went out...wait, what's that?"

Tomochika realized that something was off outside. Some sort of commotion was happening on the street below. The carriages running down the road were suddenly pulling to the side and stopping.

A shriek filled the air. The pedestrians began scattering in a panic. Searching for the source of their terror, Tomochika saw something barreling down the road at full speed.

"What is that? A truck?"

Enormous vehicles were soaring past, paying no heed to the carriages that were in their path. Those who didn't get out of the way were sent flying, crashing into the sidewalk. The pedestrians that were too slow to escape were crushed underneath.

So that's what armored military vehicles look like, said Mokomoko.

There were three of the enormous things racing noisily down the street, built in a solid, angular design. She didn't know whether there were soldiers inside or not, but they must have been carrying something.

That is...not something proper. The scent of death is strong from them.

161

"I can tell that just by looking!"

Outside, death was everywhere. The armored vehicles showed no hesitation in spreading it all around them.

No, I am speaking of the contents. Within the armored vehicles is a sense of death so overpowering that any sort of strength the vehicles themselves possess is meaningless before it.

"What is wrong with this world?! This is so not okay! Why do people die so frequently here?!"

If the natural environment of this world was just that harsh, it would be something she could understand. But this was different. Like their experience on the train, she got the impression that the people in charge simply didn't care one way or another about others being caught up in their acts of violence.

They may be related to the Sages. Those armored vehicles were clearly developed with otherworlders in mind.

Closing the curtains, Tomochika retreated to her bed and took a seat. There was no point watching any longer. It would only make her feel worse.

You said you wanted to go take a look outside, right?

"Yeah, right. I think I'll pass for now. Wow, these high-class hotel rooms are so nice, aren't they!" As expected after witnessing such a scene, her appetite for the outdoors had been thoroughly squashed.

That would indeed be the safest option. For some reason, there seemed to be some kind of undercurrent to the ghost's words.

"What? What are you trying to say? You have a problem with me enjoying my life as a shut-in from now on?"

It's impossible to stay here doing nothing forever.

"This is a world where walking down the street gets you splattered by a truck, remember?"

But can you say those trucks won't come looking for you in here?

"Sounds like you're overthinking it."

That's just an example. Actually, since not too long ago, there has been quite a bit of hostility aimed at us in here.

"What? Why? What did I do?"

Relax. Whether it was your classmates, or those thugs, or the Sage, or the bandits, or the monsters, someone always seems to be out to get you. Is it that strange that someone would be targeting you here as well? Mokomoko asked, exasperated.

Tomochika had considered all of those things to be like natural disasters, but from the attackers' perspectives, that wasn't necessarily the case at all.

"So who is it this time?"

Someone is outside the room, down the hall, waiting for us to step outside. I can't see them, though.

"If you can't see them, how do you know they're there?"

As your guardian spirit, I can sense hostility aimed at your person. While not as precise as the boy's, I can tell to some degree when there are suspicious people about. If they were just standing around waiting, it would be fine, but it seems they've grown tired of that. There's a possibility they will attack the room itself.

"Well, what can I do about it? Okay! I'm going to call Takatou!"

Awfully quick to rely on him, aren't we?

Tomochika had nothing she could do against an opponent she couldn't see. But Yogiri could probably deal with someone like that easily enough, she thought. She leaped over to the phone and called the room beside hers.

"Hello?"

"So fast! You're awake after all!"

"I just woke up. The phone rang right beside my head, so it woke me up right away."

Tomochika quickly explained the situation.

"I see. I'll head over to your room."

"I know it's kind of strange to say this, seeing as I'm the one who called you, but are you sure about that? Apparently, there's an invisible person out there."

"If they're just invisible, it's not really a problem, is it?"

There didn't seem to be any logic to his words, but Yogiri's voice alone made Tomochika feel a bit safer.

Chapter 27 — Is It Okay Not To Preserve the Crime Scene?

After hanging up the phone, the first thing Yogiri did was grab a drink of water, since he hadn't eaten anything for the past two days. He was still quite hungry but, perhaps because he had slept so well, he felt full of energy.

Yogiri stepped out of his room. The hallway was empty, but according to Tomochika there was something invisible out there. As he concentrated on the corridor in front of him, a black haze became visible, stretching out diagonally towards Tomochika's room.

It wasn't a concrete display of killing intent, and it was rather faint since it wasn't aimed at Yogiri himself, but it was enough to tell him that something was there. Despite his appearance in the hallway, though, there was no reaction from whatever it was. It likely had no idea that it had been detected.

Yogiri unleashed his power at that invisible foe. He heard the thud of something falling to the ground, and after a short while, the body of a girl appeared face down on the hallway floor. Without bothering to confirm any further details, Yogiri stepped up to Tomochika's room and knocked on the door.

"It's me."

The door immediately opened, a timid Tomochika peeking around it. "Hurry up! Get inside!" She must have been on guard against the enemy. Yogiri complied without complaint.

"You were right, there was someone out there." Yogiri lowered himself into one of the guest chairs.

"Wait, you could see them?"

"No, but I could see their killing intent. They were hiding diagonal to your door. Apparently, they weren't interested in me at all because they didn't react when I stepped outside."

"Mokomoko said something similar, that she felt some hostility aimed at me. But I don't remember doing anything that would make someone hate me that much."

All the enemies they'd encountered had been killed by Yogiri. Tomochika really hadn't done anything.

Fool. There is no way anyone could tell which of you two was responsible just by watching you.

"But in that case, it's weird for them to only be focused on her. Doesn't that make it seem like they're out for revenge or something?" While that was his best guess as to why she was being targeted, he didn't have any concrete reason for someone wanting to take revenge against Tomochika specifically.

"Well, I'm glad you came, but what do we do now?"

If you insist I leave you two in peace, then I suppose there's nothing I can do. Enjoy yourselves!

"That's not what this is about!" As Tomochika's face flushed for seemingly no reason, Yogiri cocked his head in confusion. "Anyway, what do you think we should do?" She was clearly trying to avoid a particular topic, but that was fine with him.

"Ah, right. Let me borrow your phone." Standing up, Yogiri called the front desk. "There's a woman who's collapsed in the fifth floor hallway. She might need help." After delivering that succinct message, he returned to his seat.

"What? What happened?"

"It would be weird for me to act like I didn't see anything. There's no way they'd believe that I didn't notice a body lying there."

There hadn't been anyone in the hallway to witness the death, but it was best to try and curb suspicions now. Yogiri had decided to take the most natural course of action, just to be safe.

"A body?"

"Yeah, I killed them."

"Already?!"

"If they're going to turn invisible and hide themselves, there's not much else I can do, is there? Whatever was going on, it was just too suspicious. Getting rid of them was the best course of action."

"Maybe that's true. But aren't you interested in why they were targeting me in the first place?"

Indeed, I am interested in the background of this case. It would be quite a nuisance if this was the work of an organization and not just an individual.

"That's fair, I guess, but the only thing I can do is kill. I'm not really that good at interrogating people."

As much as he had experimented with holding back his power, it really wasn't well suited to interrogation. He would need to fully show and explain his power to use it as a threat, and since the damage it inflicted couldn't be healed, there was no hope for the target to be saved in the end. And torturing someone without using his power didn't really seem like an option against an opponent who could turn invisible. Who knew what other powers they had? Putting their own safety first by killing their adversaries was simply the best option.

"Now that I think about it, it's still kind of strange to just leave her like that."

As Yogiri stepped out of the room, Tomochika followed him. The staff had yet to arrive, so the girl was lying exactly where he had left her.

"I suppose you would think she'd only collapsed if you saw her like this."

"Maybe it's not my place to say, but you're pretty cool-headed, aren't you?" Despite seeing far more gruesome corpses in their short time together, Tomochika didn't seem especially bothered by any of it.

Yogiri would have expected a girl like her to be much more shaken up by the experience.

"I guess I'm used to it. Though I think that's pretty strange too."

People eventually die. The daughter of a school of martial arts can't afford to be shaken by such trifling things.

"I don't think it's anything quite so deep as that, and I've been plenty scared — huh? Hey, do you think you should be messing around like that?" As she was looking at the body, Yogiri had crouched down by the fallen girl, casually flipping her face up. "My point is, shouldn't we preserve the crime scene?"

"Trying to help someone who's collapsed in front of you shouldn't be suspicious."

The dead girl had blonde hair, done up in twin tails.

"Huh, I thought so. This is one of Tachibana's companions," Tomochika noted. "This one was Erika, from his Bodyguard Unit."

"So the culprit is Tachibana then? Either way, this is pretty bad. Now it looks like we're picking a fight with him."

Or perhaps it would be better to say that Tachibana was picking a fight with them, although in the end, Yogiri had still thrown the first punch.

I do not know the extent of a Dominator's powers, but it would be best to assume he is aware of the status of his subordinates.

"Tachibana was staying in this hotel too, right? So the first thing we should probably do is go somewhere else."

As they were speaking, the hotel staff arrived. Someone who looked like a doctor was with them, and helped them to load Erika onto a stretcher. Since there was no sign of foul play, they didn't have any sort of law enforcement with them.

Yogiri and Tomochika decided to get out of the hotel while they had the chance.

Chapter 28 — That's What Happens When You Are Ten Times Their Level

While a Dominator could see the status of his slaves, he couldn't see them all at the same time. If that were possible, it would be a completely unmanageable amount of information. So it was an important step for him to learn to filter that information to only see the crucial things.

"Hm? Erika's signal is gone." As blade-like claws bit into him, Yuuki Tachibana received a warning from his Slave Management skill.

Standing in front of him was a four-armed monster, perhaps best described as some sort of insect-human hybrid. Covered in a lustrous black shell, it stood about three meters tall. It was more than strong enough to cut through an ordinary human with ease, but its attacks barely scratched Yuuki.

"As expected of my master! Even monsters on the one hundredth floor are no match for you!"

They were now in the depths of a ruin near Hanabusa. Yuuki had come here to test out his strength, but in the end, none of the enemies could provide enough of a challenge to actually be useful test subjects, so the entire experience was something of a letdown.

Off to the side, one of his upper-tier slaves, Stephanie, was getting excited. Her wavy brown hair framed a charming face, but Yuuki's interest was more in her sensual body.

"This guy is about level one thousand, right?" he said. "I guess this is what you would expect for being ten times their level."

Yuuki's own level had reached ten thousand. An ordinary human was typically level one to five. Those who hunted monsters for a living would make it to around level fifty, and those who trained themselves to the ultimate extreme had a limit of ninety-nine. Anything beyond that required a special class.

Dominator was one of those special cases. Yuuki had reached level ten thousand without even expending much of his own effort. He defeated monsters by using his slaves, gaining experience and money from each of them, which he then used to purchase more slaves.

Taking control of a group of bandits, he had attacked trade caravans and conquered whatever cities and villages he could find that didn't have the protection of the Sages, making their inhabitants into his slaves as well. Whenever he was able to get the defeated monsters close to death without finishing them off, he made them into familiars to boost his army as well. Even small animals and insects were drafted into his ever-growing troops.

This was all set up to happen automatically. As the cycle continued successfully, he gained more and more new slaves at an incredible rate.

"Who...are you?!" The beetle man jumped back, raising his voice in confusion. It must have found the existence of a human who could defeat it to be unbelievable.

"Interesting. I didn't know there were monsters that could speak."

"Once they surpass a certain level, monsters acquire a degree of intelligence and are able to comprehend human speech," Euphemia explained, standing beside Stephanie. For this expedition, he had brought only those two along with him.

Euphemia belonged to a race known as half-demons, characterized by their darker skin and bright silver hair. He had acquired her by raiding a village in the Haqua Forest. Among the half-demon slaves he had picked up there, she'd stood out as being particularly attractive, and so was made into an upper-tier slave.

"Ahh. Maybe it has some use as a lower-tier slave, then."

Yuuki had divided his slaves into upper, mid, lower, and labor tiers. As he couldn't manage all of the slaves on his own, he had set up this system so that the higher-level slaves could manage the lower-level ones. But his number of slaves had long since surpassed a point at which even four ranks was sufficient. He would have to overhaul the entire system soon.

"A slave?! How dare you?!"

"Uhh, Flare Bomb. How is that?" Yuuki carelessly spoke the spell.

A Dominator possessed skills only for controlling and managing slaves. But among those was a skill that allowed him to borrow his slaves' abilities. In short, Yuuki could use any skill possessed by any one of his slaves.

The beetle man spontaneously exploded, the impact tearing a hole through its chest and blowing off its limbs, leaving only its head and torso to collapse to the ground. Leisurely stepping forward, Yuuki placed his foot on the head of the creature.

"Contract." Bringing it close to death, and with his foot on the monster's head, he used the Contract skill. With that, his control was established.

"Heal." As Stephanie spoke her own magic, the creature's mangled body began to reconstitute itself. She was a Healer, whose power was further enhanced by Yuuki's own. Healing injuries like this was trivial for her.

"How many levels are there in this ruin?"

"One hundred and fifty levels," the creature responded instantly.

"All right, then. Head down to the bottom level and gather as many allies as you can along the way. If you get through all of them, return to the surface and do the same thing in the forest."

"Understood."

The monster immediately left to carry out its orders. For vague commands like these, there was room for the slaves to use their own discretion in executing the orders.

"I came here to test my strength, but it seems there isn't anything here strong enough to do that for me."

Yuuki figured if he just increased his level without getting any practical experience, he might run into problems down the line. That was the reason for his expedition into the ruins, but at this rate, the whole venture seemed completely pointless. At first, he'd been interested in seeing the ruins of a culture from a world other than his own, but after a hundred levels of the same scenery, he had grown tired of it.

"Your combat is on a completely different plane of existence, Master. Surely you would be better served reigning as a king over your troops rather than doing the fighting yourself."

"So what happened to Erika?"

Yuuki had the slaves he was particularly interested in join his Bodyguard Unit. For this expedition, he had brought only two of them. The remaining three, of which Erika was one, had been told to wait in the hotel.

Yuuki reviewed Erika's action log. Concealing her weapons, she had left the top floor of the hotel, heading to the fifth floor in search of Tomochika Dannoura's room. Using a skill to conceal herself, she had hidden near the room. The action log didn't show Erika's intentions, but she must have been waiting for Tomochika to step outside.

After waiting patiently for a significant amount of time, eventually Yogiri Takatou had come out of the neighboring room. He had looked directly at her, and nowhere else, despite the fact that she should have been invisible. At that point, Erika's consciousness had abruptly cut off.

"Hm? I have no idea what happened. She just died? Was she hit from behind?" The action log only recorded the senses of the slaves themselves, so he couldn't see anything outside of her own line of sight. It was highly likely she had been struck from behind, but if so, there had been no warning at all of such an attack.

"That is rather baffling. Erika's class was Assassin, and she was a member of the forest tribe. Furthermore, she had received even more strength from you, Master. Even if there is a faint chance she could be bested in one-on-one combat, to think that she could be assassinated this way defies belief."

Assassins possessed an Alertness skill, which allowed them to be aware of what was happening outside of their own fields of vision, and there was no way Erika would have failed to use it while waiting to launch an ambush.

"Why was she in front of Dannoura's room in the first place?"

A slave was completely unable to disobey orders, but was free to act on his or her own volition outside of that. The slave's actions were generally still in the service of his or her master, but there was no way of knowing what Erika had specifically planned to do without asking her.

"If I may share my conjecture," Euphemia said politely, waiting for permission.

"Go ahead."

"You said you intended to make Miss Dannoura your lover. I would imagine that is the reason."

"Why would she be waiting outside her room because of that?"

"One possibility is that she thought Miss Dannoura was unworthy of you, so she decided to eliminate her. Another possibility is that she intended to kidnap Miss Dannoura for you."

"But a slave isn't supposed to bring harm to their master, right? Do you really think she'd kill someone that I've shown an interest in?"

"If she believed that it was in your best interest, I imagine she would."

"I see. So if I don't specifically tell her not to, she might do things on her own that I don't actually want her to do."

"That is correct. With each individual slave's ideas of what is best for you, there is a possibility their actions may run counter to your wishes."

So not everything would always go according to plan. Yuuki made sure to keep that in mind for later.

"Well, now that she's dead, we'll never know. She was quite expensive, though."

"If you wish for more of the forest tribe, there are a number of settlements nearby. It may be prudent to launch an attack now."

"More settlements like yours, huh? Sounds like you might have a bit of an ulterior motive."

"Absolutely not. I was simply stating a fact," Euphemia bowed her head deeply as she spoke.

"Well, I don't really care. I guess I'll just get Riza or Chelsey to do Erika's job. Go retrieve Dannoura for me." Riza and Chelsey were still in the hotel. Yuuki immediately sent them their instructions.

Someone had died right in front of Tomochika's room...which meant she would likely be leaving that room behind rather soon. And whatever the method, Yuuki intended to have Tomochika Dannoura for himself.

As a Dominator, the idea that there were women beyond his grasp was unthinkable. At the same time, he felt it was unbecoming of someone of his stature to act desperate for a single woman. That was why he had stepped back for a time. But now that Erika had died, he didn't care anymore. A Dominator always had to have the best women around him. Yuuki would need to find someone to replace Erika.

"Do you believe Miss Dannoura could be responsible?"

"Who knows? But once I've got control of her, maybe we'll have a better idea. For now, just bring her outside the city."

Within the city, thanks to the protection of the Sages, the abilities of the Gift bestowed by the Sages were restricted. His contract of control could only be used beyond the city limits.

Yuuki and his entourage made their way to the elevator leading out of the ruins. By the time they reached the surface, Tomochika would be in his hands. He had no reason to doubt that would be the case.

Chapter 29 — What Does Killing Ice Even Mean?! Is This Some Philosophical Thing Again?!

As soon as she returned to her room, Tomochika began collecting her things. Seeing as all of her belongings fit into a single backpack, it didn't take all that long.

Can you wait a bit? As Tomochika turned to leave, Mokomoko stopped her.

"What? If we don't go soon, Takatou will be left waiting."

Yogiri couldn't need that much time to prepare his things either. They had agreed to meet just outside of their rooms before leaving.

A man will understand if you just tell him that a woman needs time to get ready. It won't take that long, anyway.

"Okay, fine." It seemed like an odd time to stop and have a chat, but there was probably some reason for it, so Tomochika conceded and sat down on the bed.

Although we don't know exactly what their objective was, this time the enemy targeted you specifically. Relying entirely on that boy is no longer enough. He is sensitive to danger aimed at his person, but is rather slow to notice anything aimed at you. Even I noticed it before he did.

"Okay, I already get that just because he's safe doesn't mean I am."

On top of that, you will not always be together. In short, I believe you need to find a way to survive in this world on your own.

"I agree, but what can I even do?"

Tomochika hadn't received the Gift that the rest of her classmates had, nor did she have any special powers like Yogiri did. This wasn't a situation that could be resolved simply by working hard at it.

I have been considering ways to make you stronger, but it's not something that can be done immediately. For now, you must be able to make it through on your own strength.

"That's easy to say, but how much 'strength' do I actually have?"

Tomochika's family still actively practiced their martial art, so it was something she was fairly familiar with. But she had only ever been able to practice with her own family members, and in a place as peaceful as Japan there were no practical applications for it either. She had no way of actually comparing herself to anyone else.

If it is someone entirely reliant on their own strength, it should be easy enough to defeat them. Someone like a murderer with nothing but a knife should also be simple. Against a true master, you should be able to buy enough time to find a chance to escape.

"Isn't that actually pretty impressive?"

In the context of our world, yes. But in a world like this, where your opponents have skills and magic, you don't have much recourse.

"Then what do I do about it? You wouldn't bring it up unless there was something I could do, right?"

Let us release your seal.

"And suddenly you're sounding suspicious again! I can't say I'm not intrigued, though." She was about halfway between excitement and feeling like Mokomoko was just making fun of her. But if she had her own secret power, she might actually be able to contribute something. "So what happens if we release this seal? Am I going to get some superpower or something? Normally, I would think you're just messing with me, but after seeing Takatou's abilities, maybe it's possible after all."

Sorry to burst your bubble, but this won't awaken any dormant powers within you. All it will do is allow you to feel comfortable with killing people.

"That's it?!" Of course, having the resolve to kill others was no small thing. But the gap between that and her expectations left her largely disappointed.

You shouldn't sell it so short. If you are able to attack someone with the true intention of killing them, you have already become significantly stronger. Normal people cannot kill others so easily. Even if you resolved yourself to such a goal, your subconscious would strive to avoid it.

"But that's just an issue of preparing yourself for it, right? What is the seal you're talking about?"

There is a belief that possessions run in families, correct? The Dannoura family has something like that. The nature of breaking people like they are no more than objects is something we are born with. The same goes for you.

"Really? Seems highly questionable." And it did sound unbelievable. Yes, everyone in the family practiced martial arts, but none of them were *that* extreme.

Remember when you were ten years old, you gouged out one of your grandfather's eyes? That was when I realized you were more suited to being successor than your sister.

"Except Grandpa still has both of his eyes?"

Well, that's because, umm, he had an artificial eye implanted a long time ago.

"Right, that doesn't sound insane at all! You made that story up just now, didn't you?!"

I was hoping to make it seem like there was an untamed beast living within you, but I suppose I couldn't make it convincing enough.

"Who cares about that right now?!"

At any rate, rather than any sort of unfamiliar weapon or skill, your innate talent is far more useful to you.

"Maybe, but won't it change my personality as well? I don't like the sound of that."

Your personality itself won't change. You will simply lose your hesitation when attacking. Well, I won't force you or anything. At most it will only improve your survivability by about ten percent.

After a short pause, Tomochika spoke again. "Fine. So, how do you remove this seal?" It was better than doing nothing at all, she supposed. So she steeled herself for whatever it would take.

The seal is one of mental conditioning, placed using suggestion. Removing it requires a few specific keywords.

Mokomoko then began to chant.

The mad wander the three realms ignorant of their madness,
The blind born of the four modes of birth perceive not their blindness,
Born again, and again, and again, yet birth is shrouded in darkness,
Dying again, and again, and again, yet death remains a mystery.

"Don't you think that's a bit edgy?" The whole process was getting more and more shady.

It is a verse from Kuukai's "The Precious Key to the Secret Treasury." It is often used by martial artists and by Shingon Buddhists. At any rate, all you have to do is repeat it.

"It's a bit long, though…"

You can say it as fast as you like.

"Why can't you make these things shorter?!"

Well, that's all I wanted to talk about for now. It takes some time to take effect, so make sure to do the chant well in advance of needing it.

Reluctantly, Tomochika muttered the words as she rose from the bed. She didn't feel any particular change, but that was best, she supposed. When she stepped out of the room, Yogiri was already waiting for her.

Having collected all of their belongings, the pair made their way to the emergency stairs. Hanging around would be dangerous, so their first course of action was to get out of the hotel. They could think of what came next after that.

While it is certainly better than using the elevator, it is reasonable to assume that the enemy might predict you will take the emergency stairs. Why don't you just try jumping from a window or something? Surely they won't expect that.

"You realize this is the fifth floor, right?" Tomochika was shocked by the bizarre suggestion.

I know plenty of people who could jump from this height without a problem.

"And are those people human?!"

"Well, if we had something like an emergency escape bag, it might be doable. But I don't really want to spend time looking for one, and it would be a bit too flashy for people watching from the outside. We are trying to sneak out, after all."

"The emergency stairs should be safe enough, right?"

The corridor was laid out in an L-shape. Heading right from their rooms was the elevator landing. If they went left, they would turn a corner and the emergency stairs would be at the far end of that hallway. Paying careful attention to their surroundings, the two approached that corner. Thanks to their caution, they easily heard the approaching footsteps — someone was coming from around the other side.

"My, my. Where are you going in such a hurry?" A woman with a gentle smile appeared. Wearing a soft white dress, she held a grossly over-ornamented staff in her hand.

That appearance and soft-spoken demeanor sparked something in Yogiri's memory. This was one of Yuuki's bodyguards, Riza. At the moment, she was displaying no intent to harm them, but her appearance now of all times couldn't be a coincidence.

"Do you need something?"

"Just this." With a gentle laugh, she tapped the bottom of her staff on the floor. As she did, transparent spikes appeared before them. Like a cage, icicles rose up from the floor, surrounding them on all sides. "I was told by Yuuki to take Miss Dannoura to him. If you cooperate, I have no reason to harm —"

Yogiri kicked the icicle cage around them. A number of the icicles shattered, making enough space for a person to walk through.

"Wow, how fragile are these things?" Tomochika said, smacking a nearby icicle with her hand. As her fist bounced off it, she recoiled with an exaggerated shout. "It's so cold! And why didn't it break?! Why is this one so hard?!"

"I just tried killing the part I kicked. Seems like it went fairly well."

Apparently, inanimate objects created by magic were also susceptible to Yogiri's power.

"What does killing ice even mean? Is this one of those philosophical things again?!"

As Tomochika continued to complain, Yogiri pulled her out of the cage. Riza watched them, speechless. She must not have thought escape was even possible. The fact that she was here as an assassin was plain as day, so Yogiri felt more than justified in killing her. But they wouldn't learn anything that way.

"What is going on?! I don't understand this!" Completely at a loss, Riza raised a flustered voice as she pointed her staff at the two of them. The tip glowed bright, followed by an enormous block of ice appearing in the space in front of it.

She was probably planning on throwing it at them. With its sharpness and weight, that chunk of ice would easily reduce a person to a pile of lifeless meat. Since Yogiri had been planning on talking to her, his response had been too slow. In a situation like this, even if he killed the mage now, there was no guarantee the magic she put in motion would stop. So instead he unleashed his power at the ice itself.

The frozen block immediately shattered, dissipating into mist in front of them. Riza retreated a step with a sharp cry. Since she had tried to attack them, Yogiri now had all the justification he needed to kill her, but instead he turned his eyes to her staff. It really was a large thing to be carrying around for no reason, so it was possible that it was a necessary component of her magic.

He could kill her at any time, so first he tested out his power on the staff itself. It snapped in the middle, losing its magical glow as the jeweled head fell to the floor.

Riza sank down as well, her eyes wide with fear. She was just now realizing how out of the ordinary her opponent was.

"Can you use magic without your staff?"

"N-No!" Her reply was instant. And, as it happened, it was also the correct response. Yogiri had been fully prepared to kill her if she had so much as hesitated to answer.

Chapter 30 — Why Does Our Martial Art Have Anti-Air Techniques, Anyway?

"The last time we saw someone use magic, they didn't need a staff."

He had already forgotten the guy's name, but Yogiri did recall the classmate who had destroyed the bus. He'd had nothing like a staff at all.

"I'm a Wand Master. I can draw magic from a staff, but that's it; I can't use magic without it," Riza answered from her spot crouched on the floor.

Fundamentally, using magic required some sort of energy reserve and an appropriate amount of charge time before use, depending on the strength of the magic. The amount of time needed varied based on the user's competence, the type of magic being used, and other special factors, but it was never zero. A Wand Master's staff, however, was constantly charging that magic, so it could unleash powerful attacks at terrifying speeds. The drawback was that such mages could only use the few spells that were already built into the staff itself.

"Hm, well I can deal with enemies that require items to use their powers. If only things would always be so convenient."

It had only gone this well by sheer coincidence. Yogiri couldn't expect that most of their opponents would rely on such items.

This girl may possess other hidden tools. I believe the safest option is to kill her now.

As Mokomoko cautioned them, Yogiri turned to face her. Since Riza couldn't see the spirit, it must have looked strange to see him conversing with thin air, but he wasn't especially concerned about her opinion.

"If I just killed everyone that *could* be dangerous to me, everyone around me would be dead." Yogiri wasn't especially fond of killing people. But his only way of defending himself was to kill others. He didn't hesitate when it came to killing, but that didn't mean he would go out of his way to do it. He turned back to Riza. "It seems you kind of get it already, but I'll explain it anyway. I can kill people just by thinking it, and I can detect any threats against me. If you try anything, I'll kill you instantly, so please keep that in mind. If you understand, then I'd like to ask you some questions."

"Understood," Riza replied, nerves clear in her voice. Her previous air of looking down on them as children had completely vanished. If she made the wrong choice, she would die. That fear must have felt like a physical pressure on her.

"As a Wand Master, I find it hard to believe you only carry that one staff with you. Do you have any backups?"

Reaching between her rather ample breasts, Riza pulled out a pencil-sized stick and placed it on the ground.

"Why would you hide something *there*, of all places?! And Takatou, stop staring so much!" Even in this situation, Tomochika was the same as always.

"No, I just thought it was a clever hiding spot."

An item of that size could be hidden anywhere in her clothes. Perhaps we should strip her as well?

"I've never tried, but I could probably kill just her clothes."

"Hold on, you're joking, right?" Tomochika piped up, disbelief clear in her voice.

"You haven't complained about me killing people, but making them naked is a problem?" He couldn't follow her train of thought, but he wasn't keen on having Tomochika be upset with him, so he left it alone. "Next question. You were ordered to retrieve Dannoura, right?

It seems you've given up on that, but does that mean your orders aren't absolute? From the story we heard earlier, Yuuki was using slaves in suicide attacks on monsters, right?"

"The suicide attacks were for labor-tier slaves with no other use. We upper-tier slaves are much more valuable, so we are instructed to protect ourselves above all else."

"What about your friends? There are five members of the Bodyguard Unit, right?" Erika was dead, and Riza was here, so that left three.

"Of course," she said with a chuckle, "they have received the same orders." As she spoke, something dropped from the ceiling. Whatever it was had aimed directly for Tomochika before being slammed violently into the floor. Catching it midair, she drove it straight into the ground.

Well, that paid off rather quickly, Mokomoko mused.

The thing that was now lying on the floor was a young girl, her neck bent at an entirely fatal angle. Tomochika's fingers were pressing into the fallen girl's throat, one hand ready to gouge out her eyes.

"I've wondered about this for a while, but why does our school of martial arts have anti-air techniques anyway?"

The Dannoura Way is prepared for all circumstances.

Despite her neck being broken, the girl began to stand up. Looking closer, it became clear that she wasn't human — it was an exquisitely made doll.

By the time they realized it, Tomochika and Yogiri had been completely surrounded. Stuffed animals, tin puppets, porcelain dolls...although they varied in size and construction, they were all dolls of some sort. They had moved in to block both ends of the hallway, and were even crawling over the walls and ceiling.

"Ahh. I thought you were being a bit too cooperative, but you were just buying time."

Realizing she couldn't win on her own, Riza had simply been waiting for reinforcements. She hadn't given up on her orders at all.

"I had thought that I alone would be sufficient, though," she said with a relaxed smile before suddenly collapsing. Yogiri's power had been

unleashed again. Now facing multiple opponents, leaving her alive was only a liability at this point.

Hmm. I guess you would call this a Puppeteer? Mokomoko continued her commentary. Each individual doll didn't seem all that strong, but together their numbers were enough to potentially overwhelm them.

A young girl in a black frilled dress sat on the landing in the emergency stairwell. Perhaps a reflection of her interests, she was surrounded by numerous dolls and stuffed animals.

It was Chelsey, one of Yuuki's bodyguards. In reality, there should have been no reason for her to participate — taking a single girl with no powers captive should have been easy enough for Riza by herself. Chelsey had been content to let the captain of the Bodyguard Unit take the credit for the job, coming along just in case, but things had gone in a completely unexpected direction.

Riza's magic had been totally ineffective. As shocked as she had been, Chelsey had immediately moved into action. She knew her dolls would be more than enough to get the job done. If some of the dolls themselves were destroyed, it was no real problem.

Chelsey's method of operating dolls was similar to possession. Something like a soul would inhabit the toys, allowing her to control them directly. If one body was destroyed, all she had to do was move that "soul" to another.

"She's better than I thought," Chelsey said to herself. She had figured she could grab Tomochika in a heartbeat and be done, but it seemed things wouldn't be going that smoothly.

"Owwww! What's with this girl?!" The voice came from a life-size female doll — the same kind as the one that had just attacked Tomochika.

"Start by killing Yogiri!" The teddy bear in Chelsey's arms spoke in a way that was in sharp contrast to its adorable appearance.

"Heheheh, we can take off one or two of her arms, right? As long as she's still alive!" This time it was a doll in the shape of a young boy that spoke, wearing a devilish smile and holding a large knife.

The dolls gathered around Chelsey were the leaders of her collection. Each of them could control other dolls of the same type as themselves.

"That's right. He only said to bring her to him," Chelsey said, despite having fully understood her instructions. She looked down at her own body. Though she had an endearing, fairy-like appearance, she knew there was little in the way of sex appeal there. With a body like this, she could never earn Yuuki's affection. There was no way she wouldn't be jealous of Tomochika. "Okay, everyone! Hurt them just enough that the girl doesn't die!"

"Here we go!" the bear in her arms responded.

Looking through the eyes of her small army, she watched the scene in the hallway unfold. Stuffed animals, dolls, and robots all threw themselves forward at once. As they did, they suddenly locked up in the air, flying past their targets and falling clumsily to the floor. This was as expected.

"Next...huh?" Suddenly struck by a sense of unease, she looked down at the teddy bear in her arms. It was just a normal teddy bear. "Morurun?!" Chelsey began to shake the doll in a panic, but the teddy bear neither spoke nor moved. "Jennifer! Jackie!" The girl-shaped doll had fallen to her knees, and soon after began rolling down the stairs. The boy that had been brandishing his knife was completely still, lying on the floor.

"No...no, no, no! Morurun! Jennifer! Jackie! Move! Come on! Come on!" Each of her special doll personalities was irreplaceable, like a part of her own self. Those irreplaceable companions were now being stopped forever, one after another.

Overcome by fear, Chelsey looked through the eyes of the ones that could still move. Yogiri was walking down the hallway like nothing had happened. As ordered, the remaining dolls attacked him. And once they approached him, they stopped moving.

Chelsey heard the sound of the door to the emergency stairs

opening. Looking up in terror, she saw Yogiri and Tomochika step into the stairwell. The dolls that could still move immediately made to intercept them and protect Chelsey.

"Stop! Please, stop! Don't hurt them! I'm sorry! I'm sorry!"

She finally ordered the dolls to stop their attack. Continuing the assault would only increase the number of casualties, although even that thought was beyond her in her desperation.

"Takatou, you're starting to look like the bad guy all of a sudden..."

"You say that, but all I'm doing is protecting myself," she heard an exasperated voice answer.

By the time the pair had stepped into sight, only a few of her dolls remained.

Chapter 31 — We Just Have to Kill Them Before They Can Use It

On the first floor of the ruins, Yuuki was walking towards the exit when he became aware of Riza's death.

"Is something wrong, Master?"

Stephanie and Euphemia from his Bodyguard Unit saw something change in his expression as they walked beside him.

Yuuki looked through Riza's action log. Somehow, her magic had failed, and then she had died. Not long after, Chelsey's dolls had been neutralized, and she'd completely lost the will to fight. Chelsey hadn't been killed, but had instead given up all information that was asked of her.

"Well, I guess I never told her not to say anything."

Yuuki's control over the minds of the Bodyguard Unit was quite limited. He wasn't interested in drones that only did what he told them to. And even if the details of his abilities as a Dominator were revealed, it wasn't really cause for concern. With no clear weaknesses, the more they knew about his power, the more they would despair at it.

But still, the situation was becoming unpleasant. He had thought that getting his hands on Tomochika would be a simple enough task, but it seemed he would have to really invest himself to get the job done.

He ordered the insects and other small animals within the hotel to search for the duo. It didn't take long to find them heading down the emergency stairs. Now that he was seeing them in real time, it didn't matter where they ran — he had countless eyes watching their every move.

"He said he can kill people just by willing it, but what do you think?" he asked Euphemia after explaining the situation. Yuuki personally had very little knowledge of this world, and he didn't especially care to learn about it himself. All he had to do was ask his subordinates when he needed something.

"While it is extremely hard to believe…there are a variety of possibilities. One is an intervention by someone higher in the Gift's hierarchy."

In this world, the system known as the Gift was acquired by inheriting it from someone else. To compare it to a computer, it was like a program that had to be installed. Since there was no way of knowing what power would develop when the Gift was inherited, those who gave it to others also added restrictions on the people they gave it to.

"In my case, it's the same as my power being limited by the Sages, right?"

"Correct. Normally, when the Gift is given, a restraint that prevents the inheritor from disobeying the giver is added. The exact nature of that restraint differs, but things such as nullifying their skills entirely or reducing their resistance to Instant Death to zero are both possible. However, it is difficult to believe those two are in a superior position with the Gift compared to Riza and Chelsey."

"That's what I thought. Even if they weren't actually powerless, the two of them should still be part of the Sage's lineage. But is there a way they could change their Gift?"

"While it is possible to change the Gift or to possess multiple powers, it is still very unlikely that they could be in a higher position."

"And the second possibility?"

"There could be a tremendous difference in their levels. In that case, nullifying Riza's magic or attacking with such power as to seem like Instant Death could both be possible. The issue is that both Riza and Chelsey have received power from you. Riza's level was seventy, and Chelsey's was fifty-six, so the possibility that those two have surpassed them is slim."

"Right. If they don't have a strategy like mine, leveling up so fast should be impossible."

A being's level was a numerical representation of the amount of energy contained within them. The Gift required this energy to work, so by killing others with the Gift, that power could be absorbed. Therefore, to increase one's level efficiently, one needed to kill stronger enemies in large numbers. Given that, the chances that Yogiri and Tomochika had surpassed Riza in the few days they had been in this world was just impossible. Under normal circumstances, the best they could realistically manage would be to move up a few levels.

"The third possibility is that some sort of unknown power is at work. If I were to give my honest opinion, that seems the most likely option."

"But it doesn't really answer the question at all."

"As you say. However, it is hardly reason enough to give up on Miss Dannoura, is it? There is no need to confront such a hard-to-understand, unknown ability yourself. With your power, avoiding a direct encounter with them should be quite simple."

"That's unacceptable. Why should I have to run around like a coward in the dark?" Although he said it as a joke, he was truthfully a little irritated. That wasn't how a Dominator should act. "Well, it doesn't matter how powerful their ability is. All we have to do is kill them before they use it. Do you have any ideas?"

"Yes, one could say that Riza and Chelsey were poorly matched with their opponent. Since they relied on the use of magic and puppets, their own bodies were barely different from those of ordinary humans. I believe someone with a class suited to close-quarters combat would be more effective. If their level is around fifty, an ordinary human shouldn't be able to follow their movements."

"That doesn't sound like something we can get ready immediately, though." Most of Yuuki's combat power was out hunting. As the highest priority right now was gathering resources, that was their best course of action. After all, a need to fight within the city itself had been wholly unexpected. "For now, let's get anyone who could be useful back to town. But rather than using someone who excels at something boring like hand-to-hand combat, wouldn't it be better to use someone with magic powerful enough to just blow them away from a distance?"

"Within the Sages' barrier, using magic to inflict damage on a wide area will be difficult. If we can lure them out of the city, it should be possible, but even then, injuring Miss Dannoura becomes difficult to avoid."

"That would be a problem, wouldn't it? All right, let's get them on the run then. They'll have to give up eventually." After all, Yuuki had an effectively unlimited supply of slaves. No matter how many died, there would always be replacements waiting. Even if Yogiri could kill people just by thinking it, it was doubtful he could keep it up forever. If Yuuki overwhelmed him with sheer force of numbers, he was sure to find an opening at some point.

"Kill Yogiri Takatou," he ordered all of his slaves on standby, ready to put an end to his former classmate.

Yuuki had never before failed at anything significant enough to cause him regret. No matter what twists and turns his path took, he ultimately always ended up with exactly what he wanted. So he naturally assumed that things would always go according to plan, and was always certain that he would win in the end. It was one of the driving forces behind his otherwise baseless self-confidence.

That was why he had never considered there to be any direct threat from Yogiri's power. Even if he failed with any given strategy, as long as he was in an absolutely safe place, he could try again as many times as he needed to.

As always, he gave his orders without much thought — but that would end up being a fatal error. His intention of killing now had a concrete action attached to it. As such, that line of killing intent now connected him to Yogiri.

But Yuuki himself had no idea he had made such a mistake. In the end, he never once ended up feeling that regret.

Stephanie was the more simple-minded of his two escorts. Reacting to the scene in front of her, she immediately began to wail in grief, but the deeper implications were yet beyond her. Euphemia was the only one who truly understood, and she was trembling in fear.

A being terrifying beyond belief now walked this world.

Chapter 32 — The World Isn't So Soft That It Will Let You Act Without Consequences

Tomochika let out a guttural cry that sounded like it was enough to injure her throat.

Couldn't you try to be a bit cuter when you scream?

Having finished interrogating Chelsey, they had continued their descent of the emergency stairs and were now on the second floor of the hotel.

"Oh, it's a cockroa—"

"Don't say it! If you say it out loud, it feels like they'll burrow into my brain, too!" Tomochika interrupted in a panic. On the walls of the stairwell, a huge number of bugs — mostly cockroaches — had gathered. Totally unmoving, the insects waited all around them.

"He said he used insects and small animals too, so I presume these are watching us."

Although it was impossible to tell exactly where the bugs were looking, Yogiri definitely felt like he was being watched.

"Can't we do something about them?!"

"I guess. I could just wipe them out —"

"Do it! This is exactly what your power was made for!" Tomochika once again cut him off.

"I mean, I could, but then they'd probably fall off the wall and start rolling down the stairs."

Even if they died, their bodies would remain and would probably get in the way. While Yogiri wasn't especially bothered by the idea of stepping on them, it seemed that Tomochika didn't share his indifference.

"Ugh, then things would only get worse! No killing allowed!"

"But if we leave them alive, they might jump at us or something. Even these bugs could probably kill a person if they tried."

"No, no, no, no matter how gross the..." She seemed reluctant to say the word "cockroach." "The *Georges* are, they couldn't actually kill you, could they?!"

"By 'Georges,' you mean the bugs, right? With this many, I bet they could. For example, if a whole bunch of them crawled down your throat and suffocated you, or burrowed into you and attacked your organs from the inside."

"Yuuki Tachibana...you have officially made me angry!"

Maybe because she had begun to imagine those scenarios, Tomochika became strangely tense.

"For now, it seems like they're content to just watch us, so let's get outside."

"What if they jump at us?"

"I'll kill them...but of course their dead bodies will still be flying at us."

"If that happens, I'll probably have a nervous breakdown, so thanks in advance for the help you'll have to give me."

With her eyes almost completely shut, she let him guide her carefully down the stairs. The feelers of the gathered insects turned to track their movements, so as he had thought, they were certainly being watched. For now, at least, it didn't look like the creatures planned on attacking them.

Thinking over their current situation, Yogiri came to a conclusion. "I should probably kill Tachibana."

"Yeah, I guess. Though it doesn't seem like it'll stop *them* at this point."

He was somewhat surprised by Tomochika's callous answer, but it just went to show how much sending the bugs after them had upset her.

"Dominators are a pain. At this rate, the whole world will be against us." From the Puppeteer, they had managed to gain more information about a Dominator's abilities. As Yuuki had said, he was gaining new subordinates at an accelerating rate, and he had full control over all of them. What's more, he could take any of the energy acquired by his slaves, and could even borrow their skills. Yuuki Tachibana was a terrible danger to not only Yogiri and Tomochika, but to everyone. If they left things as they were, a large portion of the world would be under his control in no time at all.

"He's waiting for me to leave the city, right? So should we?"

"If things go as I expect, we won't have to bother."

When they reached the landing between the first and second floors, the bugs all began to stir.

"I have a very bad feeling about this!"

Killing intent. Yogiri could now see countless, unavoidable lines of black stretching out from the bugs towards him. Acting as one, they seemed to be preparing to jump at him all at once.

"Seems like they're looking for a good opportunity to kill me."

"I thought so! I don't care about stepping on them anymore, please, just kill them! Though with this many of them, I might die either way!"

"Well, I don't really want them crawling on me either."

There was no hesitation when he released his power. If he left them as they were, they could gather in even greater numbers and attack him at any time. Even if he detected their killing intent, dealing with them constantly would be too much of a pain. On top of that, the more Yuuki's control expanded, the less freedom they would have to act. Eventually, their current plan of casually looking for a way back home, or even just reuniting with their classmates, wouldn't be feasible anymore.

"Die." Yogiri unleashed his power, but there was no change in the bugs.

"After all this time, *now* it doesn't work?!" Tomochika's last hope of avoiding the insects had failed, leaving her visibly shaken.

"I'm not going to claim that's impossible, but I've certainly never seen it fail before."

"Then what's going on?!"

"The situation was just right, so I killed Tachibana."

"What?!" Tomochika went stiff, his declaration catching her completely off guard.

Yogiri had merely unleashed his power at the true source of the killing intent, Yuuki himself. Suppose someone, somewhere, had the intention of killing Yogiri. That normally wasn't enough for him to target and kill them. Even if that person had sent their subordinates after him, it wouldn't change the situation. Yogiri's power could only detect the people actually carrying out the act.

But in the case of a Dominator, it was different. A Dominator's power was, at its core, the ability to create a colony. Yuuki was the head, and his slaves were the hands and feet. That was why he could use his subordinates to gather more slaves — those subordinates were like parts of Yuuki's own body.

But for the same reason, Yuuki's own killing intent filtered through his slaves and towards Yogiri. All Yogiri had to do was follow that trail back to the source.

"Since Tachibana manipulated the bugs into trying to kill me, I killed him instead."

"You can do that even when you have no idea where someone is?!"

"If they can reach me, then I can reach them. Life isn't so easy that you can attack someone with complete impunity like that."

"It seems like life is plenty easy for you!"

"Really? Japan seemed harsh enough to me."

"Anyway, that's not really important. These things are getting really active!"

The bugs along the walls had suddenly started moving. There was no more killing intent coming from them, so it seemed that Yogiri wasn't their target anymore.

"Maybe they've been released from Tachibana's control now that he's gone."

It appeared that with the person using the skill being dead, its effects had been nullified.

"No, no, no, that's bad!" Tomochika's panicked voice rose a few octaves.

The bugs were starting to jump off the walls. Whether or not they were being controlled, they were still disgusting to her.

"Let's run."

"You're not gonna kill them?!"

"Killing something just because it's gross is bad, isn't it?"

"This isn't the time for that kind of logic!"

The two of them ran down the stairs, reaching the exit at record speed.

The emergency exit opened up behind the hotel. Since they were in an alley between buildings, it was fairly dark, but they still had some time before sunset.

Tomochika immediately shut the door behind them. Somehow, they had managed to escape before the bugs swarmed them, but there was probably no need for them to have hurried. Wild bugs didn't tend to attack like that in the first place.

"Thinking about it, there isn't really a reason for us to leave the hotel anymore, is there?" Tomochika said after she had calmed down.

"Because Tachibana is dead? There's still the possibility that his human followers will come after us, though."

Yogiri had decided that running away remained their best option. For all he knew, there were those who had adored Yuuki even without being affected by his Dominator skills. At the very least, staying in the hotel would pose an unnecessary risk.

"So, we're going to run after all?"

"Maybe we should just go on ahead to the capital."

The two of them quickly agreed that it would avoid most potential problems to move on. Leaving the narrow back alley, they made their way towards the main street. But before they reached it, they realized that something was terribly wrong. The area was strangely noisy, in a way that didn't seem like the usual bustle of the city. An angry roar. The sound of something breaking, something else being smashed. Clearly, something out of the ordinary was happening. But from where they were, they couldn't see anything at all.

"What's going on? Something definitely seems off."

Stepping out onto the street, Tomochika immediately went stiff with shock. Even Yogiri was taken aback by the spectacle.

People were devouring each other.

"What...?" Tomochika muttered, dumbfounded.

Numerous bodies that had collapsed onto the ground were being greedily consumed by distorted, almost-human shapes. Those who ran were being caught, grabbed, and dragged down. The monstrous figures were even throwing themselves at the barricades set up by people who had taken shelter within the nearby buildings, trying to break their way inside.

Their skulls had been caved in.

Their guts had been ripped out and were dragging on the concrete.

Some of them crawled along the ground with no lower bodies at all.

No matter how they moaned and cried as they attacked those around them, it was hard to believe they could possibly be alive and moving. But as sluggish as their movements were, they continued to doggedly pursue their victims.

"I thought it might be some sort of fantasy parallel world thing, but a zombie apocalypse?!"

Desiccated, decomposing corpses were attacking and eating people in the street.

As one would expect, the city had fallen into chaos.

Chapter 33 — Zombie Time Is Over!

The lord of Hanabusa, Ryouta, was very much on the side of the Sages that ruled over the majority of the world. But that didn't necessarily mean his opinion of them was very high. The reason was simple — since he considered himself an upright human being, from his perspective the people that worked for the Sages were disgusting. But regardless of what he personally felt, they still came to his city.

Now, one of those unpleasant individuals was casually drinking tea right in front of him. Sitting at a low table, the man wearing a black coat over a bare chest sat with his legs spread wide. His name was Masayuki, attendant to Sage Lain and head of the Immortal Corps.

"What on earth have you done?!" Ryouta made no effort to hide his anger, slamming his hand onto the table. This room was in one of Hanabusa's governmental buildings. While Ryouta had been in here panicking over the sudden emergency outside, the cause of that tragedy had appeared before him.

"Recruiting. Zombies only last for about a day, after all."

"This isn't a joke!"

The vehicles bringing Masayuki's Immortals into Hanabusa were mowing down people in the streets. Attendants of the Sages may have had the right to eliminate anyone who got in the way of their missions, but according to reports, the vehicles were intentionally running on the sidewalks. There was no way to interpret that except as pure spite.

"Why are you even here?! Lady Lain has entrusted the management of this city to *me*. You have no right to interfere!"

"I'm not feeling all that welcome here. Didn't we survive the same battlefield together?"

"I would hardly say survive. You've been dead for ages, right? So hurry up and start acting like it!"

The two of them shared an unquestionable bond, having fought together during their time as Sage candidates in support of Lain. As such, they had both become her attendants.

"I'm looking for someone and I need your help." Seeing he wasn't getting anywhere by trying to be friendly, Masayuki got straight to the point.

"I refuse!"

"This is an order from Lain. It's not a request."

Ryouta went quiet. If that was true, he really didn't have the option of turning him down.

"I'm looking for two Sage candidates."

"Then ask the Sage in charge of them!"

"Well, about that. These two are defective candidates who never even had the Gift installed. So we don't have a way to trace them."

"So what? Why would I know where they are? There are plenty of otherworlders in Hanabusa."

"Of course, I know you don't restrict who comes and goes from the city. I don't expect you to know where they are either."

"Then what do you want from me?"

"What I want is help from the people of the city. We're hunting a pair of otherworlders. They've got to be hiding here somewhere."

"Hold on. You make it sound like you're not even sure if they *are* in the city." Ryouta felt a chill run down his spine. He couldn't believe that. There was no way Masayuki would be prepared to hunt down all the otherworlders in the city if he didn't have proof that they were actually here.

"There was a train accident nearby. We're pretty sure they were on board. So thinking about it logically, it makes sense that they'd go to the closest city, right?"

"That's the best you have?!"

"Hey, this is all on Lain's orders. She told us to get rid of Yogiri Takatou and Tomochika Dannoura. I'll do whatever it takes to get that done."

"So what do you mean about having the people cooperate with you?"

"The Immortals have already been deployed. They're waiting for my signal to attack Hanabusa."

Ryouta went stiff. Masayuki said he was hunting for two people, so why would he attack the residents of the city? He didn't understand what that would accomplish.

"Hey now," his colleague continued, "if we just politely ask them to help us look, we won't get anywhere. We've gotta make it a life or death struggle for them, or they won't take it seriously, will they? Basically, we're going to say that if they don't find those two, we'll wipe out the city."

"Are you crazy?! Who the hell would help you after an ultimatum like that?!"

"It's not like we're going to ask them to search *while* the undead are terrorizing the city. The threat is plenty clear by now, so I'll pull them back for a bit. That should be enough to get the locals excited about helping out, don't you think?"

This was all just a game to him. Masayuki was using Lain's orders as an excuse to send the Immortal Corps on a rampage, nothing more. Ryouta bit his lip in frustration. No matter how absurd the situation was, no matter how meaningless of an atrocity it would be, as an order from Sage Lain, he had no way of resisting it.

"So hurry up and give me the key to the barrier."

"What is Lady Lain doing now?"

The barrier around Hanabusa had been set up by Lain herself, and control over it was entrusted to Ryouta. The key was a symbol of that trust. With the key in hand, one could remove the barrier, strengthen it, or limit the Gifts of those who had inherited from the Sages. It wasn't something he could hand over so easily.

"Lain is off wiping Santarou's ass for him. His territory borders hers, so she's probably fairly close by. What, you can't hand it over without her permission? Don't worry about it. This is all on Lain's orders, remember?"

Even Masayuki couldn't possibly be lying about what his instructions were. Taking out the key, Ryouta reluctantly handed it over.

"Dammit! Do you have any idea how much work I've put into this city?!"

Once the Immortals moved into action, there was no way they'd stop at just searching. Visions of Hanabusa in ruins came to his mind unbidden. All he could do now was pray that they found who they were looking for as soon as possible.

Taking the key from Ryouta's hand, Masayuki stood up. "City building sims have plenty of disasters in them, right? I'm sure one of them is a zombie attack. Starting all over is part of the fun!" Stepping close, he casually patted Ryouta on the shoulder. "That said, once the genre shifts to Survival Horror, your political cheats might not help all that much!"

"This is the worst. Why did something like this have to happen…" Ryouta hung his head. His dream of building a city of one million people was crumbling before his eyes.

As the two of them stared at the hellscape before them, Yogiri was the first to regain his composure.

"They seem pretty slow. If we're careful, we can probably make it out of the city."

The things attacking the people around them were monsters, probably something like living dead or zombies. Individually, they didn't seem all that strong, but the fear they inspired was enough to throw the streets into chaos.

Monsters were a part of this world, so the existence of the undead was common knowledge. But even so, seeing a moving corpse right in front of you instinctively triggered a sense of fear. On top of that, cities protected by the Sages' barriers should have been perfectly safe from all outside enemies. For most of the city's residents, who had lived their lives entirely in peace, the sudden appearance of such creatures was something they couldn't possibly respond well to.

"Shouldn't we help them?"

"We could save like one or two people, but I don't think there's much we can do to save a whole city in a situation like this."

While Tomochika felt guilty about fleeing a city under attack, Yogiri had no obligation to protect a place that he had only just visited for the first time.

Indeed, it would be best not to get too involved. Let us escape with all haste.

As the three of them made to leave the area, a loud voice suddenly filled the air.

"Zombie time is over!"

The crackling words sounded like a public broadcast of some sort. As if that voice had been a signal, the zombies immediately stopped moving.

"Can everyone hear me? All right, people of Hanabusa. My name is Masayuki. I'm an attendant of Sage Lain and the leader of the Immortal Corps. I'm sure you've figured it out by now, but this whole situation is my doing."

The broadcast paused for a short while. With the city still in a state of chaos, he must have been waiting for things to calm down a little.

"Anyway, why the hell am I doing this? I'm gonna explain, so listen up. I want you to help me find some people. We're looking for a boy named Yogiri Takatou and a girl named Tomochika Dannoura. Both of them are about seventeen and as Japanese as it gets. Bring them to the central square, dead or alive, doesn't matter. Of course, none of you would help just because I asked nicely, right? So I figured I'd give you a taste of what'll happen if you don't. Find them quick, or the zombie apocalypse will continue!"

"Is this guy for real?!" Tomochika sounded irate.

"He does seem kind of off in the head, doesn't he?"

"I'm sure some of you have already tried, but you can't leave the city. We've changed the barrier to not let anyone through. We've also made it so that anyone who dies in the city will join the undead. The Immortal Corps is always recruiting, you know? Man or woman, young or old, we're happy to have you!"

"So…eventually everyone here will be turned into a zombie if they don't find us," Yogiri mused, "meaning the Sages will eventually get their way. But there's still a problem with that."

It was an effective strategy if they knew for sure that Yogiri and Tomochika were actually in the city. But without proof, it was nothing but pure insanity.

"Ah, right, right, the cheat that all those otherworlders have has been turned off, too. So this is also your chance to get back at those arrogant bastards. Buuuut, in one hour, the Immortal Corps starts their rampage again! So get moving while you're still alive!"

"Well, what do we do now?" Tomochika turned to Yogiri, perplexed by these developments.

"There's really nothing to do but run away, right?"

The people who had barricaded themselves inside of buildings were surging out onto the streets. Even those who had been doing their best to fight off the zombies outside were suddenly desperately looking around. Pushed into a corner by the threat of the undead, the residents of Hanabusa began a crazed search for any otherworlders they could find.

"Uh, this could actually be worse than the zombies."

There was no way they could stay hidden on the main streets. So they jumped back into the alleyway behind them.

"There's a Japanese person here!"

"This one's got black hair, take them too!"

The city had devolved into a true witch hunt. The zombie attack had struck fear into the hearts of the residents, driving them to round up anyone who even slightly resembled the characteristics mentioned.

Yogiri and Tomochika continued to walk through the back alleys. They hadn't been spotted yet, but there was no way they could remain hidden in such an obvious place. If the whole city was looking for them, it was only a matter of time before they were found.

"So what should we do?" Yogiri asked. "Even if we get out of here, the capital is kind of far to walk."

"And I'm sure the train station won't be any better than the rest of the city."

When they had decided to run from Yuuki, their objective had been to take the train to the capital. But now the situation had completely changed.

Yogiri thought for a moment. "If they've closed off the town, the train probably isn't running. And anyway, we'd be caught instantly if we tried."

"Why are they after us in the first place?"

"Probably because I killed that Sage. I guess we won't be able to get by peacefully in this world after all." Killing the Sage had been entirely in self-defense, but it was starting to look like it would cause problems for them in the future anyway. "I guess this is what happens when I use my power so recklessly." Although he said it, there was no regret in his voice. "For now, we should try to get out of the city unseen, but that looks like it'll be difficult."

While there were certainly a significant number of Japanese people in Hanabusa, the pair of them still stood out. As Yogiri tried to think of a way to move without being seen, they suddenly lost the need for stealth.

"Over here! More Japanese kids!" A group of armed men started piling into the alleyway from the street. They were all soaked in blood. Whether it was their own blood or not, they had clearly become involved in some sort of violence. Yogiri had been hiding specifically to avoid this type of situation, but all his efforts had now been put to waste.

"Die."

In response to the mob's clear intent to kill them, he unleashed his power. The men collapsed to the ground instantly. But with their position revealed, more people had already begun to gather.

"Did they do this thinking I wouldn't kill random civilians? That's kind of irritating."

Even if they were being manipulated, the locals had decided on their own to attack innocent people. But while Yogiri felt no guilt over taking revenge, he definitely preferred to avoid killing those who weren't involved as much as possible. His irritation with the person who had set all these events in motion began to grow.

Chapter 34 — I Want to See What He Can and Can't Do

Yuuki Tachibana was lying on the ground. Despite her skill as a Healer, Stephanie's magic was having no effect. With no health abnormalities, there had been no sign that he was in danger until he'd collapsed. There was no one here who could have done anything to harm him, and in fact, no one *had* done anything to him.

But he was, without a doubt, dead.

As she finally understood that, Stephanie clung to his collapsed body, wailing, heedless of the world around her. Having been purchased from a slave market, she'd probably been happier even under the disgusting power of a Dominator than she had been under her previous circumstances. Her grief was a genuine thing. She had always been quick to flatter Yuuki whenever he did something, and that was quite possibly her heartfelt impression of him.

Although she had been trembling in fear before, Euphemia slowly managed to calm down. Thinking the two of them could also die at any moment, she had been terrified, but it seemed Yogiri had no intention of killing Yuuki's slaves.

Euphemia took stock of her own body. She felt no lingering effects of Yuuki's control. All she thought when looking at his body now was "good riddance." She also felt that the energy within her, her amount of mana, had increased substantially. The mana within Yuuki had scattered upon his death, and apparently she and Stephanie, being nearby, had absorbed some. Most of it had simply dissipated, but the amount that Yuuki had possessed in the first place meant that even the small fraction they each received was enormous.

It was an immeasurable blessing.

So, what came next? Was dying enough punishment for a guy like this? Euphemia glared at her former master. She was struck by the urge to tear off his limbs, rip out his guts, and smash his remains until no semblance of his original form remained.

Euphemia's tribe traditionally held nothing but contempt for the dead. Enemy graves would be exhumed and the bodies within desecrated. They were taught that this would dispel their resentment. It was hard to imagine Stephanie would just stand by and let her do that, though.

"All right, I'll leave him to you," she shrugged. Stephanie was just as much a victim of Yuuki as Euphemia was; she had no grudge against her, nor any reason to fight her.

"Huh?" Stephanie looked up, confused by her behavior. She must have thought Euphemia would be just as sad about Yuuki's death as she herself was.

"I'm sure you've figured it out, but we're free from his control now, so I don't feel even the slightest shred of loyalty to him anymore. I'm leaving, but what about you?"

Stephanie hesitated, a conflicted expression crossing her face. But Euphemia had no obligation to take care of her either.

"See you around, then."

Leaving Stephanie behind, Euphemia made her way to the exit of the ruins. This was only the first level, and Stephanie was plenty strong on her own. There wasn't any particular danger in her being alone here.

Euphemia sank into thought as she walked to the exit. Her current objective was to reunite with her tribe and revive their village. Her tribe was rather strong, so Yuuki had valued them. They hadn't been treated as disposable like the other slaves. There was no reason to be pessimistic about their fate. They could all start over again, as many times as it took.

As these thoughts spurred her to get out of the ruins as fast as possible, she realized that something had changed. She was suddenly strangely thirsty. The area around her was bone dry, something she realized was different from when they had arrived. The ruin was in the middle of a forest. The interior had been hot and humid before, but now it was dry and dusty. Studying the floor, she saw that something like sand was scattered about.

As she came within sight of the stairs leading out, the oddities around her finally roused enough caution to bring her to a stop. Sunlight poured over the steps leading down to the ruins' basement — which should have been impossible, since the entrance was inside a two-floored structure. There was no way sunlight should be reaching the stairs.

A dry wind blew past her. Something had definitely happened above ground. But she couldn't just stay here forever. Steeling herself for whatever might come, Euphemia climbed the stairs to the outside.

As she broke through the surface, the scenery that greeted her was more or less what she had expected. As far as she could see, there was nothing but sand. There was no sign of either the ruins she had been in or the forest that had surrounded them.

"What happened here...?" The change was so drastic that it was beyond belief. Looking around, she noticed an enormous black form in the distance. It was a vague figure, a dark haze in the rough shape of a person, but with no clear or distinct edges. The sinister apparition was heading towards Hanabusa. Turning around, she could see that the forest in its path had been entirely reduced to sand. It seemed that wherever the shadowy giant walked, the land changed.

An Aggressor. Appearing out of nowhere and with an entirely unknown objective. Most people in this world regarded them with fear, but in this case, Euphemia was relieved. It wasn't paying any attention to her. Thanks to being underground when it passed by, they had been safe, and as it was heading straight for the city, she would have no problem avoiding it.

"Oh? And where did you come from? Did you actually survive the Darkness's attack?"

Turning around, Euphemia saw a woman in a red dress standing before her. At the same time, she realized that she was nowhere near safe. Just seeing her, just feeling her presence, Euphemia felt her own weakness.

This was her natural enemy, her natural predator, a violator of the soul.

"You don't seem all that strong…and you seem rather at a loss here. Could I perhaps have you explain some things for me?"

Fighting was out of the question. Her only option was to run away, but the moment she locked eyes with that woman, she lost that option as well.

Charm — permitting no resistance, her soul itself had been seized in an instant.

The woman approached. Against her own will, Euphemia tilted her head, presenting her neck for the woman to bite. And when she did, Euphemia instantly perceived that she was the highest rank of vampire, an Origin Blood — and that she was the Sage, Lain.

She was so ill-matched with that creature. It was just too vague. She couldn't even pinpoint exactly where it started and ended. Never mind whether it was actually alive or not, she couldn't even tell if it had its own will. When she tried to strike it, it was like punching fog, and the hand that touched it had crumbled to dust in an instant.

Luckily, Lain's immortality was enough to make such an attack meaningless. The lost part of her body had regenerated easily enough, but she still had no way of fighting the thing.

Lain was a vampire. By drinking blood, a vampire increased his or her number of companions and ruled over them. They possessed unbelievable regenerative power and unparalleled physical strength, and their eyes could charm their opponents just by looking at them.

They could even transform themselves and fly. With such varied abilities, they had no particular weaknesses to speak of. But even so, she had been entirely unable to defeat the Darkness.

Thinking about it, Santarou had been well-matched with their opponent given his ability to use all kinds of magic. Thanks to that ability, he had managed to find an effective means of fighting it, allowing him to drive it off once before.

But while Lain possessed an inordinate amount of magical energy, she wasn't particularly skilled in the use of magic. She could use average-level healing as well as the barrier spells of the Sages. Beyond that, all she could do was elementary-level attack spells. As a result, the Darkness had simply continued its advance, and Lain had been entirely unable to slow it down. It was hard to tell if it had even been aware of her presence.

In that helpless state, Lain had come across a silver-haired girl. She'd been standing alone, as if lost in the vast expanse of desert. She didn't seem especially useful, but curious about how she had survived unharmed, Lain had added her to her bloodline. While Charming the girl would have been enough to get her to speak, the Charm itself interfered with the target's ability to think clearly, making their answers somewhat vague and inaccurate. If she wanted a proper explanation of the circumstances, turning her was much faster.

According to her story, the girl — named Euphemia — had just been in an underground ruin. Lain was disappointed at first, but when asking about her future, she discovered that not only did the girl have a connection to the Sage candidates, but she had even come into contact with Yogiri Takatou.

"Oh? So he was able to kill without being present."

Since she had been brought into Lain's bloodline, Euphemia was unable to lie to her, meaning at least her recounting of her observations was true. This meant that Yogiri could kill people from a considerable distance.

"The city is about ten kilometers from here, isn't it?"

"That is correct."

"So at the very least, his range is about that far."

Lain continued to extract as much information from Euphemia as she could. According to Yogiri himself, he could kill simply by willing it. It worked not only against people, but against objects created by magic and animated puppets as well.

While he seemed able to kill anyone he could see, he'd apparently also killed someone that he *couldn't* see, even with that person being both underground and considerably farther away. He could also perceive potential harm to himself, with a range that had to be totally absurd. The fact that Yuuki had died immediately after ordering Yogiri's death must have been a result of that perception.

It was truly an irritating ability. Even if they tried to target him from a distance, the intent to harm him alone was enough to get them killed. In short, Yogiri's powers were nothing as simple as Instant Death Magic. It would be something much more difficult to get past.

"Now I want to see exactly what he can and can't do."

The Immortal Corps could quite possibly fail in their attack. Sending assassins after him would be a similar waste of time and resources, but even if they were going to die, it was necessary to get a handle on the limits of Yogiri's ability — its range, the scope of its power, its nature. And Yogiri's own personality. What did he like, what did he hate, what would he ignore?

"Of course, the thing I want to know most is if he can kill me."

"Did you say something, Mistress?" Euphemia responded to Lain's muttering. Even if only the two of them were there, Lain chided herself for carelessly speaking out loud.

"Don't worry about it. As much as I was able to learn about Yogiri, it might all be pointless in the end."

The Aggressor was currently heading for the very city where Yogiri was. If she left it alone, there would be no survivors. It would be nice if the city's barrier worked against it, but that had only been created to stop monsters — she had no idea how effective it would be against the Darkness.

"Now then, if the Darkness makes it into the city, we'll have more options available to us."

If she didn't mind sacrificing Hanabusa, she could think of numerous ways to handle the Darkness.

But she had no intention of doing so if she didn't have to.

Chapter 35 — Why Don't You Try to Be a Bit More of a Hero?!

After the initial commotion over them being found, people flooded into the alley. Unfortunately for them, Yogiri had no intention of holding back just because they were ordinary citizens.

"If you get any closer, I'll kill you."

At his clear threat, the people came to a halt. From the alleyway back to the main street, those in front pushed back against the ones surging forward. This of course created an even greater commotion, drawing more civilians to come and surround them.

"What are you waiting for?! Get out of the way, I'll do it!"

"You idiot! If you get any closer —"

Without understanding the situation, an overzealous young man pushed through the crowd towards Yogiri. The moment he crossed Yogiri's barrier of death, he collapsed to the ground.

"I've never seen someone make good on such an awful threat before!" Tomochika responded reflexively as she watched the clearly suicidal attack happen.

"I think it would be weirder for me not to kill them when they approach clearly intending to hurt us."

"No one would believe they'd drop dead just from getting too close, though!"

Yogiri didn't feel the need to explain himself over and over. If they were foolish enough to approach without thinking things through, that was entirely on them.

You seem rather unmoved by the deaths happening in front of you right now.

"That's because you removed the seal, right?!"

I didn't say it was a bad thing. This isn't the peaceful Japan that you know. Standing around shocked every time you see someone die would be a problem.

Yogiri had always found Tomochika to be remarkably unmoved by most of the events that had taken place since they'd been transported to this world. Given she'd had the presence of mind to keep up her snarky commentary the whole time, she seemed comfortable enough.

"Why are these people coming after us?"

The locals who had flooded into the alley were now following their movements, matching Yogiri's pace. The crowd surrounded them on all sides except at the front. Arrayed in a semicircle, they kept a distance of about ten meters.

"I guess they can't just leave now that they've found us."

Either they were chomping at the bit for a fight they couldn't have, or they were entranced by their own fear. Whatever the reason, they were neither able to approach nor able to leave, resulting in them simply tracking the pair's every movement.

As they realized Tomochika and Yogiri were just calmly walking, though, the crowd gradually calmed down.

"Hey, where exactly are you supposed to take us if you capture us?" Yogiri asked.

"Uh, right down this street, there's an open square. But what do you plan on doing?" a somewhat older man answered from their right.

"Well, I'm going there. That's why I asked."

"Wha...why didn't you do that from the start, then?! None of these people had to die!"

"Why should I care about people who just attacked me out of nowhere?"

From Yogiri's perspective, he was being accosted by random people in a city he had just arrived in. Even if they died coming after him, Masayuki was the one who had caused the whole mess, so if they were going to complain, he felt like that's who they should have been complaining to.

"Shouldn't we just leave the city if you don't care? Oh, I guess there's the barrier and all." If he didn't care about saving the people of the city, Tomochika felt it would be smarter to leave without going to the central square.

"Barrier, huh? I won't know until I try, but I might be able to just kill it."

"I'm kind of losing sight of what the word 'kill' is supposed to mean."

"What do we accomplish by leaving the city, though? Do you want to walk to the capital?"

Indeed, there is a deep ravine between here and there. Crossing it without being on board a train would be rather challenging.

"So we need to get the trains moving again somehow." If that was the case, the fastest way would be to confront the Masayuki guy who had started all of this, Yogiri thought.

"Well...umm...I'm sorry about attacking you without thinking. But what are you planning to do?" Perhaps because he had been the first to speak up, the man from before had become somewhat of a spokesperson for the crowd.

"I want to talk to him."

"He's an attendant of the Sages, and powerful enough to do all of this. I don't think you'll be able to casually talk it out," the man said, seemingly having lost sight of his own place in all of this.

"I don't want to sell him short, but if that happens, I'll just get rid of him. If he won't listen to reason then he's nothing more than an obstacle."

As Yogiri said that, they reached the central square. Under normal circumstances, it seemed like a place where plenty of people could relax. But now, the crowds of ugly monsters filling the place meant there would be no respite here. Numerous rotting corpses and clattering skeletons wandered around. Gargoyles patrolled the sky while stone giants watched from down below. This must have been the Immortal Corps.

As they made their way to the center of the square, they realized the crowd around them had vanished. The civilians had apparently stayed behind at the edge of the plaza.

"Hahaha, this is really the most fantasy-like thing we've seen since coming to this world, isn't it? Not that it looks all that fun," Tomochika said, her laugh sounding forced over the slight tremble in her voice.

Before them were a number of the armored vehicles she had seen earlier. There didn't seem to be enough to carry around all of the monsters in sight, so they couldn't have transported all the monsters that way.

"Why don't we try stealing one of those cars?" Yogiri suggested. The vehicles seemed sturdy enough. If they could secure the necessary fuel, they would be able to make it to the capital without a problem.

"Can you drive?"

"I've driven go-karts before."

"Well, that doesn't inspire much confidence…"

In front of the armored cars were numerous otherworlders, although most of them were dead. Aside from being Japanese, there was no theme as to age or gender among the bodies, all of them having been thrown unceremoniously into a heap.

Only two of the otherworlders were still alive. One was a man wearing a suit, standing beside the pile of bodies, looking bored. The other sat atop the pile itself, wearing a black coat over a bare chest as he gazed around the square. It was easy enough to determine that the latter was Masayuki — the light in his eyes spoke of an intelligence that the other undead didn't share. The fact that he was willing to walk all over the corpses was enough of a testament to his character.

"What, you came all on your own? Man, how boring. You trying to sacrifice yourselves to save the town or somethin'?" Masayuki's face twisted with displeasure. One would have expected him to be happy that his targets had shown themselves, but that didn't seem to be the case.

"Why on earth would I do that?"

"Hey, come on, what kind of answer is that?! Try to sound a bit more like a hero!" Tomochika sounded flustered by his response, but Yogiri honestly didn't care one way or another about the city.

"Well, let me make sure, then. You two are Yogiri Takatou and Tomochika Dannoura, yes?"

"Yeah. Do you feel like talking?"

"Talk? Sure. I'd also like to know exactly why you came here. I can still keep my promise by doing that. If I kill you, the game just ends."

Masayuki's irritation must have come from the fact that he no longer had the room to interpret his instructions as broadly as before. Some higher-up Sage must have told him to kill the two of them at any cost. If that was the case, if the two of them died, he wouldn't be able to continue doing as he pleased.

"We want to get on a train and head to the capital. Could you bring down the barrier and get the trains moving again?"

Masayuki stared at them, stupefied. "What?" It was as if he'd completely failed to process what Yogiri had said. It took him a while to collect himself, so Yogiri waited patiently. "Hey, hey, hey, hey! Obviously I'm not gonna do that! Can't you come up with something smarter to say? You should know you're not in a position to be asking for stuff right now! Use your head! What are you, stupid?! Is there a brain in there at all?!"

"I suppose we have something we can negotiate with. You've been really annoying, but how about, in exchange for your help, I let you live? Someone will have to set the barrier back up after we leave, anyway."

Masayuki went stiff again. Infuriated by Yogiri's casual attitude, his expression was the only part of him that changed. "If all you're gonna do is make me mad, then screw talking. Just hurry up and die!"

Masayuki jumped to his feet. As if it had been a signal, the undead wandering aimlessly around the square all turned towards Yogiri as one.

"Die."

But with one word from their target, the atmosphere of the square changed completely.

The wandering undead collapsed. The gargoyles overhead turned into stone statues and fell to the ground. The stone giants toppled over, crushing the other monsters beneath them.

In an instant, the entire Immortal Corps had been wiped out.

Chapter 36 — I'm the One Who Decides What Death Is

There were now only four people still alive in the square. Yogiri Takatou stood idly while Tomochika Dannoura looked hesitantly around them. The young man in the suit lifted his hands as if in surrender, but Masayuki was still standing on the mound of bodies, frozen in place.

"My name is Ryouta Takahashi. I'm the lord of this city. He did all of this on his own; I had nothing to do with it!" The man in the suit jumped to explain his own place in the scheme of things, a quick and shrewd act as expected of a lord.

"What...what happened? What is going on here?!" Masayuki shouted angrily, as if to cover his confusion. "Screw you, man! How did you even kill the undead? How did something that was already dead die again?!"

"Undead? I don't really know what that means, but I'm not sure you can call them dead. They were moving, so that means they were alive, right?" Yogiri asked without mockery in his voice. Even if something was a dead body, the fact that it was moving meant that it was alive in some way. Dead people didn't move. That was common sense to him.

"And now something I've been trying to ignore barges its way back in! I think a moving corpse is a pretty big contradiction already!" Apparently, Tomochika had been trying to avoid overthinking it all.

"Well, all of your friends are dead. So what are you going to do?"

"Dammit! Lain! You knew about this, didn't you?! Instant Death Magic? There's no way that's what this is!" Raising his face to the sky, Masayuki howled a string of curses. He seemed to be yelling at someone named Lain, but there didn't appear to be anyone by that name in the square.

"This doesn't seem like the best time for complaints. I'm asking what you're planning to do next. You can see what's happened here. Try using your head."

"That line got to you, huh?" Tomochika commented.

Masayuki jumped down from the pile of corpses. "What did you do?! That's not the Sage's Gift. Did you get it from a Swordmaster? Or maybe a fallen dragon? Either way, that should still be impossible! How do you kill something that's already dead?!" Unable to accept what he was seeing, Masayuki struggled to get past the basic fact that his walking dead had been destroyed.

"I'm the one who decides what death is. If it moves, it's alive. If it dies, it stops. Your opinion doesn't matter."

Confusion, bewilderment, exhaustion. As a flood of emotions washed over Masayuki's face, he finally settled on rage. Killing intent exploded from within him, filling the space around him like a miasma of hatred, imposing enough to freeze a weaker-willed person in place.

The violent emotions coursing through his mind soon manifested in his physical form. His fangs and claws began to grow. His coat merged with his body to form a pair of wings, and thick black hair covered the rest of his body.

It took almost no time at all, but he had made the wrong choice. His only chance at winning had been a swift strike, one that could take Yogiri's life faster than Yogiri could process what was happening. In the end, his decision to fight without an actual plan was the one that sealed his fate.

Yogiri responded to the killing intent reflexively.

"Couldn't you at least have let him finish transforming?!" Tomochika said, looking at the fallen Masayuki. He was now lying on the ground, in a form somewhere halfway between a person and a beast.

"Why should I have to wait?"

"It's like an unwritten rule, isn't it? Anyway, what happened to negotiating? What are we going to do about the barrier?"

"We don't need this guy anymore. Isn't that right, Ryouta Takahashi?"

"Uh, right!"

With his hands still in the air, the lord of the city nodded vigorously. They could just negotiate with Ryouta instead. He seemed far more likely to give in to them. That's why he had introduced himself in the first place — in short, he had completely cut himself off from Masayuki at that moment.

"I have no combat ability at all. I'm not sure I'll be able to talk much if I'm under threat of dying without warning, though."

"We're just protecting ourselves, so if you don't plan on fighting then you have nothing to worry about."

"Not at all! Not even a little bit! To start, would you mind if I got the key for the barrier back? Masayuki had it."

At Yogiri's nod, Ryouta approached the fallen creature, crouching down and rummaging through his clothes. In short order he had retrieved a single small key.

"Um, I think there are still zombies throughout the city," Tomochika pointed out. "What are we going to do about that?"

"Ah, that. Masayuki added his Necromancy power to the barrier. So people should stop turning into zombies when they die now that he's gone...at any rate, I'll find a way to deal with it. We have contingency plans for handling wandering zombies already."

"Leaving that alone, then, do you have any idea what's actually going on here?"

Since the one who had started the whole incident was now dead, Yogiri was still in the dark about why any of this had happened.

"Ah, well, don't get angry, okay? Sage Lain gave Masayuki orders to kill you two. Masayuki was messed up, so this is the way he chose to do it. I didn't want to let him have his way with my city, but I couldn't counteract the Sage's orders."

"So are you able to *not* carry out that order?"

"I'm an attendant like Masayuki was, but I didn't get any direct orders. So my priority is keeping the city safe."

Tomochika cocked her head, remembering her meeting with the Sage on the bus. "Wait, wasn't the Sage's name Sion or something?"

"Lady Sion is also a Sage, but her jurisdiction is elsewhere. This area is under Lady Lain's control. And this particular region has been entrusted to me."

"But Sion summoned us here and told us to work to become Sages, so why are they trying to kill us?"

They had been summoned as Sage candidates to increase the number of Sages, so it didn't make much sense for the Sages to want them dead. Although, from the opposing point of view, it made sense to get rid of Yogiri seeing as he was actively reducing the number of Sages that were currently in the world.

"I haven't heard anything about it, so I can't say. But I have no desire to get in your way, and I'll do anything I can to help you." After seeing them wipe out the Immortal Corps, he clearly had no intention of plotting against them himself. "You want to go to the capital, right? In that case, I'll just open the barrier…huh?" Touching the key he had retrieved from Masayuki's corpse, Ryouta's expression turned doubtful.

"Is something wrong?"

"It won't go back to normal…what's going on?! Is this a fake?" Flustered, Ryouta looked at Masayuki's body, but his fellow attendant wasn't someone who would bother with such trickery, nor had he had the time nor reason to do it. "No way…is Lady Lain controlling the barrier directly?!"

The key was an object for delegating control of the barrier to the local lord. In short, for Lain, there was no need for a physical key.

"That's the Sage you were talking about earlier, right? Is she coming here?"

"I don't know. I don't think she can control the barrier from that far away, though…she probably just doesn't want you two escaping."

"It looks that way, doesn't it? But to what end? The Immortal Corps is already finished." Yogiri looked around. The Immortals were strewn across the square. They would never move again. There was something else wrong that he noticed right away, too.

Killing intent. Black lines of it were now pointing at Yogiri from every direction. The sound of countless footsteps echoed from the streets leading to the square.

"What is it? More zombies? Doesn't look like it."

Their eyes were mad, but they weren't undead. They all moved like ordinary humans, and they didn't throw themselves mindlessly forward either, stopping to leave a ten-meter radius around them clear. Beyond that radius, the square was now filled to the brim with people.

Chapter 37 — If This Was Part of Her Plan, She Is Pretty Impressive

After seeing the annihilation of the Immortal Corps through Masayuki's eyes, Lain cut her connection. It was best to be safe; she knew how far away Yogiri had been from the Dominator when he killed him, so there was no guarantee that his power wouldn't reach her through Masayuki as well.

"I believe your methods are incredibly dangerous, Mistress. Just watching may have an effect on you," Euphemia advised her, standing at her side. It seemed she was being careful not to underestimate Yogiri either.

"Euphemia, how dangerous do you believe this Yogiri Takatou to be?"

"More than any Sage, Swordmaster, or mythic creature. I believe it is best not to interact with him any further. As it is now, I believe he has no interest in us."

"So you're telling me to run away? I'm afraid I can't do that."

As rulers of the world, Sages had to be an absolute, unquestionable existence. There couldn't be anything that would threaten their lives, and certainly nothing that would make the lower classes *believe* their lives could be threatened.

Fulfill your own desires. That's what the Great Sage had told them, but there were some restrictions on that. The first was that any behavior that would call the absolute power of the Sages into question was forbidden. It was fine to ignore an enemy or let them escape, so long as it didn't make the Sages look weak.

But this situation was completely different. Now that she had already made a move against him, backing down would be a mark against the Sages' honor. As such, it was necessary for her to settle things with Yogiri Takatou, one way or another.

"But what can you do?" Euphemia asked timidly.

That was a rather refreshing response for Lain. As a member of her bloodline, Euphemia's loyalty was unquestionably sincere. And she was honestly concerned about Lain's own well-being. It was the first time someone had shown such concern for her since she had become a Sage.

Which meant that Euphemia believed Yogiri Takatou was stronger than Lain.

"First, I wish to know his limits. Why don't we test that?"

From where they were, Lain could now reach the city's barrier. That would make changing the conditions in the city relatively easy.

It looks like a form of mind control. Of course, I have protected you from that attack.

Like Mokomoko said, it appeared the people of the city were being manipulated in some way.

"What about Takatou and Ryouta?"

"Maybe she's on guard against a counterattack from me."

"I am an attendant of the Sages, so I'm very high level. There's no way such a wide-ranging mental attack would have an effect on me," Ryouta said, though with an undercurrent of unease. After all, if this was an attack by Lain, as one of her subordinates, he must have felt he was in a rather dangerous position.

"But what is she planning on doing now?"

Being entirely surrounded, there was no way for them to escape.

But besides surrounding them, it didn't seem the crowd had any intention of moving in yet. Yogiri could easily kill them all if he wanted to leave, but massacring such a huge number of people who were being controlled against their will wasn't something he would be happy doing.

"Since they are being controlled, can't you just attack the person controlling them?"

"This is a bit different than with Tachibana. His case was more like a hive mind."

But standing around doing nothing wasn't an option either. As Yogiri decided to try something just to see what would happen, he was preempted by a change in the crowd.

Brandishing a knife, a single person leaped from the throng and rushed at him. Yogiri wasted no time in dispatching them, feeling their plain intent to kill. A split second later, two people broke away and rushed him from opposite directions. After dealing with them, four more came at him from all sides.

"Well, this is a familiar feeling. This is generally what happens when someone tries to test my abilities."

Sensing killing intent aimed at Tomochika, Yogiri quickly extinguished the source. The same thing happened with Ryouta, and he decided he might as well kill that one too.

"Ryouta, please get a little closer. If you stay that far away, it'll be harder to keep you safe."

"Are you sure?" Ryouta's face showed clear surprise at Yogiri's offer of protection. "I'm one of Lain's people, so I figured you were just going to kill me after all."

"I'm not interested in killing people who haven't done anything wrong. Of course, I only plan on protecting you while it's convenient for me to do so, but if you step out of line I'll probably end up killing you by reflex."

Yogiri eliminated someone expressing killing intent from far away. They must have had magic, or some sort of projectile weapon. It seemed they were testing him from a variety of ranges now.

"This is kind of getting annoying."

If Yogiri wanted to protect himself then he didn't have much choice, but using these innocent civilians to test him was getting on his nerves.

One of the people in the crowd before them exploded, chunks of meat and blood spraying towards them. Yogiri sidestepped the pieces of iron shrapnel mixed in with the gore coming his way. He wasn't able to avoid the spurt of blood, but at least he hadn't been injured.

"This is never going to end!" yelled Tomochika. "What do we do?!"

"If we just want to end it immediately, that's possible," Yogiri said, glancing over at Ryouta.

The lord of the city's face bore a twisted, bitter expression. From that expression alone, it was clear that he treasured the people of Hanabusa. For being an attendant of the Sages, he actually seemed to be a decent person.

"If that was part of her plan too, then she's pretty impressive," Yogiri muttered.

Realizing that she couldn't hurt Yogiri physically, it seemed she was now targeting his emotions. If he was up against an opponent who would take even that into account, he couldn't let down his guard for a moment — there was no way she would be satisfied with just throwing the residents of the city at him.

As Yogiri was trying to figure out what her next attempt might be, an intense intent to kill settled over them.

"Uh…what's wrong? I don't like that expression you've got at all."

"A strong killing intent suddenly appeared all around us. Normally, it's like a black line between me and the source, but now it's more like a black haze over the whole area."

It was similar to what Yogiri had felt when they had parted ways with the robot and started walking to Hanabusa. As they approached the city, it had grown weaker and weaker until he could barely feel it once they'd reached Hanabusa itself. But now they were right in the thick of it again.

"Ah, that danger forecast thing again?"

"In forecast terms, we're above fifty percent."

"That would mean it's definitely going to rain in a weather forecast, right?" Tomochika frantically began looking around.

"It feels like…things are drying out?"

It was just a subtle, uncomfortable feeling, but now that it had been put into words, it was hard to think of it any other way. The wind had turned dry, the air itself taking on a rough quality.

"Wait, what is that?!" Tomochika pointed towards the distant sky. Following her finger, Yogiri saw an enormous black figure towering in the distance, slowly approaching the city.

"No way…an Aggressor? Is that the Darkness?" Ryouta muttered, staring at the figure in dumbfounded shock.

"You know what it is? Wait, aren't Aggressors supposed to be robots?"

"The Darkness is an Aggressor that appeared recently. Sir Santarou drove it off, apparently, but…dammit. Is this what Lady Lain was fighting?!"

A scream echoed in the distance. Apparently, Lain's control didn't extend to the entirety of the city's population, as those who saw the Darkness approaching were now fleeing to the central square. Meanwhile, the Darkness casually stepped into the city, oblivious of and unaffected by the barrier. Paying no heed to the buildings in its way, the shadowy figure walked into a skyscraper, passing right through it. In an instant, the building vanished.

"Damn it! First we're trapped here by civilians, now an Aggressor?! What am I supposed to do about all this?!" Ryouta wailed under the unbearable stress of the situation.

Even if it looked like it was moving slowly, the creature was just too big. Compared to ordinary people, it was also too fast. Even if they gave an evacuation order now, there wouldn't be enough time.

The shadow of killing intent from the giant was growing steadily darker, proof enough that the monster was heading straight for the central square.

Although she had spent the time trying to test Yogiri Takatou with her attacks, all Lain had learned was that he could sense them coming before they happened. Not just those nearby, but even the ones who'd tried to target him from a distance with arrows or magic had died before they could launch their attacks. Whether he could see them or not, he was able to deal with them anywhere in the city.

"If killing him directly is impossible, how about indirectly? How about doing something that would bring about his death by happenstance, with no direct intention to kill him?"

For example, a stray bullet or an accidental shot. There would be no specific intent to kill in that case. In a similar fashion, something like an area attack that didn't target him specifically, or a time bomb could also work. In fact, the spray of blood had managed to connect, even if it hadn't actually harmed him.

"But is such a thing possible to set up at this stage?" asked Euphemia.

"I'm sure you already know, but we conveniently have an Aggressor heading towards the city. Let's make use of that."

Lain wanted to do a bit more research into exactly what constituted "killing intent," but if she was to make use of the Darkness, this was her only chance.

"Certainly, no human could survive being touched by such a thing. But do you really think it will affect *him*?" Euphemia was uncertain. She seemed to believe that Yogiri could kill even an Aggressor, despite its lack of a perceivable physical form.

"Well, I guess we can't just relax here forever."

Euphemia's eyes went wide with surprise. Lain had suddenly become two people. They were virtually identical, a sight that should have only been possible with a mirror.

"I have the ability to regenerate in an instant even after being completely annihilated. Using that power, it's easy enough to create copies of myself."

"I, umm, I understand your power is incredible, Mistress…but to what end?"

"I would like to ask that as well." It was impossible to tell the difference just by looking, but it must have been the newly created Lain who answered.

"Hm. I guess we'll call you Lain B. Though you are a copy of me, I have intentionally removed all of your memories regarding a certain person. Now, you cannot have any intention of harming that person."

This was a measure she had taken just in case. Even the thought of killing Yogiri might be enough to provoke a counterattack.

"Hmm. I don't really understand, but I suppose that's on purpose."

"Go up into the sky and wait. When I give the signal, attack the city."

Just as she was told, Lain B flew up into the sky. Even if she didn't know exactly what was happening, she'd been given instructions by Lain herself, so there was no reason to question it.

The original Lain continued to make more copies, sending them up into the air one by one. In the end, there were more than a hundred of them. Seeing so many beautiful women clad in the same red dress floating in the sky was quite a spectacle.

"Excuse me, but if you plan on attacking the city, could you not just use a magical attack of some sort?" Euphemia asked. She must have thought the plan was rather boorish.

"Unfortunately, no. I'm not all that skilled with magic, after all. Simply throwing them into the city will be more effective."

This was a plan that Lain was uniquely capable of. Her flying speed easily broke the sound barrier — no ordinary person could see it coming. With a full-power kamikaze charge, they would slam the overwhelming strength she possessed as a vampire straight into Hanabusa. Even without a clear objective, the shockwave of the attacks would be enough to destroy the city.

Lain stopped forcing the civilians to attack, instead opting to watch through their countless eyes, waiting for the precise moment that Yogiri would unleash his power against the Darkness.

Chapter 38 — Can You Please Not Enjoy My Body in a Situation Like This?!

As a dust-laden wind blew across Hanabusa, its residents continued to gather in the central square. The numerous open squares within the city were designated evacuation points. The obvious course of action was to get out of the way of the Darkness, since it was walking in a straight line, but not everyone could do that. For those who were in the middle of the city already, this was a last-ditch effort at finding protection.

"Hey, Takatou. Is there any way you can deal with that thing?" Tomochika asked, looking up at the approaching giant. They were still standing in the middle of the central square. For some reason, the crowd had stopped attacking them, but the wall of people was still thick enough to prevent their escape.

"Probably."

"Yeah, I guess that's asking too much — wait, you can?!" Tomochika reacted late to his smooth reply.

"Really?! Please! I'll do anything you ask! Please, save the city!" Ryouta cried, all but clinging to Yogiri. Matching Yogiri's previous perception of him as an actually decent person despite his position working under the Sages, it seemed Ryouta was truly concerned about the well-being of this place.

With each step it took, the Darkness destroyed more of its

surroundings. Anything its hazy body touched instantly turned to sand. They had no idea what its objective was, as it was simply walking in a straight line through the city.

"Then hurry up!" Tomochika cried.

"I don't know, I have a bad feeling about this. I guess I can't just let it go either, though."

He wasn't especially concerned about saving the people of the city, but the more damage the thing dealt, the longer it would take to get the trains running again.

Yogiri looked at the Darkness. It seemed like nothing more than a mindless black haze. Its actual body was likely incredibly small, if it even had one to speak of. In any case, if it was a single life form, there shouldn't be any problems.

"Die."

Yogiri unleashed his power. At the same time, a massive impact struck the city, and countless strands of black signifying danger suddenly appeared.

"Get down!"

Grabbing Tomochika, Yogiri threw her to the ground to avoid the lines of killing intent. Seeing them, Ryouta hurriedly dropped to the ground as well.

A moment later, something passed by overhead and screams filled the air as the people gathered around them cried out in their final moments. The wall of civilians that had trapped them in the square was destroyed. All that remained was a scattering of broken, shattered bodies.

"Wh-What was that? Was it an attack from that Darkness thing?!"

"No, I killed it," Yogiri said, pointing at the creature. The already hazy form of the giant was growing fainter, as if it were a natural fog now dissipating.

"What? So something else attacked us?!"

"Yeah. It seems like they tried to use the Darkness to hide their killing intent."

Whatever it was had punched through the buildings and crashed into the ground, creating a shockwave that had destroyed everything around it. Still more attacks were raining from the sky, seemingly intent on wiping out the entire city. An onslaught of attacks at a speed the eye couldn't follow. The problem was that they weren't aimed at Yogiri himself.

"So this is targeting us as well?"

"Yes and no. It seems like they're trying to get around my power, but I have no idea what's going on."

Although it felt like they were being carpet-bombed, he couldn't see what was actually happening. They could avoid the scattering debris, but that was only an indirect danger to them. By the time the debris struck, the attack itself had already ended.

"So what do we do now?"

"We can avoid the debris, so I guess we should just wait until it's over."

"Well, it *is* over, so could you let me go?"

"Huh, I was just thinking the ground was strangely soft."

Yogiri was still lying on top of Tomochika after having tackled her to the ground.

"Could you please not enjoy my body in a situation like this?!"

"Could you please stop holding each other like this is a Hollywood movie and do something about this?!" Ryouta shouted angrily, crawling along the ground towards them.

"We're not holding each other! This is all him!" Tomochika yelled back, her face a deep red.

"That's easy to say, but I don't even know what's attacking us."

"Uhh, I know it's kind of hard to believe, but if I tell you, can you promise not to laugh at me?" she replied.

"What is it?"

"There are a bunch of women in red dresses falling from the sky."

"Your eyes really are amazing," Yogiri was once again impressed by her eyesight. Apparently, she wasn't just good at seeing things from a distance, she also had a great eye for high-speed objects.

"Can I please stand up?"

"For now, I guess."

The city was still in the process of being destroyed, but the area immediately surrounding them hadn't been attacked for some time. Lifting himself off the ground, Yogiri set Tomochika free. Rising to her feet, she pointed up at the sky.

"They're coming from there."

"I still can't see them."

He didn't know exactly what their plan was, but it seemed like an effective strategy against Yogiri. If they had launched straight at him, he could have just killed the people responsible. But if the attacker simply threw themselves at a speed he couldn't follow, and at no particular target, there was nothing he could do. Since they weren't targeting him directly, he couldn't kill them before the attack happened, and since they moved faster than he could see, he couldn't kill them mid-attack either. The biggest problem, though, was that by the time the attack was finished, the person who had launched it had already been scattered into a million pieces.

"Dammit! If she's wearing a red dress, that must be Lady Lain! What is going on here?! Seriously, this is insane!" Ryouta was beside himself. Clearly, his superiors and his colleagues were all awful people.

"How many of these Lains are there?"

"She's probably just cloning herself. Lady Lain's regeneration is strong enough that she can easily make copies of herself."

"I see. In that case, there's something we can do." Ryouta's explanation was just the help Yogiri needed. The fact that she was willing to destroy her own city amounted to betrayal, as far as he was concerned. "But I don't have a way of getting to her. It would help if she targeted me directly." If he was personally targeted, he could counterattack, but his opponent was fighting this way specifically to avoid that outcome.

"So if she targets you directly, you can do something about it?" Ryouta asked. It seemed like he had a plan.

"My class is Mayor. I'll leave out the long explanation, but in short, I have the ability to oversee cities. Looking at the situation here, it looks like there's a pattern to the attacks. She never attacks the same place twice, and she avoids attacking places near where she has already struck as well."

Yogiri thought that may have been an unconscious decision. Even when doing something randomly, people had a tendency to add a sense of uniformity to it.

"So basically, we can make a guess as to where she'll attack next. Although even if we know that, it's not like we can get there fast enough."

"That's not a problem. I can teleport to anywhere in a city that's under my control. I can even bring a small number of people with me."

"Oh, really?! Wait, then why didn't you run away earlier?!"

If that was the case, he should have been able to escape at any point regardless of how many people were surrounding him.

"I need a wide-open space to teleport to and from. If I'd used it earlier, I would have blasted away all those people. More importantly, how could I just abandon them like that?!"

"Wow, this guy is really nice for a Sage's attendant."

Yogiri decided to go with Ryouta's plan immediately. Using the Mayor's power, they moved instantly to a part of the city that hadn't been attacked yet.

They were now in a park in a residential area. There were no signs of other people, making it seem like the area had already been evacuated. Yogiri and Tomochika stood side by side, hand in hand. Ryouta had teleported elsewhere just in case. If things didn't go well, he would come back to take them to a new location.

"There isn't really a reason for you to be here either, Dannoura. I'm sure I can figure out a way to do this by myself."

"I can see better than you, so that'll help, right?"

In addition, my powers of perception might be useful, Mokomoko added.

The attacks were happening in varying intervals, anywhere from a few seconds to half a minute apart. There was likely to be some sign of the next attack coming relatively soon.

Looking up at the sky, Tomochika squeezed Yogiri's hand. That was the signal. He immediately matched her movement as she broke into a forward sprint. Running full tilt, Yogiri felt a shiver run down his back. A pitch-black shadow appeared, drawing a line of guaranteed death straight into the ground. Turning toward the source of that danger, Yogiri unleashed his power.

"Mokomoko!"

Something slipped out of Tomochika's uniform. The object transformed into a dome, covering the two of them in an instant. The sound of something smashing into the ground nearby came immediately after. Shaking briefly from the impact, the dome fell still, and the area around them was silent.

"Man, that is not something to do on the fly. Feels bad for my heart."

I figured it was rather solid, but I wanted to test it out myself.

Even if the attacking Lain had been killed, her body had still been flying towards them. They had been protected by the object given to them by the robot Aggressor. While it was made of something similar to an artificial muscle, and therefore wasn't quite as resilient as the robot's armor, it was still tough enough to deflect a hit from a person moving at supersonic speed.

But isn't killing her clones simply a waste of time?

Mokomoko's doubt was well founded. After all, their opponent could continue to make any number of clones. But Yogiri's response was calm and natural.

"I think it's okay. I feel like it went well."

After waiting a while, no further attacks came. It appeared that his power had successfully reached the Sage's main body.

Chapter 39 — It Just Looks Like I'm Screwing Around by Myself!

The Lain Bs waiting in the sky suddenly lost their power and immediately fell to the ground. Lain didn't know exactly what had happened, as she had intentionally not been tapping into the senses of her copies. Yogiri must have used his power on them, though — there was no other explanation for why a group of immortal vampires would have died.

The smashed, sand-covered bodies of the Lain Bs disappeared almost instantly. Extensions of herself that she felt were no longer necessary always did.

"What...what on earth happened...?" Euphemia asked timidly, watching the bodies fall into the crumbling hellscape of the city.

"The Lain Bs were killed. Since they were all made from the same template, it seems killing one of them got the rest as well."

"We really shouldn't have picked a fight with this Yogiri Takatou!"

"You think so? Surely all I have to do is create them with slightly different templates this time. That way, if he kills one, the rest won't be harmed."

Despite the deaths of the Lain Bs, Lain herself wasn't affected. Clearly, Yogiri's powers did have limits after all. Even when it came to his reactions to killing intent, there were differences in that power depending on the circumstances. It might be the key she needed to take him down. With a bit more research, she should be able to find a way to break the deadlock between them.

But Lain was disappointed. In the end, Yogiri had been unable to kill an Origin Blood. She had lost her interest in him now. The Darkness had also been defeated. Was there any value in letting him continue to live? Those who opposed the Sages must be killed. There was a simple loophole to that ironclad rule, though. The rebel just had to be turned into a Sage. But that was something that could be mulled over later. Now that the Darkness had been dealt with, Lain had no reason to stay there.

But as Lain decided to return to her mansion, she noticed something strange — she couldn't move her body at all.

Did something happen?!

The unprecedented phenomenon left her bewildered. This was the first time she had been truly surprised since she had come to this world. It felt like time itself had stopped. From that feeling, a possibility came to mind, as hard as it was to believe.

Her main body had died.

The Lain that was standing here now was, like Lain B, a clone made by the true Lain. But unlike Lain B, who had been made to be disposable, this Lain was inextricably linked to the main body, and shared all of its memories as well. This was the driving force behind Lain's immortality — by leaving her main body in a safe place, she acted through the use of clones. No matter how many of them were destroyed, she could always make another one on the spot.

But now the crucial link between her and her main body had been severed. She could no longer communicate with her main body, and was no longer reflecting any changes that happened to it. Because of that, the Lain standing there now had begun to think independently.

But that wouldn't last for long. Lain's primary clone had been built with the assumption that it would have an uninterrupted connection to the main body. Should that link be severed, the unneeded body would disappear. For a dependent clone like her, that was inevitable.

The Lain standing there now was no more than a fading echo, a temporary existence, a gap between synchronizations that shouldn't even be conscious.

Like her life flashing before her eyes, her last instants stretched out as she thought over what had happened. He must have reached the main body through the Lain Bs. She was immediately filled with admiration...and relief. Lain B and her main body weren't connected directly. So Yogiri had been able to kill the main body where it waited in a supposedly safe, sealed space.

She had no idea what made that possible. His power was absurd, to the point of breaking logic. But that made it all the more likely that he would be able to save the child.

In her last few moments before disappearing, Lain's heart was filled with hope.

The next day, after that whole unpleasant chain of incidents, Yogiri and Tomochika were back in the city's central square. Numerous tents had been set up to house the survivors of the recent events, so that was where the two of them were staying as well.

The zombie attack, the bizarre behaviors of the residents, the attack from the Darkness, and finally the widespread ruin left by the Sage's own attack. Even thinking of a place to start seemed a monumental enough task, yet despite being on the edge of falling into despair, Ryouta had immediately kicked into action with the relief efforts. Take stock of the damage. Call nearby cities for aid. Provide aid to victims. Collect the necessary materials and provide a place to stay for those who had lost their homes.

"I know I'm the one who woke you up, but are you okay?"

"I'm still sleepy, but it's fine."

The two of them were heading to the Disaster Response Headquarters. Entering the building, they approached the head of the response task force, Ryouta.

"Thank you so much. You really saved us yesterday!" Though he looked exhausted from missing an entire night of rest, Ryouta greeted the two of them with a wide smile, his gratitude sincere.

"Uh, I appreciate the thanks, but that was a Sage we killed, right?" Tomochika answered, her voice tinged with unease. As an attendant of the Sages, it was odd for him to be so happy about it.

"It's fine, it's fine! That human bomb doesn't deserve respect from us." Ryouta had immediately become defiant towards his former superior.

"But the city was safe because of the Sage's barrier, right? What will happen now?"

"I'm sure a new Sage will be dispatched soon enough. Until then, we'll just have to build some walls and fend for ourselves. Anyway, did you guys need something? I said I'd do anything for you, but you see how the situation is. I might have to make you wait a bit."

"Yeah, we're thinking of leaving the city as soon as we can."

That was why Yogiri had been forced to wake up, despite wanting to sleep through the whole morning. Tomochika was strongly of the opinion that they needed to leave as soon as possible. She was concerned about all the civilians Yogiri had killed. Although he had only killed them in self-defense, the remaining civilians must have had very mixed feelings about it. It was possible some of them would try to take revenge.

"That's fine, but the trains still aren't running."

"Yeah, about that. Could we take one of those trucks in the central square?"

"The Immortal Corps' trucks? One of those will certainly get you to the capital, but are you sure that's good enough?"

"That should be fine. What do they use as fuel? Does this world have something like gasoline?"

"This world's vehicles all run on magic. They use magical stones automatically, so you don't need to be able to operate it yourself or anything. All right, please wait a little while. I'll outfit one of them for you before you go."

◇◇◇

The next morning, the two of them made their way to their new truck just as a large number of supplies were being carried inside. The rough-looking vehicle was a long, rectangular shape, with six tires. It seemed to have been developed in this world, but with the armored military trucks of their homeworld in mind.

"Are you sure you can spare all this? Even though the city is still in such rough shape..." Tomochika said, already apologizing to Ryouta as he directed the loading of the truck.

"It's fine. If you two hadn't been here, not even this much of the city would be left."

"Of course, if the two of us hadn't been here, none of this would have happened in the first place."

"Well, there's no point thinking about it like that. There is rarely a clear meaning to the actions the Sages take, so we can't know whether Lady Lain really did all of this because of you two. And Masayuki would have done what he did whether or not you were in the city. And the Aggressor likely would have attacked regardless of anything the Sages did."

Yogiri decided to leave it at that.

Ryouta gave a rough explanation of the truck and its new contents. "All right, loading is complete. I got some stuff that I thought you guys might need. I loaded it up with plenty of magic stones too, so it should easily make it to the capital." Yogiri had already boarded the truck by then, so Tomochika was the only one who heard him.

"Thank you for all of this!"

"See you around. Try not to drive off a cliff or anything." Ryouta held out a hand. After a handshake, the two parted ways.

Boarding the truck, Tomochika found Yogiri already in the passenger seat, playing on his handheld.

"Wait, aren't you going to drive? Didn't you say you were good with go-karts or something?" She had taken it for granted that the guy would want the wheel.

"I'm not good at it at all. I just said that I'd done it before. I hit the wall on just about every curve. Do you want someone like that driving for you?"

"Just hit the brakes when you go around curves!" Obviously, leaving the wheel to Yogiri wasn't an option. Climbing over him, she got into the driver's seat. "But I've never driven a truck like this before. Is it really something you can pick up without any experience?"

With my instruction in the Dannoura School of Driving Techniques, you can rest assured that all will be well!

"Can you stop making everything part of the Dannoura School, please? You make it sound so cheap!"

As an aside, the Dannoura School Flying Body Press was a specialty of her older sister.

Be it a chariot or a helicopter, I am more than capable of piloting it! Don't look down on the Dannoura name!

"What on earth has our family been doing...?" Feeling like she might strike upon a terrifying truth, Tomochika stopped that line of thought partway.

Following Mokomoko's instructions, she started the engine. Once the magic was activated, the internal system and various gauges of the truck looked mostly like any other car. As she timidly pressed down on the gas, the truck gently rolled into motion.

"Uhh, here we go!" Tomochika raised a hand into the air in an energetic declaration. "Come on, give me a response at least! You're making it look like I'm just screwing around by myself!"

"Do your best," Yogiri said, not taking his eyes off the screen of his handheld.

"I most certainly will!!"

First, she would need to head to the canyon — their ultimate goal being the capital city that lay beyond it.

Chapter 40 — Interlude: If You're Seeing This, Then…

The girl lay on her back, staring lazily at the ceiling. She didn't remember when she had started — at some point, she just realized she was there. She must have still been half asleep. She sat for a while thinking that, but no matter how much time passed, the fog over her memory didn't lift.

Finally, she decided to sit up. When she did, she realized she was sitting in a coffin. It was an ornate thing, the inner lining made of a rich satin. Compared to her body, the coffin was rather large.

"I look like a vampire," she said, surprising herself with her own voice. It was much higher and much younger than she remembered. As she went to feel her own body, she realized she was holding something in her hand. Within her hand was a round stone, but as expected, she had no idea why she was holding it.

She ran her hands all over her face and body. It was hard to call anything about her mature. She was also wearing a pink summer dress lined with frills. It appeared she was a child.

As she came to this conclusion, the room gradually became lighter. It was filled with cute-looking furniture and overflowing with stuffed animals that spoke of the tastes of a young girl. The only thing that looked out of place was the coffin. Once the room had become sufficiently bright, a woman in a red dress suddenly appeared.

"The fact that you are seeing this recording means my plan has suc-ceeded. I have died, and you have survived."

The girl was relieved that someone had appeared. She was just thinking she might be in trouble if left alone.

"Allow me to explain your true identity. You are me."

The girl cocked her head. She didn't really understand. As if seeing her confusion, the image of the woman continued to explain.

"My name is Lain. I am called a Sage by the people of this world."

The words "Sage" and "this world" were familiar enough to the girl. She just didn't understand anything about herself.

"And you are a duplicate that I created of myself. In order to provide you with maximum independence, all memories relating to my personality have been removed."

For being a duplicate, never mind her memories...even her body was completely different.

"Your body was prepared as such in order to facilitate your development as an individual. My apologies to you, but I let my own tastes run rampant. That was the form I once wished I could have had. While I was always described as cool and dignified, I was never called 'cute.' Instead, I was told that I had a hostile expression, or that I looked like someone who would become a murderer."

She wondered how the woman had responded to being told such things, but she could worry about that later. There was a chance this recording wouldn't play again. She had to make sure she heard every-thing the first time.

"The reason I have chosen such a strange, roundabout method is to avoid Yogiri Takatou's attack."

Yogiri Takatou. The moment she heard that name, her heart began to race. She knew all about him, and about his power, so she immedi-ately understood why Lain had done what she had.

"Next, allow me to explain where you are right now. This is a hidden refuge on the surface. This room and coffin belonged to me, but from now on, they are yours. You should have plenty of funds, so live however you

see fit. The two of us are entirely separate existences, so I cannot compel you to do anything."

Even being told that, the girl was still at a complete loss as to what to do. As someone artificially created, she had no proper memories at all. Even if told to live however she wanted, there was no sense of where to actually begin.

"Now that you've hopefully understood this much, I have a request to make."

It wasn't an order, no doubt in order to preserve the independence of her substitute. She was afraid of Yogiri's power reaching through to her.

Lain made her request.

"That's not fair," the girl thought out loud. Having just woken up with no memories, she had no reason for living, nor any basis on which to judge right and wrong. Given a request in that state, there was nothing for her to do but carry it out.

"Well, putting aside the request, I'll be going to meet this Yogiri."

She had a deep affection for Yogiri Takatou. No doubt that was also part of the original Lain's strategy for avoiding his power. But for the girl who understood nothing about herself, those feelings were still precious.

Or maybe that was all part of Lain's calculations, too. Either way, she didn't mind. Her feelings for Yogiri were the only thing shining within her.

The blade entered through the shoulder, exiting through the flank, cutting the human-shaped monster diagonally in half. Blood and guts sprayed as the creature collapsed, its life coming to a swift end. In short order, its Soul began to diffuse, most of it absorbed by the long-haired Ryouko Ninomiya who had cut the beast down. The leftovers were split among her remaining party members, but that only amounted to scraps.

"You're so strong, Ryouko. You must have more experience points than anyone else by now." The one who spoke was Asuha Kouriyama, the Beauty Coordinator.

They were in the middle of the forest. Yogiri's classmates were fighting to gain experience on their way to the capital. The girls here had joined as a party of four in order to level up with a simple strategy. They used the Charm Up skill on the party's strongest member, Ryouko. The aroused monsters would then rush her over and over, allowing her to cut them down as they approached. Thanks to that, the other three were able to level up in relative safety.

Of course, the amount of experience — or Soul — that each of them gained was proportional to their distance from the slain monster. Ryouko, being alone on the front lines, had risen head and shoulders above the others.

"Let's call it a day here. Charm Up is probably going to end soon, right?" Ryouko flicked the blade, handily removing the lingering blood. It wasn't just an ordinary sword. While Ryouko's overwhelming strength was in part due to her skill, the abilities of her weapon also played a major role.

"Yeah, if we keep going any longer, it'll be dark before we get back. Is that okay with everyone?" Asuha asked their other two companions.

Since the ones who weren't fighting could hardly disagree, they returned to the camp. Numerous tents had been set up in a clearing in the forest. Most of their classmates were gathered here. Having made it back to camp, they broke up the party and Ryouko made her way back to her own tent.

"Hello, Ryouko!"

She had a visitor. But this was a tent reserved specifically for her — one of those given to the high-level members of the class. Entering uninvited was against the rules.

"Could you not go inside my tent without permission?"

With her blonde hair and blue eyes, the girl inside was clearly not Japanese. Carol S. Lane. As her name and appearance suggested, she was a foreigner. Coming to Japan just in time to enter high school, she had been in Ryouko's class for two years in a row. As Ryouko looked at the smartphone she was playing with in her hands, she realized it was the phone she had lost earlier.

"Oh, sorry. Thank you for finding it for me." Ryouko immediately calmed down. She wasn't happy about Carol breaking into the tent, but coming to return the phone was probably an act of kindness. Even so, her current behavior was making Ryouko's gratitude wear thin.

"You no worry!"

"Can you not talk like that, please? It's making me angry."

"Really? All right, I'll stop." Carol slipped into fluent Japanese. Her trademark gag was to pretend she was awful at speaking it.

"Where did you find it?"

"Well, I didn't really find it. I was holding on to it the whole time. Here you go." With a smile, she handed the phone to Ryouko, who was speechless at the shameless admission of guilt. "The battery was getting low, so I decided to give it back."

Looking at the phone, she saw that the battery was below five percent. "Why on earth did you steal it?" She didn't understand Carol's motives. A smartphone was more or less useless in this world, so there was nothing to be gained from stealing it.

"I was interested in your observation tool, so I tried to brute force my way into it. Anyway, it didn't work, and the battery was just going to die, so I decided to give it back. Hey, could you actually show me how it works?"

The observation tool was a specialized app installed on her phone. There were very few people who knew about it.

"Who are you?!"

"I'm a ninja. The same as you."

Ryouko's heart leaped into her throat. The class given to her when she'd been summoned to this world was Samurai. Those who knew she was a ninja back home were vanishingly few.

"Me, American Ninja!" Carol returned to her poor, broken Japanese, but Ryouko was no longer in a state of mind to be upset by that.

It couldn't be a joke. Foreign powers were observing Yogiri Takatou — that was reasonable enough. Anyone who knew about him wouldn't be able to take their eyes off him for a moment.

"Well, it doesn't matter. It has nothing to do with me anymore," Ryouko said after a long pause. "I was surprised at first, but really, who cares about stuff from our old world?"

Those were her true feelings. If she could never return to Japan, her mission to observe Yogiri was pointless. What was most important was that she and her classmates survived.

"Yeah, I understand how you feel. So, can you show me how it works? There's no reason to keep it a secret, right?"

"If you're here to observe him too, you should already have something like that, shouldn't you?"

"We had a dedicated satellite so we could watch him at all times, but that doesn't really help us here, does it? But Japan already has a connection to Takatou, and your occult-related technology is more advanced than ours, yeah?"

Ryouko unlocked her phone. If Carol wanted to see it that badly, she didn't care enough to stop her. Opening the observation tool, she put in her personal passcode. When she did, Yogiri's current status appeared on the screen. She couldn't track his location without GPS, but it could still give her a rough estimate of which direction he was in and how far away he was. According to the tool, he was somewhere off towards the capital. In other words, he was moving faster than the rest of them.

"So he's alive after all."

"But Yogiri's power was supposed to be sealed...huh, no way...the first gate opened somehow..." Ryouko felt a chill run down her back. She had never seen the threat he posed personally, but she had heard all about the kinds of tragedies his power could cause.

"It's not really that strange, is it? He sealed it himself, so it would be easy enough for him to release it. All right, thanks." As if to say that was all she wanted, Carol made to leave the tent.

"Carol, what are you planning?" Ryouko called after her.

"Nothing in particular at the moment. At this rate, we'll meet up with him again anyway, right?"

"Aren't you scared?"

In Japan, they had been excruciatingly cautious, but back then death had seemed like a distant nightmare. With the seal released, however, it was now a reality that was creeping ever closer.

"Scared? Oh, maybe you're thinking about this in a different way than I am. Do you guys look at him as a monster or something?"

"Isn't he?" Just by thinking it, he could kill people. That was a true monster by any definition. Even when his power had been sealed, they couldn't rest easy. Just being in Japan had felt like lying on a bed of nails to her.

"I guess. But I think it's simpler than that. He's a being that rules over the deaths of all living things. What would you call that?"

"No way..." An answer so simple, and yet still astounding immediately came to mind.

"For those of us who have proof it really exists, there's nothing we can do but shed the faith we've had until now. That's just how it is."

With those words, Carol left the tent. Her new faith was something that had remained unshaken even after being sent to another world. Ryouko, who was just riding the current of her new situation, was a little envious of that unwavering belief.

MY INSTANT DEATH ABILITY IS SO OVERPOWERED, NO ONE IN THIS OTHER WORLD STANDS A CHANCE AGAINST ME!

Bonus Side Story

Side Story: AΩ

"Umm, maybe I just don't understand it properly, but will this actually do anything?"

The young woman in a black suit finally voiced the question that had been circling in her head for a while. Under her brand new suit she wore a white blouse, and her long hair was tied up behind her head. Her appearance gave a strong impression of orderliness, and as that orderly, artificial appearance suggested, she was here job hunting.

They were deep in the mountains, about three hours away from the closest bus station. But as much as it seemed they were a lone island in an ocean of wilderness, the building she had found there was strangely modern.

The Independent Higher Order Organism Research Facility. It was one of the many organizations she had applied to. After seeing the information they had provided about themselves at their recruiting seminar, she felt they should have a job for even a liberal arts student like her. And aside from employees being forced to live in company dormitories, their requirements were surprisingly lax. After how hopeless her job search had seemed until that point, she had jumped at the offer to come here immediately.

And now, she had just finished reading the documents they had put before her. Though the complicated legalese went over her head, she could get the general gist of it. Basically, it was a waiver saying if she died while working for them, they weren't responsible.

"Ah! You're wondering why we'd make you sign something that couldn't be legally binding, when we could easily make you disappear without a trace anyway, right?" the lab-coated young man across from her said happily. Aside from the chairs and table, and of course the two of them, the sparse room was completely empty.

"You just said something kind of terrifying, you know that?!" She wouldn't normally feel it was okay to talk back at a job interview, but in circumstances as suspicious as these, she couldn't help it.

"Yeah, well, the factional warfare here is kind of intense. Even small things like this are used to trip you up at every step. So it's best that you know what kind of situation you're getting into."

"Can I go home?" No matter how hard it had been for her to find a job, she wasn't interested in risking her life.

"Ahaha, after bringing you all the way here, we can't just let you leave, can we?" he replied as if it were a given. She considered just running from the room right then, but that led her to a realization — there was basically no way for her to get home on her own. She was in the middle of a remote research facility in the mountains, far removed from human civilization. Walking home when it took her three hours to get here by car was basically impossible.

"I don't understand! What is going on here?! What, am I going to be some sort of test subject or something?!"

"I guess it's easy to think a facility like this would do human experimentation, but don't worry. We're not going to make you take any strange medicine or anything. The description we wrote on the recruitment advert was an accurate summary of what you'll be doing... although maybe calling what we do just 'office work' was being a bit too liberal."

"And what happens if I don't sign this?"

"You'll just be thrown in without any explanation."

"Thrown where?!"

The contract also had a non-disclosure agreement written into it, but a facility like this would have no problem getting rid of one or two people, so any sort of contract was likely a formality. The moment she had boarded that bus for the interview, her fate had been decided.

If she couldn't run away, there was no point in opposing them either. Reluctantly, she signed the contract — Asaka Takatou.

Nodding in satisfaction, the man in the lab coat handed her an ID card.

Asaka hung her head as she walked down the stark white hallway. It reminded her of a hospital. The lack of any other people made her wonder if there were any others working in the facility at all.

"Is this a research facility for some evil organization or something?"

"Not at all. We're a proper institution, working for the betterment of humanity and the world," the man beside her responded, seemingly offended by the accusation.

"A proper institution wouldn't have such a suspicious way of recruiting people."

"Honestly, the fact that you were willing to join us properly was quite a relief. Having to brainwash everyone that comes in here is so inefficient, and it can impact their performance, too."

"So this *is* an evil organization!"

"We have pretty free rein with our methods, so I guess you could see it that way. But this facility is here to protect not only the people, but the entire country of Japan. Ah, here we are." The man tapped his ID card on the nearby card reader. As he did, the wall quietly slid open, revealing an elevator. "You need your ID card to get anywhere in here, so please don't lose it."

Following him, Asaka stepped into the elevator. Once the door closed, it quietly began to descend.

"Now, it'll take a while to get down there. Would you like me to explain anything in the meantime?"

"What do you actually want me to do here? Is there really any reason it had to be me?"

"Basically, your job will be taking care of a monster."

"What do you mean 'monster'? Is it something your evil research has created?" She had no idea what he could possibly mean by "taking care of a monster."

"It's not really something where it had to be you. We're just trying a number of different approaches."

"So what exactly are you researching at this facility?" She changed the topic, as he appeared to be avoiding the subject of the monster.

"How do I put this...are you familiar with the term 'mutually assured destruction'?"

"No, not at all."

Mutually assured destruction was a strategy used in nuclear warfare. The idea was for countries that had nuclear weapons, in the event of being hit by a nuclear attack themselves, to still have the capability of launching their own nuclear attack in response. Basically, it guaranteed that any use of nuclear weapons would result in nuclear retaliation. The theory was that this would prevent two countries from ever actually going to war.

"So wait, are you researching nuclear weapons here?!"

"That would make things easy, wouldn't it? We have the materials, after all. I feel like it would be fine to research it in secret, but the higher-ups are rather stuck on Japan's three antinuclear principles. There's no way they'd allow us to do that here. But that leaves us defenseless against other countries which *have* developed nuclear weapons. You know how dangerous a situation that is for us, right?"

"Kind of, but what can we do about it?"

"To that end, this facility is researching curses. Basically, 'if you nuke us, we'll put a curse on your country.'" Asaka was taken aback by the stupidity of his comment, but there was no sign the man was joking at all. "I also thought it sounded ridiculous when I first heard it. But even if you don't understand the principle or the logic of how it works, when you see that it does, it's hard to say anything. That's what science is."

"So, when you said I might die, that means…" Although she didn't want to believe it, after hearing this much, Asaka had basically figured it out.

"Yes, death by a curse. Oh, from the word 'curse' you might get the impression of a brutal, agonizing death from within your own body, but no, you'd just die instantly, so don't worry about it. You won't feel any pain at all; you'll literally just drop dead on the spot."

"How could I not worry about that?!"

"Okay, we need to switch elevators here, so we have a bit more walking to do." As they were talking, the elevator came to a stop. Calmly ignoring Asaka's anger, the young man opened the door.

Asaka gasped, struck speechless by the sight of the hallway beyond. It was black — not just dark, but covered in writing. The walls, the ceiling, even the floor were crowded with lettering.

"What is this?! It looks terrifying!" Upon closer inspection, it seemed they were Chinese characters written with a brush.

"They're sutras. Maybe it's just empty consolation, but it helps some people."

"I'm not sure whether I can even ask where we're going, but is it that far?"

"We're heading to your workplace right now, and we still have a ways to go. It's kind of meaningless, but the higher-ups were terrified, so they forced us deep underground. The multiple elevator changes are also just in case." The man stepped out into the hallway crowded with sutras. Asaka hurriedly followed.

After walking for a while, the man spoke again. "Are you familiar with the term 'AΩ'?" It seemed to be a continuation of their previous conversation.

"Are you making fun of me? How would I know something like that?"

"Those are the first and last letters of the Greek alphabet, Alpha and Omega. It basically means 'from beginning to end,' or something like 'everything' or 'eternity.' That's the codename of the test subject you will be responsible for."

"Is this test subject human? So this person is cursing others?" At the very least, she hoped it was human.

"I wonder, is it really human in the end?"

"What do you mean 'really' human? It's a person, right?"

"I haven't seen it, so I can't really say."

"Are you serious?"

"I mean, if you get cursed, you die. There's no way I'd want to get close to it."

Faced with his total indifference, Asaka lost the will to complain. "But it's one of your test subjects, right? Aren't there videos or something?"

"Oh, I forgot something pretty important. No one is allowed to make recordings of AΩ, video or sound. There are rumors that just watching a video of it will get you killed, after all."

"Now that you mention it, I did see a movie like that once..." Asaka's unease was continuing to grow.

"Of course, I've heard reports of exactly what it looks like and what kind of organism it is, but I don't want to give you any preconceived notions."

"If it's my job, isn't it kind of important that I know?"

"Think of it as part of your research. How will it react to meeting someone like you? Yes, recording the actions of AΩ is an important part of your job."

If digital recordings were banned, then she supposed the only option would be a handwritten journal. "Assuming I survive, right?"

"For now, I'll just say none of its caretakers have died before, so you'll probably be okay."

"Oh, do you mean I'm going to have coworkers?"

She had thought this dangerous job was being pushed onto her alone, but if she had coworkers then she would feel a lot better about the whole thing.

"It depends on how the situation develops from here, but for now you'll be by yourself. No one has died yet, but previous caretakers have dropped out due to mental health issues."

"There's no peace of mind here at all, then..." Asaka muttered.

"It's not like we make you do everything by yourself, though. There's an autonomous robot there too, so you can go ahead and put it to work as well."

"So...what exactly do I have to do? What does 'taking care of it' mean?"

"What exactly is AΩ, you mean? You won't be that worried when you find out. Ah, we've made it to the next elevator."

Boarding it, they began descending further. After going for this long, they must have made it incredibly far underground. The facility must have been regulating the airflow, but Asaka was finding it harder and harder to breathe.

"What we understand so far is that, just by thinking it, AΩ can kill anything. So far, we haven't found any way to defend against it. While we have no complaints about its strength, it's basically impossible to control, so it's hard to call it a weapon, and it can't really be used in warfare."

"If that's the case, should you really be studying it in a lab?" If something like that existed, just having it deep underground seemed dangerous enough.

"Right? That's what I think, too. But in the end, we can't kill it."

"Is it immortal or something?"

"No, its body is probably like any other person's. It's definitely possible to kill it, but there's a reason we can't — it can detect any attack coming at it before it happens and counterattack. Well, that's actually the part that made people think of using it as a means of mutually assured destruction."

"But it's already this far underground, right? Why don't you just bury it? If it's a living thing, it'll starve eventually."

"I'm surprised, Miss Takatou! That's pretty brutal of you! But we can't do that, either."

"Why not?"

"If we tried, humanity would probably be wiped out."

Asaka froze, taken off guard by that conclusion, after having skipped past the logical steps to get there.

"It kills just by thinking. So if it doesn't know you exist, it can't kill you. You get that much, right?"

"Well, you can't think to kill someone you've never heard of before, can you?"

"Right. To kill an individual, you have to know about them. But if it wants to kill indiscriminately, there's no such need. In short, if it ever decided to kill every person on Earth at once, it would be possible."

"Isn't that an obscene level of powerful?!"

"We don't really know if it's possible, but we don't know that it's *not* possible, either. So we can't really risk it."

"Well, what exactly do you want me to do?"

"We want you to give it the mentality of a Japanese person. So if Japan is attacked, it'll feel the need to respond."

"I don't know how well I'd be able to teach or train a monster..."

"You have your teaching license, don't you?"

"What? Well, yeah, I figured I'd just get all the licenses I could, just in case, but...wait, was that the reason you hired me?!"

"That's one of them, yes. We're not just hiring any old person here, you know."

"Dammit! I never should have gotten that license if I didn't plan on using it!"

As Asaka chastised herself, the elevator fell silent. They had arrived at their destination.

"Now then. From here, you'll have to go on by yourself. Just walk down the hallway," the man said, swiping his ID card to open the elevator door.

"By myself?"

"Unfortunately, I'm not authorized to go any farther. And even if I was, I wouldn't want to."

"Is it safe for me to be getting so close to something so dangerous?" Asaka asked, glaring at the man.

"Leaving it alone any longer just increases the risk. We figure it's better than nothing at all, so please just take it easy and do your best." As expected, the man had no intention of either coming with her or taking her back. "Here are your instructions. The details of your job are written inside," he finished, handing her a stack of papers.

Realizing she wouldn't accomplish anything by standing there, Asaka finally stepped into the hallway. The moment she did, the door shut behind her. Looking down the corridor, she saw a metal door not far away. It was enormous, with numerous solid-looking metal components arrayed about its surface. It reminded her of an underground vault in the center of a bank.

Can an ID card actually open this type of door?

Though she doubted it would work, she nevertheless touched her ID card to the card reader. As she did, the door emitted a loud noise as metal bolts and hinges began to move.

"Whatever! If humanity gets wiped out, it's not my problem!" With a desperate self-pep talk, Asaka stepped through the door.

The setting sun shed a blood-red light over the surroundings. The high-pitched wails of the cicadas added a melancholic feeling to the unnerving scenery.

Before Asaka was exactly the kind of scene a Japanese person would think of when told of the countryside — rice fields, a narrow river, and a small forest up on a mountainside. Red spider lilies lined the road cutting between the fields of rice, and crows flew through the sky overhead.

The twilight scenery had a somewhat sinister feeling to it. But if one went to the countryside, this kind of landscape was rather common. The only problem was that it was actually in an underground research facility.

After passing through numerous elevators and hallways lined with sutras, magic circles, and carved idols, Asaka had finally ended up here.

"It's like the scenery's been spoiled…" Asaka was filled with an overwhelming fear. While she was still half-doubting the existence of whatever it was that lived here, she could tell the fear with which it was regarded was very real.

The greatest proof of that fear was just how deep underground they were. The research facility was up on a mountain, yet she must have been far below sea level at this point. Whoever had made this place wanted to seal whatever was in here far away, where they would never have to face it.

What on earth was it?

Asaka looked at the scenery around her. There should have been a door behind her, but all she saw was the same countryside surrounding her. The door and walls showed images of that same view — in short, it was all fake. No matter how much this place put on airs, it couldn't have been all that large.

"So, what do I do now?" Up until that point, the path had more or less been a straight line. She'd seen a number of side doors on her way there, but her ID card couldn't open any of them.

Looking over her instructions, she saw that her destination was a mansion in the center of the forest. So she made her way to the small wooded mountain, the only thing standing out among the rice fields.

Passing through a shrine gate at the entrance of the forest, the mansion quickly came into view amidst the dense vegetation. It was an old-fashioned Japanese-style building. The moment Asaka saw it, she got the impression that it was haunted.

As she drew closer, it became more and more obvious that the building's age was real, and not a holographic projection of some sort.

"Hello?" Standing at the entrance, she called into the house. There was no answer, but she had expected as much. The door was unlocked, so she stepped inside. Taking off her shoes and walking into the house proper, she felt a presence inside. Tentatively, she made her way towards it.

The floor of the dark hallway creaked beneath her feet, suggesting an even greater age to the building than she had thought. Asaka did her best to ignore the unpleasant sticky sensation of the floor, gradually speeding up. After walking for a while, she saw an open sliding door. Something was clearly inside it, so she stopped in front of the door, steeling herself before peeking inside.

It was a boy.

He was in what looked like a living room. Not doing anything in particular, he sat cross-legged on the tatami floor in a white kimono.

Is that AΩ?

After all the warnings she had received, seeing him felt like a bit of an anticlimax. He looked young enough to be in the lower grades of elementary school. There was nothing scary about him at all.

The boy looked back at her with a blank stare. Seeing that plainly innocent face, Asaka began to grow angry. Perhaps merely as a result of the pressure she had felt in getting there, the anger was slowly welling up inside her.

Not knowing what to do when Asaka suddenly appeared in front of him, the boy smiled. It was a dry, ironic smile. A know-it-all, resigned smile that was decidedly unchildlike. The moment she saw that, Asaka's anger boiled over.

"Those idiots! What are they doing, keeping a kid locked away down here like this?! What on earth were they thinking, making a place like this?! What are they, stupid?! How are they so scared of a little kid?! And you too! Look how pale you are! Have you just been hiding inside this house the whole time?!"

"Huh? Yeah, I've always been in here..."

Hearing that, Asaka immediately walked into the room, grabbed the boy, and put him on her shoulders. Walking down the hallway, she ignored her shoes as she stepped out of the entranceway to the mansion. Running through the forest, she approached the rice paddy and, with a roar, threw the boy inside.

"There! You're outside! Play! Find some crayfish or shrimp or something, the ones who are transparent so you can see their insides! Put a firecracker in a frog's butt and watch it explode! Get scared as you watch a wireworm burrow its way out of a praying mantis's stomach!"

The mud-soaked boy looked back at her in shock. It was no wonder, considering Asaka's sudden outburst. But that lasted for only a moment. Sitting in the muddy water, he slowly raised his right hand to point at her.

"Die."

Asaka had, up until that moment, completely forgotten that he was supposed to be a monster that could kill people with a thought. The fact that she could be dead at any moment had completely slipped her mind.

Wait, am I going to die?!

From what she had been told, there was no way she could avoid her fate. Asaka waited for that final moment to come, struck by a sudden, stinging fear. But nothing happened.

Then she heard a thud on the ground behind her.

"What...?"

Asaka turned around. Something was lying there on the earth. It was shaped like a person, stretching out from her own shadow. She would never have believed something like it could exist, but it continued to slide out of her shadow right before her eyes.

"It's probably been hiding in your shadow this whole time."

"What is it?"

"No idea. It looks like it had trouble with the charms, so maybe it's a demon or something? Sometimes they come here and try to kill me."

"Oh, I...see..." Asaka had no idea how to respond.

"Hey. I don't mind looking for shrimps or whatever, but it's almost nighttime, so can we do it tomorrow?"

"Huh? Oh! I'm sorry! Wow, what did I just do?! I'm really sorry!" Jumping into the rice paddy, she helped the boy up.

"Are you here to replace Masaki?"

"I don't know who Masaki is, but probably, yes. I don't really know what's going on here, to be honest. My name is Asaka Takatou. What's yours?"

"The people here call me AΩ."

"No, no, no, that's just a codename. What's your actual name?"

"No idea. Before I came here they called me Lord Okakushi, because I made people disappear or something? More importantly though, I'm getting kind of hungry."

"Me too, actually...wait, do I have to cook?!"

"Masaki cooked for me, so..."

Taken in by the strange atmosphere, she hadn't thought all that hard about it, but it made sense that if her job was to take care of this boy that she would have to cook for him too.

"You're kind of funny," the boy said, laughing at Asaka's surprise.

"Yeah, I guess I can't argue with that…" She didn't have any excuse for the behavior she had shown since meeting him. She felt somehow pathetic.

Looking in the refrigerator, Asaka was at a loss. It was full of food, but it was hard to call them anything other than "ingredients." Having never cooked meals from scratch before, she had no idea how to use these seemingly high-class materials.

"All right, I give up!" Throwing in the towel immediately, she began searching other cupboards. Deep in the back of one, she found some instant ramen. "Er, well, it has to be ready by the time he gets out here, right?"

After returning to the mansion, the boy had gone to take a bath, since he had been covered head to toe in mud. Asaka was also dirty, but it was nothing that she couldn't wash off in the sink, so she had done so and then immediately set about preparing dinner. As she was boiling the water, the boy came back out.

"Hey, even if you're an elementary school kid, put some clothes on in front of other people!"

He was completely naked.

The boy's expression was puzzled. "What's elementary school?"

"Seriously?" If she had to guess, she'd say the boy had no education to speak of. Asaka's anger at the clear neglect he had been shown was beginning to resurface. "Of course, I feel like feeding him nothing but instant ramen is probably going to be called neglect too…" Without even being able to cook, she didn't have much of a right to be angry. Feeling ashamed of herself, she turned back to the stove.

As she told the boy to go get dressed, she turned off the burner. Cutting the lids of the cups, she poured the boiling water inside. After about three minutes, the boy had returned wearing the same kind of white kimono he'd had on before. Sitting him down at the low dining table, Asaka sat across from him, putting the two cups of instant ramen on the table.

"What's this?"

"You don't even know what instant ramen is, huh?" His previous caretakers must have had the utmost concern for his health. The instant ramen must have been something they saved for themselves. "Well, for now, just try eating it."

Since he seemed unsure of what to do, she removed the lid for him and handed him a pair of chopsticks. At the very least, he seemed to know how to eat noodles with chopsticks, and quickly dug in.

"Wow, this is good. I've never had something that tasted like this."

Although she had done nothing more than pour hot water into it, Asaka still felt a slight sense of pride. She started on her own food. The nostalgic everyday flavor of the noodles finally gave her a chance to breathe a relaxed sigh.

"Hey. Uhh, right, your name. Do you really not have one? What did your mom call you?"

"Mom?"

"Well, never mind. Not having a name is pretty inconvenient. Calling you AΩ all the time will be a pain."

"Really? Okay, you can call me Asaka then."

"Except we need to be able to tell ourselves apart..." Asaka muttered with a sigh. It seemed he really didn't care one way or another. "I'll just choose one for you. Is that okay?"

"Sure."

Although she had figured it would come to that, now that the moment was on her, she had no idea what to call him. As if the answer might appear there, she stared into the boy's face.

"Hmm, how about Yogiri, then?" That was the name of a dog she had once owned. Thinking he looked somewhat like a puppy, it was the first name that came to mind.

"So, Yogiri Takatou?"

"Wait, why are you taking my last name?!"

"You have to have something like that added to your name, right?"

"Geez, why is it starting to look like I'm your mom?! But if you don't even know that much...well, that's fine. So from now on, you're Yogiri Takatou. Nice to meet you." Getting past her own commentary, Asaka reached forward to offer him a handshake.

The boy stared blankly at her outstretched hand.

Seeing that he didn't seem to understand what she was doing, Asaka stepped over beside him and took his hand by force. "This is a handshake. Nice to meet you! Now, repeat!"

"Nice to meet you?" With a puzzled expression, the boy did as he was told.

While Asaka didn't fully understand what she was supposed to be doing here, it was impossible for her to think of this boy as a monster. So, however reluctantly, she decided to see how things would go.

Afterword

Thank you so much for reading "My Instant Death Ability Is So Overpowered, No One in This Other World Stands a Chance Against Me!" I was debating who to write this afterword for, so in the end, I decided to write something for each case.

【For Those Wondering Whether to Buy This Book】
The title of this book is "My Instant Death Ability Is So Overpowered, No One in This Other World Stands a Chance Against Me!" It's kind of long, isn't it? It's basically just a sentence. Titles have become something like a plot summary, so this is a case of that. The protagonist's power is to kill anything at will. There are no limits at all. Whoever his enemy is, they'll definitely die. He's going to win in the end anyway, so who needs all those annoying fight scenes in the way? That was the decision I made when writing this.

Reading about a protagonist struggling through each fight is a pain. I wanted a story where you could relax and enjoy it without any worries. I recommend this book to people looking for something like that.

【For Those Wondering Who Tsuyoshi Fujitaka Is】
Hello, my name is Tsuyoshi Fujitaka. My side job is writing light novels. I debuted as an author by winning second prize in the Seventh HJ Bunko Competition. I have written two series since then, so allow me to introduce them. I realize it's a bit blunt to be pushing my other books already, but if you've liked this book, maybe you're interested in reading more of my books, right?

"My Big Sister Lives in a Fantasy World" is a seven-volume series released through HJ Bunko. It's a modern school-life story. It's about a boy with an older sister with a case of middle-school syndrome, who forced him to go through intense training to become the strongest. He ends up fighting all sorts of things like serial killers, vampires, beastkin, monsters, demon gods, and people setting up mysterious death games.

"Unbeatable Demon Lord" is a three-volume series published by Earth Star Novels. It's an isekai fantasy. The most powerful demon lord is a young girl who, just like the title says, is unbeatable.

Both of them have overpowered protagonists, so for those of you who like that sort of thing, I highly recommend it.

【For Those Wondering About the Continuation of Unbeatable Demon Lord】
It has been more than a year since "Unbeatable Demon Lord 3" was published, and there still hasn't been an announcement about the next volume. First, I would like to apologize.

In this situation, it's understandable that some of you might think it will no longer be continuing, but to put it bluntly, the sales numbers are low enough that I was told continuing it would be difficult. But it's not like it's impossible.

If the current volumes start selling better…

If an overseas version is released and sells well…

Or if this series, "My Instant Death Ability Is So Overpowered, No One in This Other World Stands a Chance Against Me!" sells well.

If any of those happen, the possibility for a continuation will be revisited. It's kind of an unpleasant topic to talk about, but if you want to read the continuation of that series, please buy this book. Thank you in advance.

【For Those Who Read the Web Novel and Are Hesitating to Read the Print Version】
The main plot is basically the same as the web novel, but the prose itself has been entirely reviewed and improved. Fundamentally, I've tried to make it easier to understand. Of course, there has also been proofreading done, so the number of typos and other mistakes should be much smaller.

A new interlude has also been inserted into Act 2. It talks about what happens to the Hero after his appearance in the story. It also touches a little on the topic of the Great Sage.

There is also an additional short story about Yogiri while he was still living in Japan. Since the series itself is only concerned about the story in the other world, all of the stories about their original world will be in these side stories.

【For Those Involved in the Book's Production】
My thanks.

Chisato Naruse was in charge of illustrations for this book. Thank you for your many beautiful works of art. I looked forward to seeing each and every picture you finished. Seeing Yogiri's lack of motivation and Tomochika's cuteness captured so well in visual form was a delight.

Many other people were involved in the production of this novel. I would like to give my heartfelt thanks to all of them.

【For Those Curious About the Next Volume】
This book was the first in the series I wrote when I decided I wanted to become an author. So of course there is a second volume, but any continuation beyond that depends on how this volume sells. The story really begins when the world becomes aware of how terrifying the protagonist is, so I hope to be able to tell the story that far.

For those of you who enjoyed the book, please share that enjoyment as much as you can!

Let's meet again in the next volume!

Tsuyoshi Fujitaka
藤孝　剛志

Tomochika, Yogiri, Mokomoko, and even Asaka in the side story are all such attractive characters. I had a lot of fun drawing them.

What will happen to Asaka and (little) Lain from now on? As a reader, I am excited to see how their stories unfold!

Chisato Naruse

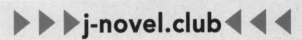